12/13/

DOUBLOON

DOUBLOON

Jay Amberg

A Tom Doherty Associates Book   New York

DOUBLOON

Copyright © 2003 by Jay Amberg

Edited by James Frenkel

Book design by Jane Adele Regina

A Forge Book
Published by Tom Doherty Associates, LLC
175 Fifth Avenue
New York, NY 10010

www.tor.com

Forge® is a registered trademark of Tom Doherty Associates, LLC.

Library of Congress Cataloging-in-Publication Data

Amberg, Jay.
    Doubloon / Jay Amberg.—1st ed.
        p.   cm.
    "A Tom Doherty Associates book."
    ISBN 0-765-30100-8 (acid-free paper)
      1. Key West (Fla.)—Fiction.   2. Treasure trove—Fiction.   3. Shipwrecks—
Fiction.   4. Divers—Fiction.   I. Title.

PS3551.M19 D68   2002
813'.54—dc21

                                                                    2001058980

First Edition: January 2003

Printed in the United States of America

0 9 8 7 6 5 4 3 2 1

For my father,
Thomas H. Amberg

And in memory of my mother,
Khrybel Travers Amberg

Acknowledgments

Thanks again to John Manos for his editorial guidance.
And thanks, once more,
to Andrew H. Zack for his support.

DOUBLOON

Prologue

THE STRAITS OF FLORIDA
AUGUST 23, 1642

Santa María Magdalena's lanterns carved arcs of light as the galleon pitched through the horrific storm. Whipping rain and salt spray slashed across her decks in horizontal sheets. Foaming twenty-five-foot waves struck her sterncastle with such force that the caulking popped loose. Bartólome de Alcala, *Magdalena*'s captain and admiral of the Spanish treasure fleet, stood on the deck outside his cabin on the sterncastle. His round face and protruding nose were not handsome, but the intensity in his dark eyes had attracted women in his native Seville and compelled men to obey his orders aboard ship and in the Spanish empire's farflung ports from Cartagena to Manila. Bracing himself with his ebony cane, he watched as the crew struggled to heave overboard the bales of indigo and copper slabs he had ordered jettisoned. *Magdalena* was top-heavy and cumbersome—a plodding, heavily armed treasure trove. Her thirty bronze cannons made her one of the mightiest ships afloat, but her wide beam and high sterncastle made her one of the least maneuverable.

Glancing up at the shredded pennants flapping on the mastheads, de Alcala shouted to his first mate, "Hoist the sheet anchor to the deck! Cast off the wooden chests!"

The governor of Cuba, a tall, emaciated man, led a Jesuit

priest in a black cassock toward the sterncastle. They clung to the ornate blue and gold railing as they climbed the ship's ladder. While the governor stumbled toward de Alcala, the Jesuit slumped to his knees in front of a two-foot-high solid gold statue of Mary Magdalene washing Christ's feet. Bolted to the deck at the base of the mizzenmast, the statue glistened in the rain. The Jesuit took an exquisite red coral and gold rosary from beneath his cassock, prostrated himself, and chanted in Latin.

The governor slipped on the deck, grabbed a stay, and yelled, "Where are we, Captain?" His drenched doublet clung to his narrow frame, rivulets of water streamed down his sallow face, and his thin gray hair was matted to his skull.

"Somewhere near Florida's Martyrs, your Excellency," de Alcala shouted over the din of the storm.

"Islands?" the governor yelled as he clutched the stay. "Land. . . . We must make land."

"Only sea-room is safety," de Alcala shouted. "The reefs would tear . . ."

The mainmast's yardarm splintered. Rigging and torn sails hurtled onto the quarterdeck, entangling the sailors raising the massive sheet anchor and stock. Struck by the yardarm, one of the wooden chests disintegrated, spewing silver coins across the deck and into the sea. Clasping the transom, de Alcala shouted to his crew to help their mates.

"Not the chests!" the governor yelled. "You must not dump the chests!" He wiped away the water pouring down his face and into his pointed beard.

De Alcala did not answer.

"You must save the bronze chests!" the governor screamed.

"I will do what's necessary to save my ship and crew," de Alcala answered.

"I order you to save those chests!" The governor drew his swept-hilt rapier halfway from its scabbard.

De Alcala glowered at the governor. "Your cargo is cursed," he shouted. "We are double blood-cursed by your cargo."

Noting the look in de Alcala's eyes, the governor jammed the rapier back into the scabbard and yelled, "Your impertinence, Captain, will be reported when we reach Spain."

"If we reach Spain, Don Pedro. *If...*," de Alcala shouted as he turned again toward the tumult of demolished rigging and spars on the deck below.

The governor wheeled, pulled a leather pouch from his doublet, and shook out two gold coins. When he stooped and thrust the coins in front of the Jesuit's face, the priest shook his head. His hand quivering, the governor held the coins under the Jesuit's nose until the priest reached up, snatched them, and began to wail, *"Absolvo te..."*

Magdalena's foremast cracked and plunged into the sea. Dragged by its halyards and stays, the broken mast acted like a rudder. *Magdalena* swung around and broached to the huge waves that crashed over her railing amidship, engulfing the crew and wreckage on the quarterdeck. As *Magdalena* reeled from side to side, cannons smashed through the gun ports. Water poured through the gaping holes and sluiced into the hold. A wave broke against the sterncastle, shattering the railing, dousing the lanterns, and flooding the deck. The Jesuit vanished in the foam. Flung against the mizzenmast, de Alcala hooked his arm around a halyard and then quickly looped a safety line over his oilskin slicker. The governor lunged for the gold statue as the deck tilted to port. Terror in his eyes, he clung to the statue when *Magdalena* lurched back toward starboard. One of his hands slipped from the statue, and he clawed at the deck and shrieked. Then, his mouth open in a wordless cry, he slid across the deck and plummeted into the ocean.

Rain whipped *Magdalena*'s decks, and wind whistled shrilly in what was left of her rigging. The thundering waves continued to buffet her, eventually sweeping even the enormous sheet anchor into the sea. De Alcala stood tangled in the halyard and lines, willing his ship to stay afloat. The gold statue gleamed darkly in the driving rain.

In the half-light of the false dawn, *Sea Devil* was alone, a dark mote on the vast tract of ocean. The wind was calm, and the water's surface barely rippled. Resting at anchor, the old tugboat listed to port. Nick Gallagher, asleep on the lower starboard bunk in the forward cabin, woke abruptly when a flashlight left on the upper bunk rolled off and clattered to the deck. He raked his hand through his thinning blond hair fringed with gray, rose groggily, got his balance on the tilting deck, and muttered, "What the hell?"

He hustled through the galley and clambered down the ship's ladder into the hold. Seawater poured through an intake valve in the engine room and swirled around his knees as he hunched over the bilge pump. He grabbed a rag and stuffed it into the pipe's mouth. Then, looking for a wrench, he swore softly to himself. The boat lurched farther to port, spilling equipment from the steel shelving into the water. The generator sputtered, and the lights blinked.

"Busted valve," he said aloud, his voice calm and even. "And the goddamn pump's frozen." The rag blew out, and water spewed through the valve again. "Hey, Dewey!" he shouted over his shoulder. "Get your sleepy ass down here and give me a hand!"

As he reached up for a towel hanging from a nylon line, the engine room spun wildly. He tumbled sideways, his head striking the bulkhead. Silver lights wove around him. The generator screeched, blue sparks arced into the water, and the hold went black. Partially buried by lines, he groped for something stationary. When he tried to stand, he toppled backward. Water shot up his nose. Coughing and choking, he got to his feet and disentangled himself from the lines. "Shit," he shouted into the blackness.

Water roared, churning around his waist. The air smelled of fuel oil.

His scalp above his ear was warm and sticky; his breathing was fast and harsh. Holding his hands in front of him, he turned in a circle until he touched something large and steel. As he ran his hands across and under the object, he could not at first imagine what it was. Then, he stepped back and murmured, "Holy shit." Up was down: the tugboat had flipped over, and he was fifteen feet below the ocean's surface with a diesel engine hanging next to him.

He swallowed the welling fear and yelled, "Dewey!"

When he heard no answer but the water raging into the hold, he felt around in the darkness trying to get his bearings. He opened his mouth wide and slowed his breathing. He then shut his eyes, ground the heels of his hands against his lids, and visualized the engine room upside down. Though he had lived on farms until he was forty, he'd spent the last twenty-three years on salvage boats, and he'd come to feel more at home aboard them than anywhere else. Even in the rising water below deck in an overturned boat, he began to feel a cool objectivity. Aware that the stern hatch had to be directly below the engine, he felt around with his bare feet until his toes bumped an anchor. Placing one hand against the engine housing, he held his breath, ducked under the water, and pulled the anchor out of his way. He then swept his free hand back and forth over the steel until he located the hatch cover.

When he surfaced, he exhaled, wiped his face, shook his head, and muttered to himself, "Okay. . . . This is it."

As the water reached his shoulders, he took a series of breaths, each one deeper than the one before. The water rose to his neck. He submerged, turned, and kicked downward. He lost time clearing the lines and springs that cluttered the area. Exhaling slowly, he let the air bubbles drift past his chin and cheeks. When he pushed on the hatch cover, he floated up. Bracing his feet against the engine housing, he tried again. The cover opened a few inches, and water streamed through the crack. He lost his grip, slid away, and twisted around.

Breaking the water's surface, he drew in the engine room's stale air. He had to stand on his toes and tilt his head back to keep his mouth above the water. Though in utter darkness, he opened his eyes wide. Clinging to the housing, he tried to regain control of his breathing. He knew he'd have only one more shot, and his heart was racing too fast for him to breathe slowly and deeply. Above him, he heard scraping on the hull. Pounding the bulkhead, he shouted, "Dewey!" a third time.

He sucked in air, plunged under the water, braced his feet on the engine housing, and thrust his hands against the hatch cover. As the cover began to open, he straightened his legs, driving downward until the cover swung away. The surging water tugged him backward. His body scraped against the housing, and his open eyes burned in the blackness. His fingers caught the edge of the hatch; his breath burst from his mouth. With one hand he yanked himself halfway through the hatch. As he stroked hard against the surge, his other arm caught in a snarl of lines being sucked toward him. His heart palpitated, and his head thundered. Stifling an urge to inhale, he writhed until his head was also snared. *This,* he thought, *is no time to die. I'm so close. So close to the goddamned motherlode.* His heart beat erratically, and a darkness deeper than the blackness of *Sea Devil*'s hold began to close in on him despite his gaping eyes. *Only a few more days, a couple weeks at most. Hell, today could be the day.* He took one final involuntary breath. And then he hung there, entangled, as water filled his lungs. *So close.*

In the gathering light, *Sea Devil*'s deep, humped hull looked like a dark turtle shell. Air bubbles boiled from beneath the boat, and the water was iridescent black with diesel fuel. Life preservers, bench planking, and rubber buoys floated in the muck. A solitary figure, panting, his hands cut by barnacles and blood clotting the white streak in his long black hair, pulled himself toward the hull's peak. The sun rose, spilling light like wine across the water.

L anding," Jack Gallagher said, three hundred feet out. His right hand held the Super 80's yoke, his left the airliner's dual throttles. He was proceeding visually, having turned off the autopilot and autothrottle five minutes earlier. He checked the localizer glide slope, altimeter, and air speed indicator.

The captain, seated in the cockpit to Gallagher's left, continued his callouts: "Two hundred feet . . . one hundred feet . . ."

Gallagher checked the engine gauges.

"Fifty feet . . . forty feet . . . thirty feet . . ."

The convective turbulence and a ten-knot crosswind jostled the Super 80, and Gallagher, constantly working the throttles, kicked the plane's nose around to the runway's centerline.

"Twenty feet . . . ten feet."

Gallagher kept his eye on the center line, felt the smooth touch of the landing gear's wheels on O'Hare International's 22-Right runway, lowered the nose, deployed the thrust reversers, and started the braking. The landing, he knew, was as good as any veteran could do, but there was no adrenaline rush—nothing like dropping an F-18 onto a carrier's pitching deck in thick soup. The Super 80 drove like a big old truck.

When the spoiler lever came out, the captain said, "Deployed."

Gallagher brought the plane down to taxi speed, stowed the thrust reversers, and then, as American Airline procedures required, let the captain take over the controls. After a career as a navy fighter pilot, he couldn't quite get used to not being in command. He missed the camaraderie, too. With the airline, he was doing three-day trips, six legs each trip, but never with exactly the same crew and, in his first few months, only once with the same captain. His training class had been mostly younger guys with whom he'd felt out of sync, and the company itself was cold—simply a business. He was settling into the routine well enough, just as he had aboard ship and in port, but the change from active duty to civilian life hadn't been easy.

During the eight-minute taxi to the gate, Gallagher was busy talking on the radio with Chicago ground clearance, doing his checklist, and looking out for other aircraft. When they reached the gate and the Super 80 came to a full stop, he straightened his tie, turned, and opened the cockpit door. As the passengers filed toward the jet bridge, he completed his checklist and then stood to greet them. He was forty-two but looked younger. Just under six feet tall, he weighed one hundred and ninety pounds. His uniform shirt fit snugly over his muscular frame. His skin was ruddy, his eyes were pale green, and his sandy hair was cut short.

When the last passenger had deplaned, Gallagher grabbed his hat from the hook on the cockpit's back wall and hefted his black leather kit bag. "Nice trip," he said to the captain. "Nice flying with you."

"Yeah, we're home," the captain answered. "See ya next time."

Gallagher nodded. Chicago had been his base for four months, but the two-bedroom apartment near the Cumberland "L" stop that he shared with three other pilots he barely knew was nothing more than a crash pad. His things were still in a storage unit, and he'd hung only a calendar on the wall. He took his Purdy suitcase from the forward closet, attached his kit bag to it, and wheeled it up the jet bridge.

As Gallagher entered O'Hare's terminal, he saw John Davis leaning against a white pillar. Though they'd been shipmates intermittently over the years and Davis, too, was now flying for American and based in Chicago, Gallagher hadn't seen him in six weeks.

"Hey, Wolf," Davis said, pushing away from the pillar. He was still built like the wrestler he'd been at Annapolis: stocky, with no neck and thick, sloping shoulders.

Looking into his buddy's eyes, Gallagher knew this wasn't a social visit.

"I've got some bad news from Florida," Davis began.

Gallagher stopped rolling the Purdy.

"Your father's wife called Susan in D.C., who, when she couldn't reach you, got in touch with me. She figured better me than somebody you didn't know." Davis shrugged.

Gallagher took off his hat and brushed his hand through his hair. Shaking his head, he took a deep breath. "When?" he asked. "How?"

Sweat slid from Jack Gallagher's temples and streamed down his back as he climbed the stone steps of Our Lady of the Sea Catholic Church in Key West. The blistering August sunlight flashed off the church's white stucco facade and bell tower. As he squinted in the glare, the air shimmered with heat. He pulled open one of the heavy wooden doors and entered the church. The temperature inside, hovering at ninety-three degrees, was slightly cooler than the temperature outside, but the air was no less humid. The funeral had already begun, and more than two hundred people were seated in the pews as he made his way up the nave. A large circular fan, four feet across, stood in front of each side altar, blowing sultry air over the congregation. Some of the women waved fans shaped like seashells.

As Gallagher slipped into a pew, an elderly Hispanic man, meticulously attired in a black suit, brown tie, and starched white shirt with gold cuff links, turned and nodded gravely. Soft light diffused through the stained-glass windows above the high altar. Below the right window, a stout woman in an aquamarine dress was playing "Amazing Grace" on an ebony grand piano. At the foot of the altar, a short priest in white vestments stood between two dark-haired altar boys in red cassocks. Between them and the first pew, the closed casket containing the body of Gallagher's father rested on a mahogany stand. A bouquet of red and pink hibiscus lay on the coffin's lid.

"We are gathered here today to honor the memory of our friend, Nicholas Gallagher," the priest said. His English was perfect, but he spoke with a heavy Cuban accent.

As the priest spoke, Gallagher scanned the pews in front of him. The thin, auburn-haired woman in the first pew was his father's second wife, Rita. Next to her, the tall, gangling young man with the stringy red-blond ponytail had to be Tim, her son and Gallagher's half brother. Gallagher hadn't seen Tim in years, and he barely recognized the young man, so different from the boy he remembered. Six pallbearers wearing identical short-sleeved green and blue tropical shirts sat in the pew behind Rita and Tim.

"Nicholas Gallagher loved the ocean," the priest was saying, "and he knew full well that at any moment she can take as well as give, deny as well as provide, destroy as well as create." He took a handkerchief from beneath his vestments and wiped his forehead. "Nicholas loved life far too much to ever wish for death. But of this we can be sure: he would have rather died at sea than on land, rather aboard a boat than in a hospital . . ."

As memories flooded over Gallagher, the ceremony washed away from him. He glanced up at the tubular lights hanging from cables. He had seen his father only four times in the previous twenty-three years. During his final exams his plebe year at the U.S. Naval Academy, he had learned that his father had abandoned his mother in West Branch, Iowa, and bolted to South Florida to pursue his dream of Spanish galleons and sunken treasure. His father had hunted for gold, remarried, and found and lost a fortune. His mother, at first irate and later embittered, had run the family farm alone for eight years before finally selling out, marrying a schoolteacher, and settling in as an assistant librarian at the Hoover Memorial Library. Gallagher himself had stayed in the navy, flown carrier-based interceptors, and let the service replace the family that no longer existed.

Once the priest finished speaking, he sat down in a high-backed chair to the right of the altar. One of the pallbearers, a man in his middle thirties with a tapering white streak in his long black hair, stood, left his pew, and walked toward the piano. His hands and arms were cut and scraped. As he picked up a guitar with a woven, multicolored strap, the large round gold earring hanging from his left ear winked in the light. He and the pianist played a sad, almost melancholy duet with a slow Caribbean rhythm. His deep voice reedy, he sang, "Listen to de ocean . . . Listen to her call . . ." The music echoed around the church. "She holds de treasure beyond your dreams . . . beyond de dreams of all . . ."

As the pianist and guitarist segued into a more upbeat tune, the congregation rose. The guitarist sang, "De island's gonna rock ya . . . and de waves, dey gonna roll ya. De ocean's in your veins . . . you'll sail de Spanish Main . . ." The other pallbearers clapped to the music, and by the second refrain the church was thundering. Gallagher couldn't quite fathom what was happening. The elderly man in Gallagher's pew swayed quietly with the music, but most of the others in the congregation were clapping and singing. The pianist leaned forward and pounded the keys. The pallbearer strummed the guitar so hard that one of the scabs near his wrist broke and drops of blood sprayed the worn face of the guitar.

When the funeral ended, the pallbearers carried Nick Gallagher's casket from the church. The sun's glare temporarily blinded Jack Gallagher as he stepped from the vestibule. Rita and Tim Gallagher stood on the top step, nodding to people who offered their condolences. Rita's eyes welled, but she didn't cry. The deep-red blotches on Tim's sunburned face held vestiges of acne.

As Gallagher approached, Rita turned toward him. "Jack, it's . . . Sorry about not letting you know sooner," she said, her voice hoarse, almost gravelly. "Had trouble locating . . . reaching you." She bit her lip. "But it's good you made it."

"Yeah." He ran his index finger around the inside of his collar. "Just. I dropped my bag at the hotel and hustled over here."

"You're coming to the cemetery?" Though she was only forty-eight, the skin of her face was lined from too much time spent out in the sun. Crow's-feet spread from the corners of her deep-blue eyes as she watched the casket being hefted into the hearse.

"I was hoping I could ride with you," he answered.

Hesitating, she glanced at Tim, who stood silently, his hands folded in front of him. "Of course," she said, her tone distant.

At first no one spoke as they rode in the limousine along Margaret Street. Rita shook her head slowly; Tim stared down at his hands; and Gallagher gazed out the window. Away from the tourist bars and T-shirt shops on Duval Street, Key West was dormant. Traveller's palms and banana trees shaded the yards of the wood-frame Conch Cottages. Balustrades, slender columns, and gingerbread adorned the second-story galleries of the larger houses. Cats curled in a midday torpor in the shade of the porches, and orange-red hibiscus bloomed behind the white picket fences. As Gallagher thought about his father, he felt sad and empty. Even though he had seldom seen his father in the previous two decades, the thought of never again being swept up by the man's expansive smile and enthusiastic ramblings about the sea and Spanish treasure was causing an ache he hadn't anticipated.

"How'd it happen?" Gallagher asked.

Tim glanced at his mother before turning to Gallagher. "An accident out on the dive site," he answered. "Salvage boat flipped and sank. Dad . . . he was below in the engine room . . ."

"Jesus," Gallagher said as the motorcade slowed near the cemetery. "Were you aboard?"

"No, uh-uh." His eyes tearing, Tim shook his head. "Maybe if I was . . ."

"We never even had a chance to say good-bye," Rita said.

Just inside the cemetery gate, a brass band—six elderly men wearing dark uniforms and peaked caps—came to attention as the hearse passed. After the cortege stopped along the main drive, Gallagher stepped out into the heat rising in waves from the concrete. As the band struck up a tinny version of "When the Saints Come Marching In," the pallbearers pulled the casket from the hearse and carried it along the roadway. Only a few trees dotted the sea of vaults surrounding the procession. A gray-black thunderhead rose in the southwestern sky, but the bright sun directly overhead scoured the white and aqua burial vaults separated by low walls and wrought-iron fences. The mourners passed the silver-painted fence of the battleship *Maine* cemetery plot. The tall statue of a sailor, holding an oar upright in his right hand and shading his eyes with his left, stared mutely over the gravestones of those who had died when the warship exploded in Havana Harbor a century before.

The procession stopped near a royal poinciana. Only a few flaming red flowers remained in the tree's wide, flat canopy. Long, pale green seed pods hung from its branches. The newly finished vault—three cinder blocks high with a concrete roof— lay open. The area had been cleared, and a blue tarp had been placed in front of the vault. As the pallbearers lowered the casket onto the tarp, the mourners gathered in a loose circle around the priest. The band stopped playing and let their instruments rest like outmoded weapons at their sides. The priest wiped his face with his handkerchief, blessed himself, and began a litany of prayers. Gallagher stood, his back straight, and blinked away the sweat that rolled into his eyes. His mind was back in the white farmhouse where he had grown up. He was sitting at the dining room table on a winter's night with his father, who was jotting notes in a dark hardcover notebook. Spread out on the table were books about treasure diving, goldsmithing, the Spanish Main, and the conquistadors; pamphlets on gold coins and galleons; and maps, antiquated and modern, of Florida and the Caribbean—the "Spanish Lake" as his father called it. His father shuffled paper and scribbled, and all the while talked of treasure, sunken treasure, Spanish treasure . . .

The priest said, "Dust thou art, and to dust thou shalt return." He scooped up a chunk of the hard coral earth and flipped it onto the casket where it cracked and slid off onto the tarp. Rita tossed another clod of dirt onto the casket. The priest led the mourners in a final litany, made the sign of the cross over the casket, bowed his head, and turned away.

The band took up their instruments and played "Taps." A jet roared overhead. The pallbearers milled about, seemingly unsure if their task was complete. As the mourners began to disperse, Rita stood rigidly by the casket, her hands at her sides and her thumbs rubbing against her index fingers, glaring across the grave site at a stocky, fiftyish man talking with a portly older man in a seersucker suit. The top of the stocky man's head was bald and sunburnt, but long blond hair curled over his ears. Though he looked as though he had once been muscular, he had a heavy paunch, and his neck was fleshy above the sweat-drenched collar of his white shirt. The older man held a straw boater in one pudgy hand and kneaded a white handkerchief with his other.

Tim walked off by himself toward a row of stunted palms.

Rita's eyes welled again as she murmured, "Those bastards . . . How could . . . ?"

The two men suddenly stopped speaking as a svelte Hispanic woman in her early thirties approached them. Her black hair was short, and, to Gallagher's eye, the curved line of her oval face was exquisite.

"Oh, terrific. . . . Just f . . . ," Rita mumbled. A black and yellow bee circled above her head as she took a deep breath, gnawed her lower lip, turned, and said, "We need to talk, Jack."

Gallagher nodded but didn't answer. He had been on a training cruise the summer after his junior year at Annapolis when she had married his father. He'd met her twice over the years, and both times he'd found her pleasant enough—but she was the second wife, the woman who had taken his mother's place, and he felt a chasm between them. They had only his father in common, and they had known the man at different times in his life.

"It's Nick's will," she said. "There's stuff you need to know."

4

Late that afternoon, Gallagher walked by the Jalous Trailer Court toward the Key West Bight docks. Tourists browsed at the ramshackle wooden sheds that sold T-shirts and wind chimes and conch shells. The sky had become hazy; the heat and humidity spread palpably along the waterfront. The patchy breeze of earlier in the day had died completely, and he had already sweated through his blue cotton shirt.

Glancing at the sheet of paper on which Rita had written directions, he passed the low-slung white wall of a tavern festooned with fishnets and multicolored wooden buoys. The red and gold Doubloon, Inc., sign hung above the door of the white two-story building just beyond the tavern. He knocked on the door and pushed it open. The odor of cigarette smoke permeated the thirty-by-forty-foot office. A rattling window air conditioner cooled the room only to the mid-eighties, but, compared to the street, the office felt good. In the far corner, Rita sat facing a computer terminal on her desk. A round oak conference table standing on a frayed Oriental rug dominated the center of the room. As he stepped into the office and shut the door, she turned toward him. Reaching for the cigarette burning in the ashtray on her desk, she said, "There you are."

She dragged deeply on the cigarette and exhaled through her nose. "Can I get you anything? Coke? Beer?"

He shook his head, walked over to the table, and ran his hand along the top of one of the six pressed-back wooden chairs spaced around it.

Without taking her eyes off Gallagher, she took another drag from the cigarette, stubbed it out on the lip of the ashtray, and picked up a glass half filled with dark rum and ice. "Have a seat," she said, waving her hand toward the table. Neither of them said anything as she carried her drink over and sat at the opposite side of the table. Her eyes seemed an even deeper blue in the light from the fluorescent lamps overhead. The skin beneath her eyes was puffy. "How're you taking it, Nick's death?" she asked.

He shrugged. "I feel kind of . . . at loose ends," he said, brushing his fingers along the table's polished veneer. His eyes welled, and he rubbed his nose. "Even though he wasn't much a part of my life the last . . . recently . . . there's this deep emptiness I can't explain . . . or shake."

Rita nodded. "Nick still mentioned you. A lot. Followed your career in the service as best he could. Worried over Kosovo and all." She stood quickly, went over to the desk, and brought back the ashtray, a pack of Marlboros, and a gold lighter with a gold coin affixed to it. When she lit a cigarette, her hand trembled.

Before she sat down again, Gallagher said, "Maybe I will have a beer." He watched as she pulled a Dixie from a small refrigerator under a table to the right of her desk. She was still lithe, her figure almost girlish; her auburn hair fell across her shoulders. "How about you?" he asked. "How are you doing?"

She twisted the cap off the bottle and flipped it into the wastebasket. "It was so sudden, the accident and all. So completely . . . unexpected." She handed him the beer, sat down, and took another drag from the cigarette. "I don't know. It's just starting to sink in. I'm just starting to miss him. Deeply." She smiled sadly. "It's rough, Jack. Real rough. And it's only gonna get harder."

They sat silently again for a moment. Listening to the air conditioner, he gazed at his father's collection of books on Christopher Columbus in the glass-fronted bookcases that lined the wall. "But you're back at work right away," he said.

"Yeah," she answered, looking him in the eye. "There's too damn much to do." She pinched the filter of the cigarette and then rolled it between her thumb and forefinger. "It probably looks bad. Sort of, I don't know, disrespectful . . . unfeeling . . . to an outsider. But Nick would've wanted me to. Would've wanted me to keep going."

He glanced at the large beige conch on her desk and then at the swept-hilt rapier, restored and glistening, that hung on the wall above the computer.

"Here's the thing, Jack," she said. "I needed to talk to you right away, today because . . . It's important." She mashed the tip of the cigarette in the ashtray. "Nick left ten percent of the company to you."

"What?" he asked, startled.

She turned the lighter over in her hand, gazed at the coin, and then stared across the table at him. "You own ten percent of Doubloon."

"Why?" It made no sense to him that his father had left a

percentage of the marine salvage operation to him. Their relationship hadn't been close over the last twenty-three years, and he'd never shared his father's dream of sunken treasure.

She shook her head. "Damned if I know. Nick changed his will a couple of months ago. Never told me." Her lower lip quivered for a moment until she began to bite it. "Hell, maybe he thought he owed you something. Does your mother know he's . . . gone?"

"I called." He swigged half the beer. "In her mind, he died a long time ago." He stared across the table at her before taking another drink of beer. "Ten percent of the company?"

She nodded. "Nick had thirty percent, I had twenty, and Tim five. Various board members and stockholders control the rest. He left a third of his shares to each of us—me and Tim and you."

Gallagher finished the beer and tilted the bottle in the light. *What the hell*, he wondered, *was going through the man's mind?*

She stood, walked to the refrigerator, and lifted out another beer. As she twisted the cap, she said, "Look, Jack, I'm no good at beating around the bush." She handed him the beer and, still standing, leaned forward with her hands pressed on the tabletop. "With Nick gone, Doubloon's in deep trouble. We've got over a million in treasure as collateral in a Miami bank, but we're half a million in hock beyond that. Some of the investors have gotten cold feet. Bailed out on us." She picked up her glass and drained the rum. Sliding the glass back onto the table, she added, "But that's not the problem. We've been in over our heads before, and I can handle it." She reached for her cigarettes. "It's the salvage itself." She lit a cigarette and sat down. "The State Office of . . . the god-damned government's trying to shut us down."

Aware that his ten percent could shift control of the company, he took a deep breath and exhaled slowly. "My father didn't owe me anything, Rita," he said. "I left for Annapolis a year before he came down here."

Rita slouched in her chair and looked away for a moment at the bookcases. "Well, you've got the ten percent," she said dryly. "It's yours."

"Okay," he answered. Assuming he knew where the meeting was headed, he added, "And you want to buy it."

"With what?" She laughed bitterly. "I just told you we're 500K in the red."

He thought about his father's death out on the ocean, wondered what it must have been like, that first inhalation of seawater, drowning alone in the utter darkness of a salvage boat's hold.

"The thing is, Jack," she said, "we're so damn close." She leaned forward, rested her elbows on the table, and stared into his eyes again. "So damn close to finding the motherlode. Nick could feel it . . ."

He brushed his hand through his hair. "The motherlode?"

"That's what Nick always called it." She stood, went over to her desk, pulled the drawer open, palmed a gold coin, and brought it back to the table. She held the coin in front of his eyes. "This is the first gold coin Nick found out on the sites this year. He kept it for luck." She slid the coin onto the table. "He didn't have it with him when . . . He left it here in the drawer last Thursday."

Gallagher looked down at the face of the coin. In its center,

a castle stood out on a shield scored with vertical lines. Two
lions faced each other at the foot of the castle. To the left of
the shield was an 'H'; to the right was the Roman numeral
VIII. Two concentric circles of raised dots ringed the coin's
periphery. The words "Dei Gratias" and "Rex" were inscribed
between the circles. He wiped his hand, damp from the condensation on the beer bottle, and picked up the coin. A little
larger than a quarter, it weighed far more. He ran his thumb
over the face and then turned the coin over. The date 1642
stood out at the base of the coin. A double floral border en-
compassed a Jerusalem cross with a castle in each of its quad-
rants. Holding the coin between his forefinger and thumb, he
turned it so that the light reflected from it. *This was my father's
obsession*, he thought, *the thing that uprooted him, yanked him
away from his wife . . . finally cost him his life. Here's the
dream—treasure.* Pulling his eyes from the coin, which seemed
to him as though it were in mint condition, he asked, "A piece
of eight?"

"A doubloon, Jack," she answered, her voice low. "Nick
only found three of 'em, but he was betting there are thousands
more . . ." She waved her hand toward the ocean. ". . . out
there." She picked up her glass, saw that it was empty, and
put it back on the table. "Jack, your father wasn't perfect, God
knows. Our books are, well . . ." She shrugged. "He sometimes
cut corners. The business didn't always run smooth. Things
sometimes got away from us. But he had this . . . gift." She
pointed to the doubloon. "And we're close, damn it. All we
need is a little more time . . ." Her voice trailed off.

They both remained quiet for a moment. He put the coin
on the table; she lit a cigarette from the butt of the one burning

in the ashtray. He looked down at the glinting doubloon, listened to the air conditioner rattle, sipped the Dixie, and then scraped the bottle's label with his thumbnail as he thought about what she'd told him. "I'll hold onto the stock," he said finally. "Not sell it to anyone." Then, still mulling his father's death, he added, "Maybe I'll stay on for a couple of days. See how the operation runs."

She raised her empty glass, gazed into it as though it held some portent, and said, "That's really not necessary, Jack. You don't have to do that."

He looked into her eyes. "Actually, I'd like to," he said. He wasn't sure that he wanted to get involved with his father's obsession, but something had compelled the man to change his will without telling even his wife. He had almost certainly intended it as some sort of signal—a cryptic message cast across the gulf that separated father and son, a gulf now permanent.

"Have you ever done any diving?" she asked.

"A little. In the Mediterranean and the Red Sea."

"Okay," she said. "Visit the salvage sites if you want. But I can't have you hanging around the office. There's too much to do for the frigging state board hearing. I just can't have it. It won't work if you're . . ." She stopped speaking, picked up the doubloon, and stared at it.

The coin's face gleamed in her hand, and he, too, couldn't draw his eyes from it.

5

Just before eight the next morning, Gallagher carried a small duffel toward the Key West Bight dock two hundred yards from the Doubloon, Inc., office. The sky was clear, and despite a strong southeasterly breeze, the day was already stifling. The shops along the wharf were not yet open, but a group of Japanese tourists, all dressed in matching white tennis shoes, white shorts, and bright red short-sleeved shirts, gathered near the catamaran *Stars and Stripes*. Its twin fiberglass hulls were spotless, and both its mainsail and jib were neatly furled. A barefoot young woman stood on the aft deck sorting through fins and snorkels.

Gallagher stopped near the bow of *Intrepid*, one of Doubloon's salvage boats. Rita had arranged for the crew to take him out on what she'd called the "treasure run." He'd wanted to check out his father's business and talk with the people who knew his father best, and this staged adventure, though not at all what he'd had in mind, seemed a necessary first step, a start to his reconnaissance. The steel hull of the forty-six-foot converted tug was painted marine green, and the cabin, bridge, and superstructure were beige. The wheelhouse's six sliding windows were open, and aerials and electronic gear protruded along its signal mast. One of the pallbearers, a burly fifty-year-old black man whose hair was flecked with gray, stepped out of the wheelhouse and placed his huge hands on the railing. His thick torso loomed against the expanse of pale sky behind him. "*Buenos días, amigo*," he shouted to Gallagher, raising his hand to wave him aboard. As Gallagher hopped the boat's gunwale near the stern, the man descended the ship's ladder at the back of the wheelhouse. He extended his hand, which seemed the size of a toilet seat, and clapped Gallagher on the shoulder.

"Jack, I am Ozzie Millan," he said with a pronounced Cuban accent, "one of your father's oldest compadres in the Keys." His smile revealed a gold upper front tooth.

"Nice to meet you, Ozzie," Gallagher answered.

"Nick . . ." Millan began, but his eyes clouded and he looked out toward the ocean. After a moment, he shrugged, hammered on the bulkhead, and shouted, "Dewey, we got us a Doubloon stockholder aboard." His tone was more upbeat, as though he was trying to put behind him whatever he'd been about to say.

The guitarist stuck his head out of the cabin's hatch and nodded to Gallagher. He wore cutoff jeans and no shirt; he was wiry and darkly tanned. His prominent nose was framed by black sideburns that extended to the bottoms of his ears. The gold earring Gallagher had noticed at the funeral was a coin about half as large as the doubloon Rita had shown him.

The three men met on the stern deck. The black steel braces of the stern lifting rig crisscrossed above them. Behind them, two huge rusted red tubes, bent at ninety-degree angles, jutted out over the stern beyond the lifting rig. The boat was old and jury-rigged to perform tasks for which it had not been designed, but it was carefully maintained. Every line was coiled, each piece of equipment in its place.

"Jack Gallagher," Millan said, "this is Dewey Thibodeaux, our mapper. A Cajun from South Louisiana, and Doubloon's luckiest diver."

As Thibodeaux shook Gallagher's hand, he said, "Where y'at?" When he withdrew his hand, he added, "I hear we're gonna take ya out for a little treasure huntin' today." His tone was cool, and his accent, a gumbo of Southern drawl and South Bronx, reminded Gallagher of some of the hawkers he had heard during lost weekends in New Orleans's French Quarter early in his naval career.

"We'll push off in ten minutes or so," Millan said to Gallagher.

Looking past Gallagher along the dock, Thibodeaux muttered, "Oh, shee-it." Then, taking Gallagher's duffel bag, he said, "I'll stow dis for ya," and slipped through the hatchway into the cabin.

The Hispanic woman Gallagher had seen accost the two men at the cemetery sauntered along the pier toward *Intrepid*. When she reached the boat's bow, she squinted at Millan and said, "*Buenos días*, Ozzie, *Qué pasa?*"

"Struggling, Señorita," Millan answered. "But getting by." He smiled at her, his gold tooth shining. "Always getting by."

The woman smiled at Gallagher, brushed her hair back from her eyes, and asked Millan, "Is Dewey aboard? I thought I saw him a minute ago." Her perfect English held no hint of an accent.

"He's aboard, Señorita," Millan answered. "But he's busy." Millan turned to climb the ship's ladder to the wheelhouse.

"I've got some questions I need to ask him," the woman said.

Millan tugged at his earlobe. Cocking his head, he said, "The engine's been running bad, and he's probably up to his elbows in grease."

"Ozzie," she said, rubbing her index finger along the edge of her notebook, "he needs to talk to me. I've got a copy of the marine investigator's preliminary report on *Sea Devil*. He's got to comment on the report. It'll look a lot worse if he doesn't."

Millan ran his tongue over his gold tooth.

"Get him for me, okay, Ozzie?" she said.

As Millan ambled over to the hatchway and disappeared, the woman turned toward Gallagher, extended her right hand, and said, "You must be Nick's son, Jack." Her dark eyes gleamed.

He shook her hand. "And you are?"

"María José Hernández." She let go of his hand. "Josie, to my friends. I'm a reporter for the *Key West Tribune*." She smiled again. "You're staying on in town?" The wide sleeves of her loose white blouse luffed in the wind, the fabric pressing across her breasts.

"Just for a couple of days," he answered.

She nodded toward the boat's cabin. "You heading out?"

He wondered what Millan and Thibodeaux were doing. "Yep. The grand tour of the Keys." A gull circled and landed on a pylon near *Intrepid*'s stern. Feeling somehow as though he shouldn't say anything more, Gallagher laughed and added, "You know, taking in the sights as long as I'm down here."

Pulling a black pen from her shoulder bag, she said, "You and I should have a talk before you leave town."

"What . . . what do you mean?" he asked, taken aback.

She glanced out at the open water and then looked at him. "Something's rotten here in paradise, Jack Gallagher," she said, "and your tour guides keep acting like everything's fine."

"Something's . . . ," he began, ". . . you mean, with my father?"

Millan poked his head out of the hatchway and said, "Dewey's slopping around in engine oil, Señorita. Can you come back in a half hour?"

Hernández glanced at her diver's watch, gazed at Millan for a moment, and then smiled ironically at the captain. "*Sí, sí*," she said. "But tell Dewey it's his loss. He'd be better off if he'd gone on record. The *Trib* is running the story tomorrow, and blowing me off won't do him any good." She turned toward Gallagher. "What are the odds," she asked him, "of this tub still being here in half an hour?" Her smile softened. "Nice to meet you, Jack Gallagher," she added. "Like I said, let's have a chat sometime."

As she turned to leave, he nodded and answered, "Yeah. Good idea, Ms. Hernández."

She glanced back over her shoulder and smiled again. "Josie," she said, and then strolled off along the pier.

When she was about fifty feet away, Thibodeaux stepped out of the hatch. He was sweating profusely, but his hands and arms showed no signs of engine oil. As all three men watched her sensual gait, Thibodeaux said, "Nice ass on dat li'l darlin', podna. But I'm tellin' ya, Josie's fuckin' poison. Pure fuckin' poison, dat one."

Without making any comment, Millan climbed the ladder to the wheelhouse.

"What was that all about?" Gallagher asked Thibodeaux.

As Thibodeaux shook his head, the small gold coin danced at the base of his ear. "She's got dis t'ing about Nick's deat'. And dat stuff she's been writin', it's total shit, I'm tellin' ya."

"What?"

"She t'inks it wasn't no fuckin' accident."

Gallagher stared into the diver's eyes. "What the hell does that mean?"

Thibodeaux looked away, scratched his sideburn, and then flicked his earring. "I was on *Sea Devil* wit' Nick when she sank, ya know dat." He snapped his fingers. "She turned turtle like dat, I'm tellin' ya. If I wasn't sleepin' out on de deck, I'da never . . ." He held up his arms, showing Gallagher the cuts and bruises. "After she flipped, I had ta climb de fuckin' barnacles on de hull."

Millan fired *Intrepid*'s engines, and the gull on the pylon flapped away.

Thibodeaux looked up at Millan on the bridge, nodded, and raised his thumb. "De t'ing is, I just can't fuckin' talk about it yet, podna," he said to Gallagher, "Not wit' her or nobody. But Josie, she keeps harassin' me." He began to scuttle forward to cast off the bowlines. "She just won't fuckin' let up."

Gallagher stood by the gunwale, Thibodeaux's words echoing in his mind. The gull glided off, a dark fading dot in the sky. Gallagher stared at Thibodeaux on the bow and then caught sight of Hernández for a moment among the tourists near *Stars and Stripes*.

6

On the ride out toward the Marquesas Keys, Gallagher spent part of the time sitting alone on the tug's bow squinting at the shimmering water and wondering about both Hernández's and Thibodeaux's statements. At one point, he saw a pair of sea turtles, and another time he thought he glimpsed a stingray rising from the sand. When it became too hot in the sun, he retreated to the stern, where a tarp Thibodeaux had stretched over the lifting rig's braces provided shade but only scant relief from the heat. Sitting on a fifteen-gallon cooler listening to the engines rumble, he concluded that, as an outsider, he'd likely learn little if he confronted the others about what had happened to his father. He'd have to bide his time, wait for his moment.

Fifty-five miles due west of Key West, Millan swung *Intrepid* around a series of coral reefs shaped like crooked claws, and Thibodeaux used the bow winch to drop the starboard anchor near a red buoy in the water. Like fists thrust in the air, cumulus clouds climbed the western sky toward the sun. Millan raised the red and white dive flag and then flipped the dive ladder over the port side and dropped a weighted nylon line. Thibodeaux dipped the dive harnesses into the sea and strapped them on the tanks. "Dere's not'in' ta worry about," he said to Gallagher as though he were a guide who'd led this particular tour too often. "We're only goin' ta be down eighteen ta twenty feet." He set the regulators on the tanks. "Ya really only gotta remember one t'ing."

"What's that?" Gallagher asked.

"Breat'e."

Gallagher laughed. "That much, I can remember."

"As long as ya breat'e, dere's not'in' else ta it, podna," Thibodeaux said as he tested each regulator's second stage, letting the air hiss out for a moment. "Your buoyancy'll be pretty much neutral."

"You're diving on a site we worked last summer," Millan said, helping Gallagher pull on the harness and tank. "Found a dozen cannon and so many silver coins we nicknamed the spot *Banco de Havana*. Most of the cannon are still down there because our lab's only got space to clean one at a time."

Gallagher put the regulator's second stage into his mouth and sucked the dry compressed air for a second.

"De site's been worked over pretty good, and storms've shifted de sand," Thibodeaux said, "but we could still find a oreo or two around de cannon."

Before Gallagher could ask, Millan said, "Pieces of eight, amigo. Silver coins encrusted with sulfide. They look like chocolate cookies." He tapped his temple with his forefinger. "The divers are all loco." Yanking at Gallagher's harness, he added, "You're all set."

Thibodeaux spat in his mask and, after he rubbed the saliva around, reviewed the basic hand signals with Gallagher. Then he said, "Ta equalize on de way down, pop your ears. Once we're on de bottom, just stick close ta me."

Gallagher tried to spit in his mask, but his mouth was dry. He felt a little of the excitement and nervousness he had felt whenever he had climbed into the cockpit of a plane he hadn't flown before.

Before pulling on his mask, Thibodeaux took off his earring. "Barry may still be around down dere," he said as he handed the earring to Millan. Thibodeaux then slipped on his fins, tested his regulator again, adjusted his mask, and made a circle of his index finger and thumb. Standing on the deck where the gunwale had been cut down to form a narrow dive platform, he held onto his mask, took a long scissors step outward, and slid gracefully into the water.

Gallagher glanced at Millan and burst out laughing.

"*Adiós, amigo*," Millan said as he waved his hand toward the ocean.

Gallagher stepped to the dive platform and clenched the regulator's rubber mouthpiece between his teeth.

"Go on, amigo," Millan said.

Gallagher held onto his mask, tucked his head, took a long stride forward, and found himself doing a shoulder roll beneath the waves. He glanced at the light glistening above, righted himself, and began to sink slowly. It was quiet except for the sound of his own breathing. Thibodeaux's air bubbles expanded like chrome mushrooms as they rose past him. Holding his nose and blowing out to clear his ears, he looked down at the diver hovering below.

When Gallagher reached the sandy bottom, Thibodeaux pointed to some cylindrical shadows sixty feet away. Farther east, coral heads rose like dark, distant ridges. Thibodeaux checked his compass and motioned for Gallagher to follow.

Gallagher popped his ears a second time, slowed his breathing, and, as he began to swim, tested his buoyancy. He had to kick only a little to keep from sinking. Light reflected from the motes floating in the water, and off to his left a school of small fish swirled like a silver cloud.

The cannons, long, green-black, and covered with algae, looked like sections of discarded sewer pipe. A four-and-a-half-foot barracuda, all mouth and muscle, circled above the cannons. When Gallagher pointed to the fish, Thibodeaux nodded and swam over to a cannon that lay tilted across another cannon. *This must be Barry*, Gallagher thought as he stared at the barracuda's sleek silver body and flat round eye.

After taking his dive knife from the plastic sheath strapped to his calf, Thibodeaux waved Gallagher closer. The diver scraped a spot near the cannon's reinforcing ring and wiped it with his hand. Gallagher peered at the ornately rendered image of two dolphins rising from the sea. Thibodeaux sheathed his knife, swam forward to the cannon's muzzle, and fanned the sand, which rose like fine dust.

Gallagher mimicked the diver's actions, and they worked their way along the base of the lower cannon and then away from both cannons. As Gallagher got into the rhythm of the work, the barracuda became simply a natural part of the place. Time receded, and the events of the previous few days—the news of his father's death, the hurried flight to Key West, the funeral, the conversation with Rita, the encounter with the reporter, and Thibodeaux's revelation—all seemed to fade, leaving him floating in this tranquil world admiring the small aquatic sand devils he was creating.

Suddenly, Thibodeaux was tapping his knife's haft against

his tank and gesturing to Gallagher. In his other hand, the diver held a flat black object. Gallagher breathed more rapidly as he moved closer and fanned the sand. Less than a minute later, Gallagher uncovered a black disk. He turned it over in his hand and then held it up toward the diffused light. The coin did, in fact, look far more like a cookie than a piece of silver.

When they had discovered three more coins, Thibodeaux checked his gauge and watch and compass and then pointed back at the dive line, a vertical filament hanging in the distance. Clutching three of the oreos in his left hand, Gallagher followed Thibodeaux's fins toward the line. As he swam, a bright splinter caught his eye. He turned and waved his right hand over the sand. Beneath the swirl of sand lay a small, tangled, red and gold heap. He lifted it from the sand, realizing only as its beads slid between his fingers that he was staring at a finely wrought rosary. The gold crucifix, although only an inch in length, held an ornately detailed image of the dying Christ. Only a few of the red coral beads on the rosary's intricately worked chain were encrusted with sand and shells. His trembling hand caused the gold to coruscate. For a moment, he forgot to breathe.

7

The next thing Gallagher knew he was standing at *Intrepid*'s stern holding the rosary, the dive equipment strewn on the deck around him. His skin prickled, and everything seemed to be happening in slow motion.

"I been over dat spot a hundred times," Thibodeaux said, shaking his head. "But dat's de t'ing about treasure." He glanced at Millan. "Ya just never fuckin' know. D'ya, Ozzie?"

Millan nodded. He stood quietly staring at the rosary until Gallagher handed it to him. "*Diós mio*," he whispered. The beads were tiny and bright in his hand. "Some hombre drowned with this. And nobody's touched it for more than three hundred and fifty years." He passed the rosary back to Gallagher. "You are Nick's son," he said smiling, his tooth gleaming. "Definitely Nick's son."

While Gallagher showered off the saltwater and Thibodeaux stowed the dive equipment, Millan radioed news of Gallagher's discovery to Key West. As the sun slipped behind the western cloud bank, *Sea Rover*, Doubloon, Inc.'s other remaining salvage boat, arrived at the dive site. A Mississippi tug six feet shorter than *Intrepid* and even older, *Sea Rover* was a less tightly run boat. Lines lay about on the deck, and fins and masks and snorkels were piled haphazardly against the bulkhead. As Tim Gallagher shut down the engines and climbed down from the wheelhouse, his two divers tied off *Sea Rover* and set bumpers between the two boats. One of the divers was lanky, with long brown hair, and the other was stocky, with tattoos on his biceps and forearms. As the divers boarded *Intrepid*, they held aloft fresh spiny lobsters.

Passing a round of Dixies to the newcomers, Thibodeaux shouted, "Hot damn, de boys've been bug huntin'!" He turned to Gallagher and pointed at the lobsters. "Dat's good eatin', dere, I'm tellin' ya."

Tim and the two divers huddled around Gallagher admiring the rosary. Gallagher still felt an odd euphoria that he had not experienced since he had flown sorties in the Balkans. Tim ran his fingers through his long, stringy hair, glanced back and forth between the crucifix and Gallagher's face, and repeated, "Fuckin' A. Holy fuckin' A!"

Millan picked up the tub of lobsters and motioned for Gallagher, who still held the rosary, to follow him. "Lend me a hand, amigo," he said as they entered the galley, a narrow cabin with a stove, refrigerator, sink, and butcherblock counter against one bulkhead and a small table and cabinets and storage bins along the other. Millan placed the tub on the counter, glanced at the lobsters, and said to Gallagher, "Ah, *langosta*, amigo. Dinner tonight will be *muy grande*." Millan wiped the sweat from his face and neck with a paper towel, took a bottle of dark Tortuga rum from a cabinet, and poured each of them two fingers over ice. He then took a small blue airtight plastic container from another cabinet, dipped it into the seawater in the tub, and said, "Give me the rosary, amigo."

Gallagher rubbed his forefinger lightly over the crucifix and handed him the rosary.

As Millan slipped it into the plastic container, he said, "The water's better for it than the air until it gets to the lab." He sealed the plastic lid, wiped the container, took down a half-filled can of flour, buried the plastic container in it, and set the can up high in the cabinet. "And it'll be safe up here," he added. He passed one glass to Gallagher and raised his own in toast. "To treasure," he said, "to *tesoro* and to *la mar*, who gives up some of her secrets to us." He swigged the rum and then ran his tongue over his gold tooth. "But only some of her secrets, amigo. Only some."

"What do you mean?" Gallagher asked. "Are you talking . . . my father's . . . ?"

Millan set his glass on the counter and took a deep breath. "No, Jack," he said. "A long time ago I gave up asking why somebody dies." He shrugged. "Something like what happened to Nick, there is no why. Asking why helps nobody and nothing."

"What then?" Gallagher persisted.

"I was only thinking of you and that rosary." Millan stared into his glass on the counter. "When you think you've got the best of *la mar*, you can be sure you are wrong. It's something Nick understood." He smiled sadly to himself. "The more you get to know her, the more there is to know. That's all I meant, amigo." He lifted his glass again and waited until Gallagher raised his as well. "And now, Jack," he added, "we've got work to do."

Millan stunned the lobsters with the wooden handle of his

knife, split their shells, and took the meat from their tails. While he set a pot of black beans to simmer on the stove's back burner, Gallagher squeezed limes over the lobster meat and then sliced the meat into large chunks.

When calls from the stern interrupted their work, Gallagher stepped from the hatchway. Thibodeaux and the two divers were facing west where the sun, the color of blood, was slipping below the cloud bank. Tim, who stood off to one side, also faced west. Rills of red and pink light permeated the underbelly of the clouds, and a deeper red spread across the water. Millan leaned against the railing near Gallagher, and the younger men fell silent as the sun dipped into the water. Just as the sun disappeared, its corona flashed green. Thibodeaux and the two divers thrust their beer bottles above their heads and hooted, but Tim remained silent.

Back in the galley, Millan poured cooking oil into a large black skillet. He then finished his rum and refilled both of their glasses. While they waited for the oil to heat, he said, "I've known Nick since the beginning, Jack, since just after he came to the Keys." He took a long sip of rum and swiped his mouth with the back of his hand. "There was good times and bad. But no matter what, there was always *la mar*, the water and the sun and the stars." He dropped garlic cloves into the pan and shook it to douse them with the hot oil. "There was money and no money, treasure and no treasure, but *la mar*, she was always there." He scooped up a handful of the lobster meat and spread it in the skillet where the oil was sizzling. "That's what you really got to know, amigo."

Gallagher nodded, but he wasn't sure he understood. He'd spent more than a fourth of his adult life at sea, but aboard

aircraft carriers—mammoth floating cities with airports on top.
He hadn't often, he realized, been as close to the water as he
had been all that day.

After dinner, Thibodeaux got out his guitar, and, sitting
against the stern bulkhead near the ship's ladder, began to
play songs and parts of songs that flowed into each other. He
sang Cajun and Zydeco songs in French, Caribbean tunes in
patois and pidgin English, and country rock in his Creole accent. The streak in his hair was pale in the dying light. Thibodeaux and the two divers shared a joint; Tim swigged his
beer and listened to Thibodeaux's songs and the divers' me-
andering stories about their Key West exploits. Millan cleaned
up the galley and then climbed to the wheelhouse.

The divers began to talk about diving for Nick Gallagher
and Doubloon, Inc. Their stories, rambling and desultory, became bittersweet. Isolated from the others by his memories,
Tim didn't speak at all. Gallagher listened to the stories and
the guitar for a while and then, when the gray emptiness he'd
felt at the funeral started to close in on him, wandered up to
Intrepid's bow, where he sat on a hatch cover behind the anchor winch. He was cooler there in the light breeze, which
carried away the music and the divers' voices. The sky had
become clear again except for wisps of high clouds that caused
the stars to wink. The stars and the boat's red and green bow
lights cast shimmering shadows across the water.

After a few minutes, Tim came forward and leaned against
the bulkhead. He had his hands in the pockets of his cutoffs,

and his red hair stuck out from beneath his Miami Hurricanes cap.

"Man, finding that rosary is something, Jack," he said. His tone, though friendly, was tinged with jealousy. "You got the golden touch. Just like Dad."

Unsure how to answer, Gallagher gazed at the stars. He'd been about Tim's age when he'd learned that his father had deserted his mother. And, although they shared that father, he wondered how their upbringings—on an Iowa farm and on a South Florida salvage boat—could have been more different. Tim, he knew, had never gone to college, had probably never left the Keys except to work on the boats.

After a few moments, Tim sat down on the deck facing Gallagher. Tim was barefoot, and his feet were callused and scarred. His eyes were bloodshot, the acne scars purple. "When I was nine," he said, his speech halting and his voice almost cracking, "for my birthday, Dad gave me a mitt. It was great, a Steve Carlton." He picked at a callus on his heel for a moment. "I was pretty tall and a lefty, so I was a pitcher. Dad was gone a lot, but when he wasn't away or on a boat he'd play catch with me. We didn't have much of a yard so we played in the street under the trees. He had this old catcher's mitt . . ." He rubbed his nose with the back of his hand. "D'you know the mitt I mean?"

"Yeah, Tim, I do," Gallagher answered. He remembered the mitt and pitching to his father after the evening chores were finished. Football had been his sport, and being fast enough to play flanker had probably, he knew, gotten him into Annapolis. But his father, who had always loved baseball, had taken him every summer to Wrigley Field in Chicago for a Cubs game. "The annual pilgrimage to the Friendly Confines," his father had called it. And his father had pounded that catcher's mitt and thrown the ball back hard.

"Well," Tim said, "I used to think, you know, that I had this older brother who was away in the navy. I mean, who was a fuckin' fighter pilot and all . . ." He stopped speaking and began to gnaw at his lip like his mother had. "But, you know, you weren't . . . I only met you one time before Dad's . . . before yesterday." He leaned over and tugged at the spring line set between *Intrepid* and *Sea Rover*. "I felt like Dad . . . I don't know . . . was sorta comparing me. He never said so . . ." His voice cracked again and grew strident, as though he wanted to remain amicable but wasn't quite able to. "But he talked about how you'd played football at Navy. Flown fuckin' F-18s." He shook his head. "And now Dad's, uh, gone. And you show up. And on your first day, on your first fuckin' dive, you find that rosary. I mean, it's the day after the funeral, and I'm back workin'. Just like Dad woulda wanted. Captain of my own boat. In charge of the divers. Workin' the sites he'd been arguin' for at . . . What the hell am I supposed . . ." As he stood up, his knee joints cracked. "Shit, I don't know what I mean." He gazed up at the sky where a sliver of moon hung below an impossibly bright Venus. Waving his hand toward the stern, he said, his voice softening, "I'm gonna get a brew. You want one?"

"Maybe later," Gallagher answered. "But thanks anyway, Tim."

"Yeah, okay," Tim said.

As Tim started to turn away, Gallagher asked, "What do you think about Dad's death?"

Tim's eyes began to tear as they had during the ride to the cemetery. "I feel like there's somethin' I shoulda done . . . even though I know there wasn't nothin' anybody could do."

"You're sure about that?" Gallagher asked.

Tim looked down at him. "What d'ya mean?"

"I don't know. I've been hearing stuff." Gallagher shook his head. "You sure it was an accident?"

"What? You mean, that crap in the *Trib*?" Tim removed his cap, ran his hand through his hair, and put the cap back on. "Dad's bein' gone is awful, Jack," he said. "I feel like I've been kicked in the balls and the stomach both. But Mom and me, at least we know it just happened. Nobody did it." He exhaled and bit his lip. "Shit happens. Specially on boats." He tapped the bulkhead with the side of his bare foot. "Old fuckin' boats, with lots of equipment that's used way harder than it's supposed to. Dad . . ." He rubbed his eye with the back of his hand. "I dunno. I guess Dad was just in the wrong place . . ." His voice became a whisper. ". . . at the wrong time."

Gallagher nodded, and Tim stuck his hands in his back pockets, took a deep breath, and looked out over the dark, shining water.

8

As *Intrepid* approached Key West late the next morning, the sky was clear, and it was less muggy than it had been the previous two days. *Sea Rover* had cast off just before midnight so that Tim's divers could be back in the water early at the site they were working. Thibodeaux had offered Gallagher a bunk in the forward cabin, but Gallagher, preferring the open air and night sky, had taken an air mattress out to the stern deck. He had dozed off with *Intrepid*'s rocking and the hum of the bilge pump, but he had slept fitfully. Years before, he had set his life on a clear and stable course, and everything that had occurred since he had heard about his father's death seemed to be pointing him off that course. Tim's talking with him, telling him about playing catch with their father, had further opened a mental hatch, and his mind had flooded with images—of his father riding the tractor in the cornfields as Gallagher waited for the schoolbus in the gathering light; of his father pulling up in the family's red pickup and standing on the sidelines watching football drills, his face chafed and sweating and his thick arms folded across his chest; of his father hunched late at night in his wingback chair poring over Samuel Eliot Morison's biography of Columbus.

At dawn, Millan had started *Intrepid*'s engines and, wearing only baggy blue shorts, hoisted the anchor. A gnarled scar the size of a fist had shown on his belly even in the scant light. Now, both Millan and Thibodeaux were in the wheelhouse. Millan steered the boat as Thibodeaux shouted into the marine radio telephone. Gallagher stood on deck gazing at the island, where radio towers jutted into the sky to the right of the white expanse of hotels and condos on the waterfront. Along the Bight, the rusted lookout tower rose above the turtle kraals, the fat civil defense blimp hovered above the naval dock, and the red and white smokestacks rose over the monolithic pink stone power station.

Thibodeaux left the wheelhouse and slid down to the deck on the railing of the ship's ladder. "More fuckin' trouble, podna," he said as he set a bumper off *Intrepid*'s starboard gunwale.

"What?" Gallagher asked.

"De *Trib* published Josie's story dis morning. Front page." He slipped a half-hitch on the bumper's line and pulled it taut. "Saying again dat Nick's accident was no fuckin' accident." He turned and punched the side of the compressor with his fist. "And dis time practically accusin' me a offin' de guy."

Gallagher stared at the diver. Although a half-dozen questions ran through his mind, he said, "She tried to talk to you yesterday."

Thibodeaux didn't answer.

"What's going on, Dewey?" Gallagher asked.

Thibodeaux stared at him but still did not answer. His knuckles bleeding, he stooped over the stern cleat and unwound a length of line.

Gallagher said, "I'm going to read it in a few minutes, Dewey."

Thibodeaux let go of the line and glanced toward the waterfront and then out to sea. He raked his fingers through the unruly white streak in his hair, spotting it with red. His shoulders slumped as he exhaled. "I'm tellin' ya, I still don't know what de fuck happened. I've tried ta figure it out, but . . ." He shook his head. "*Sea Devil* was my boat, podna. I was de captain. And I almost died, too, when she flipped, ya know dat." He picked up the stern line again. "Only me and Nick was aboard."

"Just the two of you?" Gallagher asked. "Is that normal?" He looked over at the navy's hydrofoil moored at the Trumbo Point dock. A jet skier in a bright pink life vest whipped spin-turns just outside the pale granite seawall.

"Yeah, just de two a us. And, no, it ain't normal. Dere'd been dis heavy fuckin' meetin' on board dat afternoon. Ozzie'd already took de divers inta town for some R and R." He cocked his head and yanked at the loop in the line. "And Tim took all de honchos back on *Sea Rover* after de meetin'. Nick, he was supposed ta go, too, but he decided ta stay aboard for de night." He paused for a moment. "Ozzie was gonna bring de divers back in de mornin'."

As *Intrepid* approached the cut in the outer seawall, squawking gulls circled the salvage boat. Both Thibodeaux and Gallagher glanced at them.

"Dey t'ink we're a fuckin' fishin' boat," Thibodeaux said.

"So you and Nick were the only ones aboard *Sea Devil* after the meeting?" Gallagher asked.

"Yeah. T'ings didn't go too good at de meetin'. Dere was

some shit about which a de dive sites ta work. And I t'ink dat Nick, he just wanted ta get away from all de land sharks for a while. Me and him talked for a long time after dinner. Ya know, about de dives we'd done over de years, de treasure we'd found. Den, I sacked out on deck." He waved at the bulkhead. "I can sleep anywhere. Like a fuckin' log. De divers, dey rag me about it all de time, I'm tellin' ya." He fiddled with his earring. "Nick, he was still out on deck, like he wanted ta talk ta de ocean or somet'ing. Nick was like dat wit' de ocean, podna. It was like he knew somet'ing dat none a de resta us would ever get, I'm tellin' ya. I got no fuckin' idea what time he went below. But way after midnight."

Thibodeaux stopped speaking for a moment. His hands worked back and forth on the line. "I woke up in de water when *Sea Devil* turned turtle." He wiped his knuckles on his T-shirt and then fingered a scab at the base of the white streak in his hair. "I musta hit my head on de gunwale or somet'ing. It was gettin light out, but I didn't know what de fuck was goin' on. Or even where de fuck I was. Almost got sucked under myself. All kinds a shit from de deck was floatin' around."

"And what makes Hernández think it wasn't an accident?" Gallagher asked.

Thibodeaux stared at him. "Dat report. De fuckin' marine investigation report." The gulls swooped low over the stern and rose again in a flurry of gray and white wings. "De water supposedly ran in t'rough de head's intake valve. De housing had tore free, and dere was no way ta shut it off. And de bilge pump was froze, too." He kicked *Intrepid*'s gunwale. "*Sea Devil* was old. Almost ten fuckin' years older dan dis tub. And maybe t'ings didn't always work right." He looked into Gallagher's eyes. "But dere's no fuckin' way dat intake valve coulda blown out like dat . . . all by itself," he said.

The back of Gallagher's neck bristled. He wasn't exactly sure what Thibodeaux was saying, but the muscles in his stomach were tightening. "What do you mean?" he asked.

"I mean dat I fixed dat valve myself a mont' ago. Less dan a mont' ago. It was fuckin' watertight, I'm tellin' ya. And de pump freezin' up at de same time. I mean, it could happen, but it's like lightnin' strikin' de same spot. Somebody musta been dickin' wit' 'em."

Two pelicans stood like sentinels on the granite blocks as Millan guided *Intrepid* through the cut between the breakwall and the naval docks. Gallagher rolled his neck to relieve the tension, exhaled slowly, and asked, "Who?"

"How de hell do I know? I'm tellin' ya, mosta de fuckin' company was on board at one time or anot'er dat day. Board members, stockholders, divers, even Braxton Finch and Rita. Nick, he wanted dat meetin' on board de boats so dat everybody could check out what de fuck was goin' down. Dey had ta actually see what it fuckin' took to work two sites at de same time, ya know dat."

"Okay," Gallagher said. "Okay." He leaned forward with both of his hands flat against the top of the compressor. "Did you hear my father at all?" he asked. "At any time?"

Thibodeaux turned and looked out at the ocean. A coast guard whaler passed *Intrepid*, and the two crew members waved to Millan in the wheelhouse.

"You never saw or heard my father after the boat flipped?" Gallagher asked, trying to keep his voice even.

"I don't know, Jack. I t'ink I mighta heard Nick once. When I was climbin' de fuckin' hull. Dere was dis poundin' below me. Like where de engine room'd be. I t'ink dere mighta been, anyway."

Gallagher sat down on the ice chest and rubbed the palms of his hands together.

"I tried ta get him, Jack. I did. But dere was not'in' I could do. I was too outa it. I couldn't hold my breat' for shit. *Sea Devil* sank in less dan five minutes. I held onta a cushion 'til Ozzie found me. I was scared. I was bleedin' from de barnacles, and all I could t'ink about was fuckin' sharks. When Ozzie brought me . . ." Glancing over at the dock that *Intrepid* was approaching, he muttered, "Jesus fuckin' Christ."

The stocky man Gallagher had seen talking in the cemetery leaned against a piling. His arms crossed and his head cocked, he stared out at *Intrepid*.

Gallagher looked back at the cuts and scrapes on Thibodeaux's arms and asked, "So my father must've been down in the hold trying to fix the problem when the boat capsized?"

"I guess." Thibodeaux tugged at his earring. "Yeah. Right. He musta been."

"Why didn't he get you to help him, Dewey?"

"I don't know. Maybe he t'ought it wasn't dat bad."

Gallagher stared up at the diver.

Thibodeaux shrugged uneasily. "Look, Jack, I tole ya everyt'ing I remember. Like I said, I woke up in de fuckin' water, almost drownin' myself, I'm tellin' ya." He exhaled and looked up into the wide pale sky above Key West. "When de coast guard divers pulled Nick's body out de next day, he was all tangled in lines. And de side a his head was cut. He musta banged his head on de engine or de bulkhead or a empty air tank. I don't know."

"But you're positive you fixed that valve? That it was working before the meeting?"

"Abso-fuckin'-lutely. Dat's somet'ing I'm sure a." Thibodeaux's voice was harsh for the first time. "Like I told ya, somebody musta fucked wit' it. And wit' de bilge pump. Dey may notta planned ta kill Nick, but dey sure as hell wanted ta sink my boat."

9

While Millan shut down *Intrepid*'s engines and Thibodeaux tied off the spring lines, Gallagher, preoccupied by what Thibodeaux had just told him, took the blue plastic container from the flour can, rinsed it off, and brought it out onto the deck. The stocky man sidled toward *Intrepid*'s stern. His hands stuffed in his pockets, he said to Gallagher, "Hey, flyboy, whatcha got there?" His tone was contentious, his voice harsh and raspy as though his vocal cords were damaged.

Gallagher gazed at the man and asked, "Do I know you?"

"Name's Vogel, Pete Vogel," the man said. He stepped on the gunwale and dropped to the deck a foot from Gallagher. "Maybe Nick mentioned me to ya." His face was leathery, a long scar wound above his left eyebrow, and he smelled of bourbon. His wrinkled shirt was open except for the bottom three buttons, and the diamonds studding the pointed gold cross that hung on a gold chain around his neck gleamed in the sunlight. His faded baggy denims, belted tight under his overhanging paunch, were rolled up at his ankles.

"No, Pete," Gallagher answered, "but I didn't talk to my father much."

Millan peered out of the wheelhouse. Thibodeaux, who

stood on the bow, shouted, "Hey, Pete, dere's no way ya . . . Get de fuck outa here, I'm tellin' ya."

Vogel ignored Thibodeaux. "Yeah, I know you didn't talk to Nick much," he said to Gallagher. "But he talked about you." He cleared his throat and spat into the water.

Gallagher stared at the man. Vogel's light blue eyes were bloodshot, and the skin under his eyes was dark and swollen.

"Me and him was partners," Vogel said. "Had a falling-out. A misunderstanding. And a douche-bag judge fucked me over." He pulled his right hand from his pocket and tapped Gallagher on the chest with his forefinger. His ring and little fingers, truncated above the knuckles, were stumps less than an inch long. "But I'm still gonna get what's mine."

Gallagher pushed Vogel's hand away, squared his shoulders, and said, "I don't know who you are, Pete, or what the hell you're talking about. So, if you'll excuse me . . ." He brushed by Vogel and hopped onto the dock.

Spinning around, Vogel yelled, "Hey, flyboy." He wiped the back of his maimed hand across his mouth, cocked his head, and nodded at the container. "Whatever you brought up, I got a right to a piece of it."

Gallagher shook his head, turned, and left Vogel standing on *Intrepid*'s deck. "Ozzie," he shouted up to the wheelhouse, "I'll meet you in the office." He strode along the finger pier without looking back until he reached the wharf. When he turned, Vogel still slouched on the salvage boat's deck glowering at him. Squinting, Gallagher scanned the rest of the area. The tourist boats hadn't returned from their morning runs, but two piers to the right of *Intrepid*'s mooring, the elderly Hispanic man who'd shared his pew at the funeral stood in the cockpit of *Maestro III*, a sleek forty-foot Sea Ray express cruiser. Framed by the cruiser's swept-back radar arch, the man looked incongruous in his white dress shirt and dark slacks. He lowered the binoculars he had been using, picked up a drink, and gazed across the water and docks as though he owned the Bight.

When Gallagher entered the Doubloon, Inc., office, Rita sat at the conference table flanked by two of his father's pallbearers. The older man, heavyset, with thick white hair, was saying in a resonant voice, "And I'm telling you, we have no case. There's no preponderance of evidence. Hell, all we've got is Dewey's word—and we all know what that's worth. The police . . ." He paused, tapping the ash of his cigar into a silver ashtray and turning to gaze at Gallagher. The second man, tall and lean and fit, had been spinning a gold pen between his thumb and index finger as he listened. A little younger than Gallagher, he had shaggy brown hair and a neatly trimmed beard that was blond and red as well as brown. A blue cloud of smoke hovered above three copies of the *Key West Tribune* lying in the middle of the table.

"This must be Jack Gallagher," the older man said, "safely returned from the wind and sea and stars." He heaved his bulk from the chair and shook Gallagher's hand. "I'm Braxton Finch, Doubloon's attorney. Welcome aboard." His large gold bishop's ring, set with a twenty-five-karat octagonal emerald, glinted in the light. "Where are your comrades in arms?"

"They'll be along in a minute," Gallagher answered.

"And this," Rita said, motioning toward the younger man,

"is Doctor Hugh Whitaker, our archeologist-historian."

Whitaker put down his pen, leaned forward, clasped Gallagher's hand, glanced at the blue plastic container, and said, "What have we here—a gift from the sea?"

Gallagher handed the container to Rita, who placed it in front of Whitaker. "A surprise for you," she said to the archeologist. "Jack's first contribution to Doubloon." She looked at Gallagher and added, "I haven't told either of them what it is."

The archeologist took off the lid, gazed into the container, and abruptly glanced up wide-eyed at Gallagher. He fumbled for his glasses, which lay next to a legal pad on the table, then took a white handkerchief and a small leather case from the pocket of his corduroys. He removed a loupe from the case, attached it to his glasses, and spread the handkerchief on the table. Gently, almost reverently, he pulled the rosary from the container and laid it out on the handkerchief.

"I'll be damned!" the lawyer exclaimed.

Looking at Gallagher, Rita said, "It's beautiful, Jack. Gorgeous."

His hands still dripping with saltwater, the archeologist turned the small crucifix over, adjusted the loupe's magnifying lens, and inspected the figure and the floral design. Letting his breath out slowly between his teeth, he said, "Definitely late sixteenth or early seventeenth century." He rolled one of the red coral beads between his thumb and forefinger. Speaking as much to himself as to the others, he added, "The red coral came from the Mediterranean or the Far East, perhaps India." He looked up at Gallagher. "The Spanish believed that red coral had special magical powers."

There was shouting outside, and a moment later Thibodeaux followed Millan into the office.

As Rita glanced anxiously at the two newcomers, Finch said, "Captain Millan, my amigo. And Dewey, our rambling rogue."

Sucking in his breath, Whitaker held the crucifix in the palm of his hand so that the overhead light reflected from it. "Where'd you find it?" he asked Gallagher.

"Near some cannon," he answered.

"Out dere by de Havana Bank," Thibodeaux said.

"Really?" the archeologist asked. "In what, fifteen feet of water?"

"Twenty," Thibodeaux answered.

Rita took the rosary from the archeologist. "Somebody," she said, "must've clung to this in a galleon's last horrible minutes." She drifted away for a moment, her eyes on the crucifix, before nodding toward the door and asking, "What was going on outside?"

"Pete was waiting on de dock when we got in," Thibodeaux said. "Den de bastard followed us here." He scratched his ear, causing his gold earring to jiggle. "It's like he already knew about de rosary or somet'ing."

Finch looked at Millan rather than Thibodeaux as he asked, "He boarded the boat despite the court order?"

Millan shrugged. "*Sí.* Of course," he answered. "I radioed in that Jack'd found something. Something valuable." He shrugged again. "He must've thought we were onto the motherlode. Or maybe the *Magdalena* statue."

"Dat means de bastard's monitoring us," Thibodeaux said. "Probably Beecham, too." He exhaled. "De chicken inspector wouldn't want nobody ta sneak no treasure by him either, ya know what I mean."

"Everybody's after treasure," Whitaker said. He glanced at the rosary in Rita's hands and smiled ironically. "The sharks are everywhere."

Rita nodded. "You got that right," she said, replacing the rosary on the handkerchief. She picked up one of the newspapers and looked over at Millan. "When you came in, we were just trying to figure out what to do about this." She unfolded the paper and flattened it on the table. "Close Castro Aide Faces Firing Squad in Drug Case" was the banner headline; toward the bottom of the page, the three-column headline read: "More Questions Arise About Treasure Salvor's Death." She handed Thibodeaux a copy of the paper and then turned to Gallagher and said, "Have a seat if you want, Jack. As a stockholder, you might as well see what we're up against."

While Thibodeaux stood reading the article, Rita lit a Marlboro and smoked it silently. Whitaker's hands quivered as he meticulously wiped each bead of the rosary to get rid of any residual grains of sand. Finch sat back, his elbow hooked over the corner of the chair, his head cocked, and his eyes focused on Thibodeaux. Millan turned a chair around and sat so that his forearms rested on the chair back. He read the story about the drug case in Cuba before scanning the piece on Doubloon. Gallagher first gazed at each of the others and then took the third newspaper and began to read.

Thibodeaux rolled the newspaper and slapped it on the table. "I'm tellin' ya, I fixed dat valve myself," he said. Shifting his weight from foot to foot, he turned to Rita. "It was watertight, ya know dat."

His tone dry, Finch said, "Sit down, will ya, Dewey, so we can hash this out rationally." He dragged on the cigar. "Ya make me nervous jitterbugging there." Smoke escaped from his mouth as he spoke.

Gallagher continued to read the newspaper story. The first three paragraphs presented the circumstances surrounding Nick Gallagher's death, a summary of the investigation, and the police chief's comments that there was no tangible evidence to refute the coroner's report of accidental death. The article then went on to discuss not only the State of Florida Marine Antiquity Board's impending review of Doubloon's salvage record but also other salvors' allegations that Doubloon was both cheating the government and destroying the environment. The article ended with comments by an anonymous source close to Doubloon suggesting that Nick Gallagher had, in fact, broken numerous laws and asserting that with his death the company was now leaderless. "Doubloon, Inc.," the article concluded, "is like a loose cannon careening across the deck of a sinking galleon."

As Gallagher finished the article, Thibodeaux hissed, "Goddamn it, I'm sure as hell not de unnamed source. Ask Ozzie. I didn't even talk ta Josie. Dat's de trut'. And dat crap about de cannon and de galleon sounds like somet'ing you'd say, Braxton."

Ignoring the comment, Finch rolled the cigar between his thumb and index finger. "We need to separate the issues here, Rita," he said. "Nick's death is not something we're equipped to deal with. I spoke with Chief Enright for twenty minutes this morning. Whatever Dewey's views, there exists no evidence that Nick's death was anything but . . ."

"I tell ya," Thibodeaux interrupted, his voice strident, "somebody messed wit' dat fuckin' intake valve."

Whitaker looked up from the rosary. "Even if you're right," he said, "it doesn't mean it was murder." His voice was authoritative; his eyes behind his glasses were clear and bright. "If someone tampered with the valve, how could he know that Nick—or you, for that matter—would be trapped below?"

Gallagher realized that Thibodeaux had already admitted that possibility aboard *Intrepid* on the way into the dock.

"Yeah, yeah," Thibodeaux answered. "But I don't know if ya get de whole picture, Hugh. While you were off sippin' sangria in Seville, some weird shit was goin' down here." He glanced at Rita. "Everyt'ing from fuckin' seances ta us gettin' accused a counterfeitin' de doubloons, I'm tellin' ya."

"Dewey," Finch broke in, "try listening for once in your life." He waved the tip of his cigar at the diver. "There's neither evidence nor motive—and hence, no case."

Thibodeaux leaned back in his chair, ran his hand through the white streak in his hair, and fidgeted with his earring.

"More importantly," Finch went on, "getting hung up on what happened to Nick isn't going to save this company or Nick's dream of finding the motherlode." He looked over at Rita and Millan. "Of far more pressing concern is our chances of getting our salvage licenses renewed at the MAB hearing."

"But the article can't help," Rita said. She turned the cigarette lighter repeatedly in her hand.

"No, you wouldn't think so." Finch paused and then began to speak more slowly. "Not unless we can show that the allegations are not only groundless but also an attempt to bias the board's proceedings."

Rita's eyes shone. "You mean, hold a light to it?"

"Exactly," the lawyer answered. "If we're being pilloried in the media—and we sure as hell are—we've got a strong card to play." He put his cigar in the ashtray, leaned forward, and folded his hands on the table. "If we can show prejudice against Doubloon exists, even if we lose in the board hearings, we'll be able to obtain an injunction to keep other salvors off the sites. And we'll eventually—and inevitably—win on appeal."

Whitaker stared at Finch. He let go of the rosary, pulled off his glasses, and tapped the frames on the legal pad in front of him. "But that won't find the motherlode," he said. He laid the glasses on the paper and then held up the rosary. "This makes me more sure than ever that we'll find the treasure in the shallows around the Havana Bank." The rosary's crucifix swung like a pendulum as he spoke.

Rita, who seemed not to have heard a word that the archeologist had said, jammed out her cigarette. "I'd still like to know who the hell Josie's source is," she said.

"Rita," Finch said, his voice low and his tone resigned, "it doesn't matter. Anyway, you know the señorita. You could drag her halfway to hell, and she wouldn't divulge her source."

Millan patted the top of his chair with his huge hands. "You know, amigos," he said, "Josie's been fair to us before. When we first found the *Banco de Havana*, she got the story right." He wrapped his hands around the slats of the chair back. "She did a better job than those reporters from Miami and New York."

Rita lit another Marlboro and gazed quizzically at Millan.

"Dat bitch is out ta sink us, I'm tellin' ya," Thibodeaux said.

Finch stubbed out his cigar, stood up, and leaned forward with his hands on the table so that he loomed over the others. "Jesus H. Christ, folks," he said, shaking his head. "Could we focus for three measly minutes on the MAB hearings?"

Gallagher smiled wryly, gazed across the table at the rosary still swinging in Whitaker's hand, and thought, *This company is sinking fast.*

10

An hour and a half later, Gallagher strolled by the mock depot where tourists were boarding the yellow and orange cars of the Conch Tour train and settling into the shade of the cars' fringed canvas roofs. The tour conductor, standing at the rear of the train's ersatz black engine, had already begun his spiel extolling the pleasures of the island paradise they were visiting. Gallagher had just showered and shaved, and his face, sunburnt from the previous day on the ocean, tingled. As he crossed Front Street, he dodged a bicycle ridden by a potbellied old man wearing only a purple tank suit and flip-flop sandals.

Gallagher waited on the curb under a palm tree for a group of jabbering Italian tourists to pass before entering the doorway of the red-brick office building. He climbed the stairs to a lobby that opened into a large office. The track lighting and the expanse of steel desks, keyboards, and glowing computer terminals clashed with the office's oak paneling, columns, and window frames. Gleaming five-foot chrome and molded-plastic partitions separated the office's periphery into carrels.

The receptionist, a thin, tan young man with bleached, razor-cut hair and a neatly trimmed mustache, sat at a desk that held only a telephone console and a notepad. "Welcome to the *Key West Tribune*," the man said in a high voice with a British accent. "How may I help you?"

"I need to see María José Hernández," Gallagher answered.

"Oh, yes, Josie," the man said. "Do you have an appointment?"

"No," Gallagher answered. He scratched his eyebrow.

"Oh, I see," the man said. "And your name is?"

"Jack Gallagher."

The receptionist smiled, lifted the phone, pressed four buttons, and said, "Josie, honey, there's a gentleman in the foyer." He paused. "Jack Gallagher." He nodded. "Okay. Will do, Josie." Still smiling, he turned and pointed theatrically toward the far right corner of the office.

When Gallagher approached Hernández's desk, she was speaking into the telephone tucked between her ear and shoulder. As she stood and waved at him, she tapped her computer's mouse with her other hand, closing the file on the screen. She then took a stack of papers from a molded plastic chair and motioned for him to sit. The lighting played on her face as she moved. Her small nose and high cheekbones were perfect. "Yes. I told you, everything is okay," she said to the person on the phone. "Yes. Bye." She hung up the phone and sat down in the swivel chair by her desk. "Jack Gallagher," she said, smiling. "It's nice to see you again."

He smiled back at her but said nothing.

"I expected someone from Doubloon, Braxton Finch perhaps, but not you." She brushed her short hair back from her forehead. "Is this an official visit? Should I have our lawyers present?"

"No. Not at all." He shook his head. Having dealt with

reporters at various times in his career, he realized that he and Hernández were going to have to do a little social dancing before they could talk candidly. "Your story caused a stir at the Doubloon office, but no one from the company knows I'm here."

She crossed her legs and nodded. "Okay," she said. "That's probably just as well."

He looked her in the eye. "You suggested that we talk."

She rubbed her hands on her jeans. "I did, didn't I?"

He smiled. "And I wanted to ask you some questions about Doubloon."

She folded her hands across her knee, and her eyes sparkled as she said, "But let's save some time, shall we? I'm not under any circumstances going to tell you my source for the story."

"I expected as much," he answered, leaning back in the chair. If he were to discover the source, he knew, it would take time—and likely be caused by her inadvertently letting some detail slip.

She leaned toward him, her smile warm. The top two buttons of her white blouse were unfastened. "It's good you came." She slapped her thigh. "I'm not much of a host, though. Can I get you coffee? Iced tea?"

He shook his head.

"You don't drink coffee, do you?"

"No."

"Not into the caffeine fix, huh?" She played with her gold rope necklace, the only jewelry she wore besides small gold earrings. "Well, what can I help you with, Jack Gallagher?"

He gazed at her for a moment. "You've read the various investigators' reports."

She nodded. "The police report. The coroner's report. The marine investigation report. Read all of them and interviewed everyone who'd talk to me."

He leaned forward, almost in a crouch, with his forearms on his thighs. He stared at her as he asked, "And you think my father was murdered?"

She leaned back and looked away from him. "The cops don't think so. It looks like an accident so they've closed the case. And they're right. Even Nick's . . . your father's . . . head wound appears to've been inflicted when he fell against something. Maybe when the boat capsized." She turned back. "But *Sea Devil* sinking like that still doesn't add up. Whatever happened out there on the water, Jack, something's not right. And somebody's to blame."

"Who?" He continued to stare at her.

She stood up and put her hands on her hips. "I honestly don't know."

"But you intend to find out."

She met his gaze. "Yes, I do."

"Good," he said, nodding. "What can you tell me about Pete Vogel and Doubloon?"

She sat down again and took a deep breath. "You met Pete?"

"Yeah. At the dock when we got in this morning."

She fingered her necklace thoughtfully. "Drunk or sober?"

"He wasn't falling down. But, yeah, he'd been drinking."

She shook her head. "Pete was Nick's partner until . . ." She paused, glancing at her desk calendar. ". . . until about this time last year. Pete'd been holding out treasure, pieces of eight. And Nick had Braxton Finch haul him into admiralty court."

She smiled ironically. "The judge, who'd already made Pete's acquaintance, not only dissolved the partnership but set an injunction against Pete's having any dealings with Doubloon. Pete's appealed, and he thinks he's got a chance. But there's no way the decision'll be overturned."

Gallagher scratched his scalp. "Why the hell would my father take on somebody like Vogel as a partner in the first place?"

"Pete's okay when he's dry. Rough around the edges, maybe, but . . ." She drummed her desk with her fingernails, glanced at him, looked away, and then stared into his eyes. "Jack, the truth, at least as I see it, is that a couple of years ago Nick wanted to work some salvage sites Pete had leases on so he got in bed with him." She smiled again. "At first Pete liked the arrangement, especially because Nick was doing most of the work. But once the divers started finding all those coins, greed got the best of Pete."

"And Pete rubbed off on my father?"

"No. Nick was never greedy." She hesitated as though she was trying to edit what she was about to tell him. "Look, Jack," she said finally, "I've covered Doubloon for a while now. Nick always made good copy. And I liked the guy. But you're a pivotal stockholder in a company that's not exactly repu . . . that has, at the very least, bent the rules a lot. That's why I suggested we talk in the first place." She paused, wiping her palms on her jeans. "Rita thinks I have a thing about Doubloon, an obsession. That I'm trying to wreck the company. But all I've ever really done is reported what the company was up to—and not all of it, I admit, was flattering. I tried to be fair. Nick, I think, understood that. But Rita . . ." She looked directly at him. "I'm not obsessed with Doubloon, Jack. Interested, but not obsessed. And I've gotten to know the salvage scene pretty well. Something's been brewing all summer, something with the salvage sites and the state. And the story . . ."

"And you intend to break the story," he interrupted.

She paused, glancing over at the green glowing menu on her computer screen. She then looked straight at him again. "Yes, damn it. Of course, I do. But, Jack, that's not why I wrote today's article." She shook her head. "Or only part of the reason, anyway."

"What's the other part?" he asked.

"I do have an obsession, Jack," she answered, "but it's not Doubloon or treasure. And I'll tell you . . ." She turned, flipped the page of the calendar on her desk, and gazed at him. "Hell, I'll show you. Are you still in town tomorrow?"

"Yeah," he said. He'd called his chief pilot and arranged an emergency leave. "Rita and the others don't know it yet, but I'm going to stick around until I find out what happened to my father."

"Good." She smiled at him. "Dewey already took you on the standard Doubloon oreo adventure, right?"

He smiled and nodded.

"Hooked you with pieces of eight?"

His smile broadened, but he didn't mention the rosary.

"Well, tomorrow, Jack Gallagher, I'll show you the ocean's real treasure. Borrow some scuba gear and meet me at the Bight dock near the Doubloon office at six sharp."

11

Gallagher knocked a second time on Doubloon's door. Though it was past six-thirty in the evening, both the temperature and the humidity were still well into the nineties. With no wind at all, the air felt heavy and close. Jimmy Buffet's "Changes in Latitudes" throbbed from the bar down the Bight, but the customers seated at the outdoor tables looked like they were wilting in the heat.

When Rita opened the door, she said, "Oh, Jack, I was just thinking about that rosary you found." Her hair was pulled back in a loose ponytail, and the collar of her blue blouse was askew. She locked the door behind him and reset the alarm. The air conditioner clattered; the smell of stale smoke hung in the air. "There must be some psychic bond between you . . . and Nick . . ." Her tone was warm, as though finding the rosary had proved his worth. "Come on up," she added. "I'm working in the lab."

The wooden stairs squeaked as he followed her. The second floor of the building was also one large room, but with four windows the lighting was better. The desk nearest to the stairs held a computer and reams of piled paper; intricate drawings of artifacts hung on the wall near a second desk. On a third desk along the far wall, another computer's screen was filled with a strange scrawling cursive script. A dozen six-foot electrochemical reduction tanks filled the center of the room. Each was a fiberglass water vat with stainless-steel plates at both ends connected by copper wiring to battery chargers.

Rita led Gallagher past a tank that contained six partially encrusted sabers. Musket barrels lined the tray in a second tank, cannonballs and bar shot rested in a third, and ship's hardware lay in a fourth. She stopped the other side of a fifth tank in which silver goblets and candlesticks were spread on copper meshing. Pursing her lips, she stared at the goblets. Her eyes were watery, glowing. "You've got the touch, Jack," she said. "The boys worked the Havana Bank site most of last and part of this summer, found thousands of silver coins, thousands—but nothing as precious as that rosary." She slipped her hand into her pocket and took out the doubloon she had shown him two days before. She gazed at the coin for a moment—and then abruptly flipped it to him.

At its apogee, the coin sparked with light.

Startled, he caught the doubloon, glanced at the coat of arms and the inscription, and stared at her. He then shook his head and reached across the tank to give back the coin.

"Take it, Jack," she said. "Nick always gave the divers a bonus whenever they found anything special." Her smile was sad. "And . . . he'd want you to have it."

He turned the doubloon over in his palm. He neither expected nor wanted payment for finding the rosary, but he had a feeling he should accept the coin. It had obviously meant something to his father, and giving it to him just as obviously meant something to Rita.

"It brought him luck," she said. "I wish to hell he'd had it when . . ." Her voice trailed off.

He gazed at her as he held the doubloon. Then, glancing at the coin again, he asked, "The 'H' is a mint mark? Havana?"

Frowning, she said, "Yeah. And the experts are giving us a goddamned hard time about that. There was no known mint in Havana—just Potosí and Mexico City." She sucked in her breath and bit her lip. "In fact, the numismatists have no evidence of any gold coins struck in the Americas until the 1700s. One of 'em even accused us of counterfeiting the doubloons. Melting down other treasure in order to mint the things ourselves. Went to the damn State Antiquities Board with his allegations."

He lifted the coin, gazed at the date, and looked up at her.

She leaned forward and pointed at the doubloon. "It's got to be one of the first gold coins ever minted in the New World, Jack. When we find the rest of 'em, we'll have added our footnote to history." She turned and gestured toward the computer on the desk against the far wall.

Gallagher closed his fingers over the doubloon and squinted at the screen. The script seemed to be all one endless word, arcane and more Oriental than Western in appearance.

"That's a ship's manifest and lading summary," she said. "Hugh dug up some stuff in the Spanish Archive of the Indies over in Seville. Had copies made and transferred to disk."

"Can you actually read it?" he asked.

She smiled, the lines near her eyes crinkling. "The Spanish is pretty much like Spanish today. But it's written in *procesal*, a record keeper's script that's a chain of words and sentences.

You sort of have to supply the punctuation as you go. I've been teaching myself since Hugh got back." She shook her head, then tapped the tank's rim with her fingers. "Hugh couldn't find any mention of gold coins anywhere on the manifests of the treasure galleons that sailed in 1642 or 1643, so I've been going back through the records. All I've been able to find is something called the *Gobernadora Carga* on one of the 1642 galleons, the *Santa María Magdalena*." She looked into his eyes. "She was supposed to have sunk in the Keys, but for the last year or so Nick'd been betting that *Magdalena*'s somewhere out near the Tortugas." She gazed down at the goblets again. "The Havana Bank discovery and Nick's doubloons sort of confirmed his guess and all."

"What do you think about what Dewey says?" he asked.

"About Nick's accident? I don't know, Jack." She bit the corner of her lip. "Somebody could've sabotaged the boat, I guess, but nobody . . . except Dewey himself . . . could've known that Nick would even be aboard when the boat went down."

"Who would stand to gain from his death?" he asked.

"Nobody," she answered, bitterness creeping into her voice for the first time. "That's just it. Over the years everybody from the divers to Hugh and Braxton has taken shares of stock when there was no cash. Hell, we're ten months behind on Braxton's retainer right now." She strolled over to the central tank, more than twice as long as the others, in which a cannon like the ones from the Havana Bank lay submerged. Small silver bubbles clung to the cannon's barrel and muzzle. Turning toward Gallagher, she laughed sardonically. "Nick's only beneficiaries," she said, "are Tim and me . . . and you."

Gallagher didn't speak for a moment. Finally, he held up the doubloon and said, "Thanks. I wasn't really expecting anything."

"I know that," she said, staring into the tank, seeming to follow the paths of the bubbles that intermittently rose from the cannon.

"Actually, Rita," he said, "the reason I came by was to borrow some dive equipment." He had stopped in a number of the dive shops in town, but no one would rent him equipment without a diver's certification card.

"Of course," she said, still gazing at the cannon. Then she frowned at him, her eyes narrowing, and the lines from their edges furrowing. "Why?"

"I'm doing some diving in the morning."

"With who?"

"Ms. Hernández. She wants to show me . . ."

"With Josie?" Her eyes flashed, and the warmth vanished from her voice as she spat the question at him.

"I met her at the dock yesterday when she was trying to interview Dewey. She asked me to . . ."

"Jesus, Jack," Rita interrupted. "Trust me on this. Josie's not your friend."

"She's been straight with me so far, Rita," he answered. He did not add, *Straighter, probably, than most of the other people I've met here.*

Rita glanced at the doubloon as though she might want to take it back. "She may pretend to be, Jack, but she'll stab you in the back the first chance she gets."

"Rita," he said, "I may learn something that'll help." He shrugged. "And who knows—I may even get her to see things a little differently."

12

At first light the next morning, Gallagher walked along the sidewalk away from the Doubloon, Inc., office carrying fins, a mask, and a regulator in a mesh bag. Thibodeaux, at Rita's grudging request, had left the dive gear with Whitaker before setting out again on *Intrepid*. Gallagher, using a key Whitaker had given him, had just retrieved the gear from the office. The temperature was in the low eighties, and a southeasterly breeze riffled the navy-blue Conch Republic T-shirt he had bought at one of the street-corner sheds near Mallory Dock the evening before. The vendor, a sprightly old lady with dark, wrinkled skin and crooked teeth, had bent his ear about how Conchs, the Key West natives among whom she was proud to number herself, had gotten their name because the early settlers had subsisted on conchs whenever other food was scarce. As she'd begun to expound on Key West's attempts to secede from the United States and form the Conch Republic, he'd smiled, nodded, and slipped away.

He passed a refrigeration truck delivering produce to the Waterfront Market; the motor hummed as its driver unloaded cardboard boxes onto a wooden skid. A skinny man with long, greasy blond hair, a beard, and bare feet lay curled on the cement by the first finger pier. His hands were tucked into his crotch, and the bottoms of his feet were black. Gallagher stopped near the end of the pier, put down the bag, stretched, and watched the chubby parrotfish, blue shadows in the gathering light, meander around the pilings.

A twelve-foot Boston Whaler cut around the breakwater and slowed so that it produced no wake. As Hernández swung the whaler broadside to the dock, she smiled and shouted, "Morning, Jack Gallagher." Her bright yellow pullover was almost the color of the rising sun.

"Morning, Ms. Hernández," he said as he handed his gear down to her. The whaler, outfitted for diving, had a tank rack with four green compressed-air tanks in front of the steering console and varnished wooden benches that ran the length of the port and starboard gunwales. He hopped into the whaler and sat on the starboard bench near the steering console.

Hernández took his gear and stowed it under the port bench. She then raised her thumb, grinned at him, and spun the whaler away from the dock. Outside the breakwater, she gunned the motor, pointed the whaler between Tank and Wistaria Islands, where the scrub pines were red-gold in the light, and turned the wheel so that the whaler took off westward. The whaler's hull bounced on the water with a staccato rhythm. Spray hurtled around and behind the low-slung boat.

The roaring air and pungent ocean refreshed Gallagher. He smiled at Hernández and shouted over the motor and beating hull, "Where we headed, Captain?"

"The Western Dry Rocks," she answered, grinning back at him. "Diving for treasure. Real treasure."

He stretched his arms out and leaned back against the vibrating gunwale. "How long have you been diving?" he shouted.

"Ten, eleven years," she answered. The wind blew her hair back from her face and pressed the pullover against her body. "I needed a gut class for a change so I took a diving-certification course my senior year at Miami—and fell in love with it." She shook her head and smiled. "One of life's little ironies."

"Did you grow up in Miami?"

She nodded. "In Biscayne Bay, actually. My father was a doctor in Havana. He left Cuba in '57 when he saw that no matter who won the civil war, the island, the country he knew, was going to be destroyed. I was born here." She laughed. "My parents have always considered me a little too *americano*."

"Both your parents were born in Cuba?"

"Yes, and they still live among the émigrés." She shook her head. "They even hate the word *émigré*." Her smile became pensive. "They still think of themselves as exiles even though they've been here more than forty years. But even if Castro were gone, my parents and most of their friends wouldn't go back except for vacations."

Salt spray beaded on Gallagher's arms, and the sun was already warm on his face and neck. "And you came to Key West to write for the *Tribune*?" he asked.

"Yes," she answered, "and to get away from . . . the hassles in Miami . . ." She turned the wheel so that the whaler's heading was west-southwesterly. ". . . And to dive the reefs."

A few minutes later, as they passed Sand Key, Gallagher

turned to gaze at the red iron lighthouse jutting from the small island.

Hernández said, "In a couple of hours there'll be close to a dozen boats and hundreds of divers and snorkelers swarming that reef." She shook her head. "And this is low season."

"You're against diving on the reefs?" Gallagher asked.

"No. Not at all," she answered. "That's what we're going to do." She paused. "I am for *protecting* the reefs, Jack. And once people see . . . experience . . . their beauty, it's a lot easier to convince them to do something about the problem."

The water in front of them sparkled like a sliding tray of gems, and they rode along in silence for five minutes before she asked, "And what about you, Jack Gallagher?"

"What about me?" he answered.

"Well, I know that you found a priceless gold rosary the day before yesterday."

Startled, he stared at her. Doubloon hadn't yet gone public with the discovery, and he wondered who'd leaked the information to her.

"News travels fast in Key West, Jack, especially among the salvors. You might as well get used to it." She smiled. "Nick'd been known to salt dive sites with a few pieces of eight to hook investors, so Dewey was probably setting you up with that little oreo gambit of his. But the rosary's the real thing. Congratulations."

Still wondering who'd told her about the rosary, he nodded but didn't say anything.

"I know that you're an Annapolis grad," she went on, "that you flew navy F-18s, that you retired last winter, and that you're now flying for American out of Chicago." She eased off on the throttle and cocked her head. "And I know that you didn't much keep in touch with your father. But I don't know anything else—like what makes you tick."

Smiling, he asked, "Does the reporter in you ever take the day off?"

"Seldom." She grinned at him. "And does the fighter pilot in you ever let down his guard?"

He patted the gunwale with both hands and said, "Touché."

"You married, Jack?" she asked.

"I was." He shook his head. "My ex lives in D.C."

"Any children?"

"No. Uh-uh. I guess we never settled down enough."

She looked at him for a moment before asking, "You're not one of those ironmen lunatics, are you?"

His smile was almost shy as he answered, "No. I haven't even run a marathon in a couple of years." Rubbing his knees, he added, "The wheels aren't what they used to be."

"I had to ask," she said. "It's the haircut." She reached out suddenly and swept her palm across the top of his head.

He smiled and rubbed his hand over his scalp. "I guess I got used to it in the navy."

Laughing, she punched his arm. "But you're still pretty fit, huh?"

He squinted across the dazzling water. "Fit enough, I guess. And what about you . . . Josie?"

She laughed again. "Not nuts enough to run marathons, that's for sure." Then, looking straight at him, she asked, "What's your call sign, Jack?"

He looked away, shook his head, and smiled at her again. "Wolf," he answered.

"Wolf!" she chortled. "Why Wolf? No, don't tell me."

He began to laugh, too. "It had less to do with the ladies and more to do with my keeping to myself. Going my own way—a lone wolf, I guess."

"Sure," she said, still laughing. "Right." She threw her head back, showing the graceful line of her neck, and gazed up at the sky. "Now that I need them," she shouted, "where are all those chaperones my father used to threaten me with?"

Three miles beyond Sand Key, Hernández slowed the whaler, circled a shallow reef, and had Gallagher snag a white buoy set above a sandbar west of the coral heads. The wind barely rippled the ocean; the sun, well up, sparked the aquamarine water. To the east of the whaler, white sand gullies were visible between long fingers of coral cliffs rising almost to the water's surface. No other boats were anywhere around the reef.

Hernández took gear from the bins under both benches. As she handed him a red and black inflatable life vest, she said, "Try this BC on."

Frowning, he held it up and inspected the tank brace and straps on the vest's back. During his naval water safety training he had worn life vests, but he'd always found them cumbersome. "BC?" he asked.

"*Buoyancy Control*," she said. "Once you're in the water, you won't know you're wearing it. And it'll keep you afloat when you're on the surface."

Still uncertain he wanted to wear the BC, he asked, "You just happened to have this aboard?"

She dipped her green and black BC into the water and then began to strap it onto one of the air tanks. "It was a friend's," she answered. "He left it with me for safekeeping." She took off her pullover to reveal a bright green tank suit that stretched over her svelte figure. As Gallagher stared at her, she tossed him his mask and snorkel. "During the dive we'll use the buddy system," she said. "Stay to my right, and let me lead." She put her hand on her hip and smiled. "Got that, Wolf?"

"Yep," he answered, cinching the strap on the baggy red and blue nylon swimsuit he'd bought at a shop on Duval Street. He grinned at her. "I'll fly your wing during the dive."

Her mask and fins were the color of her tank suit. Her BC fit snugly, and her regulator had four hoses attached—a second mouthpiece, a depth gauge, and an air hose she attached to a valve on her BC. His BC fit him well also, and, as he fastened the clips, he speculated about who'd left it with her. When they had both put on all of their equipment except for their masks, she reviewed the dive plan and signals with him. Then she said, "There's only one rule you have to remember."

"Breathe," he said.

She laughed. "Well, that too," she answered, "but I meant—never touch the coral."

They entered the water by sitting facing inward on the whaler's gunwale and, legs tucked close to their chests, rolling backward. As they righted themselves in twelve feet of water and headed toward the first long finger of coral, Gallagher popped his ears, let some air out of his BC to become neutrally buoyant, slowed his breathing, and felt almost immediately the floating tranquility he'd experienced two days before. The water was limpid, the visibility even better than it had been at the Havana Bank. As he and Hernández glided above the coral cliff, they dispersed a school of blue tangs. When the two divers circled a large stand of elkhorn coral shaped like a tree of green antlers, a yellowtail snapper almost touched Gallagher's mask.

Hernández pointed to a spot on the coral wall below where eight princess parrotfish were grazing on algae. Gallagher nodded but didn't notice anything until the spotted moray eel turned its head and retreated into a crevice in the overhanging sheet coral. Farther on near a purple and green sea fan, a pair of queen angelfish, spectacularly multihued and shimmering, transfixed Gallagher. He watched the angelfish and the sea fan waver with the surge until Hernández tapped him on the shoulder and gestured toward some dark, distant shadows. Five blacktip sharks, between six and eight feet long, circled above the coral cliff. They had long gray snouts, and their dorsal and pectoral fins were tipped with black. When he looked quizzically at her dark eyes, large behind the mask, she shook her head and pointed down to the sandy gully between the coral fingers.

As he followed her slow, graceful descent, he passed pairs of foureye butterfly fish with their false eyes, black spots ringed with white, in front of their caudal fins. A trumpetfish, spindly and thin with an elongated snout, stood on its head above a giant brain coral. Just before the divers reached the bottom, they paused near three pairs of yellowtail damselfish whose iridescent blue spots glowed even at a depth of forty feet.

Hernández and Gallagher swam away from the sharks through a gradually deepening gully. They passed under a low arch and drifted through a chimneylike canyon. Following her through a tunnel too narrow for the two of them to swim side by side, he felt as though he really was flying a buddy's wing over mountainous terrain. At fifty-five feet, they headed into another serpentine tunnel.

As Gallagher took a deep breath, his regulator's second stage froze open. The abrupt rush of air through the mouthpiece gagged him. Silver bubbles streaming around his face blinded him. He stopped swimming, held his breath, and struck the mouthpiece, jarring it from his mouth. Bubbles continued to stream all around him as he held the free-flowing mouthpiece. His tank hit the overhang, metal scraping against coral. Bubbles trapped under the coral arch shot about his head.

13

Gallagher shook and slapped at the regulator's mouthpiece until he felt a hand grasping his elbow. Through the wall of bubbles he saw Hernández waving her regulator's auxiliary mouthpiece. She let go of his elbow for a moment and signaled for him to drop his mouthpiece and breathe out. Nodding to her, he exhaled slowly and slipped the mouthpiece under his arm so that the bubbles surged behind him. She held his left arm just above the elbow, turned the auxiliary mouthpiece, and inserted it into his mouth. As he grabbed her left elbow, he gulped the dry compressed air.

Holding each other in that loose embrace, they swam out from under the coral arch and drifted down until they were kneeling on the gully's sandy bottom. Bubbles still gushed from the mouthpiece behind him as she flashed him the circular "okay" signal, and he returned it. She made a twisting motion with her hand and then pressed against him while she reached over his shoulder and turned off his regulator's valve. Still holding each other, they slowly ascended. At fifteen feet, they paused while she checked her watch and depth gauge. Tiny gold-brown particles floated around them in the blue light.

As soon as they reached the surface, she inflated her BC

and, after taking out her mouthpiece, orally inflated his. They hung onto each other silently for a moment, rising and falling with the surge in light that seemed impossibly bright.

Gallagher removed the auxiliary mouthpiece and said, "Thanks, buddy."

"Are you okay?" she asked.

"Yep," he answered, leaning back and squinting up at the wide azure sky. "A-okay."

Still holding him, she smiled. "Thought I might lose you there for a second, Wolf," she said.

"Yeah, me too," he answered as they finally let go of each other.

They swam on their backs to the whaler and clung to the gunwale as they removed their fins, masks, and BCs. He swung himself onto the deck and lifted aboard first her BC and tank and then his. They clasped each other's forearms, and he pulled her aboard. He sat on the starboard bench, ran his hands through his wet hair, took a deep breath, and again said, "Thanks, Josie."

As she turned off the valve on her tank, she smiled at him but didn't answer. She inspected his regulator, took a diver's knife from the sheath strapped to her calf, and fiddled with the mouthpiece until the intake valve popped closed. "You were pretty cool down there, Wolf," she said. "A lot of novice divers would've panicked."

He smiled, rubbed the palms of his hands together, cocked his head, and gazed at her. "I guess I had a buddy I could trust."

"Good," she answered, smiling down at him. She put down the regulator and stood there bathed in light, her green suit and wet skin aglow in the sunshine. "You know, Jack," she said, "I brought you out here because this is the ocean's real treasure . . ." She sat beside him on the bench, her arm grazing his. ". . . the elkhorn coral and angelfish and sea fans . . . even the moray and the sharks. This is it, Jack." She looked into his eyes with an intensity that startled him. "Right here and now. This . . ." She waved her hand over toward the reef. ". . . is worth more than any rosary . . . more than all the Spanish gold ever mined. And we're destroying it so fast." Placing her hand lightly on his forearm, she added, "If you ever do have kids, there probably won't be any reef for their children. For your grandchildren."

They sat silently for a minute, and then she stood up and, leaning over near him, pulled from under the bench a five-gallon cooler. The muscles of her thin arms rippled as she worked. She opened the cooler, which was filled with water, and dipped her regulator into it. After shaking the water from the regulator, she stowed it under the port bench, picked up her mask and fins, rinsed them, and put them in a bin. "It's our carelessness, Jack, our mindlessness, that's wrecking the reefs."

"And Doubloon's part of that mindlessness," he said, finishing her thought.

She picked up his regulator and, looking at it rather than at him, said, "This is the sort of attitude the company's got. Giving a novice a regulator that hasn't been maintained."

He stood up and looked into her eyes. "Josie," he asked, "you don't think someone deliberately . . . ?"

"Damaged the valve?" She lifted the regulator, pushed the valve open, and watched it stick for a second before it closed again. "Why? To keep you from diving with me?"

He shrugged.

"I don't know, Jack. Most divers know that the deeper you go the more likely the equipment . . ." She shook the regulator. "The whole company's run this way—lax to the point of negligence."

Without any rancor, he said, "And you blame my father."

She looked out over the glistening water. "No." She turned back and gazed at him. "Well, yes, kind of. It was that damned pirate image he was always foisting off on the media. Nick Gallagher, world's greatest treasure hunter. He didn't keep up with the dive technology because it got in the way of that image. Even liked to brag that you need instinct, not high-tech equipment, to find treasure. He just sometimes let his image . . ."

He cocked his head, waiting for her to continue. His skin was drying, and his back was starting to itch.

"Jack, despite that image he cultivated, Nick was okay," she said. "He was good to his own people. Treated his employees, if not his investors, honestly. And he never hit on me—unlike almost every other salvor around here." She shrugged. "He was pretty careful himself most of the time. And in his own way, he had a lot of respect for the ocean. But he still abused it when it suited his purposes. He's the one who gave his divers the idea that anything goes. He never really trained anybody. Just gave them gear and called them divers. And the boats . . ." Her cheeks were beginning to color with anger. "Those rusted tubes sticking out the back of the boats?"

Gallagher nodded. "We didn't use them when I was out on *Intrepid*."

"Nick cooked them up to shoot the boat's propwash down-ward to blow the sand away from a salvage site," she contin-ued, ire rising in her voice. "They're hard on any plant life, and they play havoc—absolute hell—with the coral when they're working near a reef." She stared vehemently into his eyes. "That makes me unhappy, Jack."

He glanced at the regulator, and she followed his gaze.

"I don't know if somebody sabotaged *Sea Devil*," she said, shaking her head. "Dewey wouldn't talk to me, so I don't know exactly what makes him think so." She held up the reg-ulator again. "But here's the thing—either somebody did, or else the equipment was just like this, so badly maintained that Nick himself was responsible . . ."

"So you want me to get Doubloon to clean up its act," he interrupted her. "That's why you brought me out here."

"No, Jack," she answered, putting down the regulator. "Be-lieve me, Doubloon will clean up its act, or it'll be out of business." Though her anger had diminished, her smile was still pensive. "I just wanted you to see what was at stake." She reached over and touched his arm. "What's your take on Dou-bloon?"

"Too soon to tell."

"Come on, Jack," she said. "What's your gut tell you?"

"That something's not right." He shook his head. "That Doubloon's a ship without a captain."

"And?"

"And that whatever's happening isn't over."

She nodded but didn't say anything more.

While she finished stowing the equipment, he mulled over what she had said. The more he learned about his father and

Doubloon, the more unfathomable the man's life and business seemed. The man he had known growing up had certainly dreamed of Spanish treasure, but he had also worked long, hard hours on the farm, paid his bills on time, and, as far as Gallagher knew, treated everyone from farmhands to co-op partners fairly. He didn't want to think about his father cutting corners, duping investors, and making devious deals. *Does the search for treasure inevitably corrupt you?* he wondered. Shading his eyes with his hand, he gazed out over the water. The whaler swayed in the surge, and the ocean was an infinite glimmering field. He guessed from the height of the sun that it was still early, some time before eight. There were still no other boats in sight.

As he scanned the horizon, she dipped two sponges into the cooler and tossed one to him, saying, "Better rinse off so that the salt doesn't drive you crazy on the ride back."

He washed his face with the lukewarm water. As he glanced over at her, she lifted her head and squeezed the sponge so that the water ran down her neck and between her breasts. She then turned partially away, pulled down the left strap of her tank suit, and sponged off her shoulder and breast. Her skin below the oval tan line halfway down her breast was pale ivory, and her aureole and nipple were brown-gold. She turned fully away, pulled the other strap off, and sponged her right breast and stomach. And then she reached for her pullover, shimmied it over her head and shoulders, slipped her suit down, and stepped out of it as the pullover slid down around her hips. He had been with a lot of women in different parts of the world, but none of them had ever done anything quite so naturally sensual.

Gallagher spent most of that afternoon in the *Key West Trib-une*'s morgue sifting through articles from the past twenty years about his father, Mel Fisher, Burt Webber, Bob Marx, and the other South Florida treasure salvors and their inter-mittent discoveries of Spanish galleons' gold and silver. He also scanned the *Trib*'s more recent pieces on the Marine Antiquity Board's myriad proceedings and the incessant and sometimes byzantine lawsuits involving the salvors and the state.

That evening, he took Hernández to dinner at Bagatelle. They sat outside on the second-story balcony overlooking Du-val Street. As they ate broiled lobster tails, they watched the people streaming along the street. Among the throng of tourists and Conchs, a bald woman in a tight red mini-dress strutted toward Mallory Dock. A bow-legged man in a tank top and baseball cap turned backward loped back and forth. A legless man in sunglasses and a striped sailor shirt wheeled his chair up and down the strip. As Hernández and Gallagher finished their wine and shared a piece of key lime pie, the sun sparked and vanished behind a wall of clouds building over the water. A single western star shone in the darkening sky.

After dinner, she took him back to her condominium in Truman Annex overlooking the ocean. The rich fragrance of frangipani and poinciana permeated the air, and her skin smelled of lilacs. She brought a bottle of cabernet and a cork-screw from the kitchen, leaned up to him, and kissed him. He gathered her to him. As she let the bottle and corkscrew slip onto the sofa, he lifted her blouse and camisole over her head. Her nipples rose under his fingers. She unzipped his pants and felt him harden. And then they were suddenly clawing at each other, tearing at each other's clothing, their hands and mouths roaming. He ripped away her panties. His tongue lingered for a moment on her flat stomach where a vertical scar marred her otherwise perfect skin. She bit his shoulder, swirled her tongue through his chest hair, licked his nipples. He carried her into the bedroom, and they made love ardently, overeagerly, rolling ecstatically off her futon onto the floor.

Later, she spread bath towels on her balcony, and they lay naked together sipping the wine and watching a rain squall blow in toward the island. The clouds extinguished the stars, and the waves rose with the wind. Silver-white bolts of lightning lit the sky; thunder clashed. The cool drops pelted them, mingled with their sweat, bathed them. At the height of the storm, he let his tongue rove again down her abdomen below the scar—until he was drenched, trembling, dizzy, awash, almost drowning in heat and wetness. And then they made love once more amid the strobing light, rolling thunder, and crashing surf. Her fingernails raked his back and neck. Her sighs gave way to murmured Spanish. He became breathless, and his skin tingled as though he had been electrified.

14

Just after two the next afternoon, Gallagher entered the Chart House Bar, a dark rectangular room with peanut shells and popcorn strewn across the floor. The lunch crowd was gone, but a man in a blue and yellow flowered shirt sat alone at one end of the bar and a young couple huddled at a corner table. Gallagher sat at the other end of the bar facing the television, which was perched atop an old Wells Fargo safe, playing a silent video of the Sugar Ray Robinson–Jake La Motta fight. He waved to the bartender, swept the peanut shells onto the floor, and gazed at the low cork ceiling haphazardly covered with college and pro football pennants and stapled postcards and notes. The bartender, a small, grizzled old man in a dirty white shirt, took his order for a cheeseburger and a Corona and then yelled back into the kitchen before pulling a bottle from the cooler.

Gallagher lifted the bottle from the cardboard coaster, pressed it against each of his temples, and tilted it to his mouth. The lime the bartender had wedged into its neck caused the beer to trickle for a moment before gushing out. Thirstier than he'd thought, he downed most of the beer. His morning at the Key West Library rummaging through the vertical files in the local history collection hadn't been especially productive, but he'd gotten a better feel for the place and the salvage operations. Between the *Tribune*'s morgue and the library's files, his reconnaissance, he knew, was about as complete as it was going to be. And his sense that he had to discover why his father had died and deal with whatever had happened aboard *Sea Devil* had deepened with each passing hour.

He took the doubloon from his pocket and looked at the shield and the two lions at the foot of the castle. As he turned the coin over and rubbed his thumb along the Jerusalem cross, he felt anchored to the island, pulled by treasure. Hernández had told him that the reefs were the ocean's real treasure, and he knew exactly what she'd meant. But the sensation, the light-blasted, time-stopping thrill of finding the rosary still gave him chills like those he had experienced only occasionally as a fighter pilot. "Flying the zone," one of his wing commanders had called it, and, when he had mustered out of the navy, he hadn't expected ever to fly the zone again. And then there was Hernández herself. By the time he had left her apartment, he had already missed being in her, hearing her murmured Spanish. The scent of lilacs had lingered with him all that morning.

As the bartender hobbled over with a cheeseburger and Tater Tots on a Styrofoam plate, Gallagher slipped the doubloon back into his pocket. He ate quickly, watching Robinson and La Motta silently pummel each other—and thinking about what he had to do.

When Gallagher dropped the mesh bag with the dive gear inside the Doubloon door, Rita and Braxton Finch, seated at the conference table, looked up from the legal briefs they were perusing. Rita's white sleeveless blouse and blue jeans were freshly pressed, but her face looked haggard. She glanced at the dive gear, grimaced, snubbed out a Marlboro in the ashtray, and forced a smile. "You must be the luck, Jack," she said. "Tim radioed this morning that he found a gold goblet and a huge hog—a silver bar of sixty or seventy pounds."

The volume of the marine radio on the counter in the corner had been raised, and a marine operator's call mixed with the noise of the air conditioner. As Gallagher walked to the table, he glanced at the computer on Rita's desk. The screen displayed the same arcane script he'd seen up in the lab. "Congratulations," he said. "Where'd they find it?"

"West of the Havana Bank, a mile or so." She tapped the tabletop with both hands, and her smile became more natural, the deep lines around her eyes crinkling. "The hog's got markings that may match *Magdalena*'s manifest."

"The 1642 galleon you were researching?"

"Yeah. The *Santa María Magdalena*," she said, fanning the pages of the brief in front of her. "It's the motherlode, Jack. I know it. I started to check the manifest, but Braxton said we had to deal with this state board crapola first."

Finch caught Gallagher's eye, lifted a Dixie, tilted the bottle in an ironic salute, and finished off the beer.

Rita reached for her cigarettes, hesitated, and then drummed her fingers on the table. "Anyway, Hugh's at his place checking his printouts of all of the manifests and lading summaries. If he can identify the hog, it'll be the first positive proof we're onto the motherlode." She bit the corner of her lip. "Even if it isn't," she added, her tone more somber, "it'll still keep the sharks away awhile."

"Are Ozzie and Dewey out there, too?" Gallagher asked.

"Yeah. Ozzie headed *Intrepid* farther west to where Tim's working." As she grabbed her pack and lit a cigarette, her hand trembled. "Tim's bringing the bar and goblet in this afternoon." She glanced at her watch. "He ought to be here any minute." Her hand quavering, she raised a glass, swirled the ice, and sipped her rum and Coke.

Finch picked up the remnant of a corned beef and rye sandwich lying on white deli paper next to the empty Dixie, tucked in a loose slice, and popped the sandwich into his mouth.

"Late lunch?" Gallagher asked as he sat down.

Nodding, Finch crumpled the deli paper. Rita went over to the refrigerator, got two more beers, and gave one to each of the men. She then raised her glass again and said, "To *Magdalena*'s treasure."

Still chewing, Finch said, "To treasure." He swilled two-thirds of the beer and wiped his mouth with the back of his hand. "Today's the day."

"Doubloon business keep you from lunch?" Gallagher asked Finch.

"Very much so." Finch nodded. "Things were more than a little crazed at the office. The very soul of insanity." He took a thick cigar from the inside pocket of his jacket and inspected it. "The government's been nipping at our tail even worse than usual. I spent an hour on the phone with that imbecilic chicken inspector, Beecham. And near as I can tell, that intransigent cretin isn't going to budge." He unwrapped the cigar and ran it under his nose, sniffing it. "Havana, rum-soaked," he said to Gallagher. "Would you like one?"

Gallagher shook his head and said, "No thanks."

Rita passed her gold lighter to Finch and then turned toward Gallagher and said slowly, her accent exaggerated, "Robert Lee Beecham, III, the gentleman in charge of Florida's Office of Antiquities, is a pompous ass."

Finch snorted. "Beecham parlayed a career as an agriculture department pooh-bah and one term as lieutenant governor into an appointment as director of antiquities. And the fairy knows nothing, I mean diddly-squat, about admiralty law." He rolled the cigar between his forefinger and thumb as he lit it. The tip of the cigar burned brightly when he drew on it. "Beecham's expertise runs the gamut from fodder to manure."

"Braxton's never lost in court to the Gov," Rita said, "or to any other public official."

"That's right," Finch said. "But I still have to drag their corpulent derrières into court every time something comes up." As he raised his cigar to punctuate the point, his emerald ring glinted. "Jurisdiction disputes, salvage contracts, it doesn't matter."

"What's going to happen during the hearing?" Gallagher asked Finch.

"The government has to show just cause as to why our salvage contracts should not be renewed when they expire the end of the month," Finch answered. "And Beecham is picking every goddamned nit he can."

"Does he make the decision?" Gallagher asked.

"No," Finch answered. "The three-man, ah, excuse me, three-person, Marine Antiquities Board does, but he'll submit

a report making a recommendation at the end of the week—
and it doesn't look good."

Gallagher set his beer on the table. "Is this guy on the take
or what?" he asked.

Rita shook her head. "No," she answered, "he may be the
only politician in South Florida who's not." She pulled another
Marlboro from her pack, retrieved her lighter, and lit the cigarette. "Power's his trip. It's like he gets off on screwin' people
over."

"Beecham haggles with everyone," Finch explained, "but
Nick showed him up jaw-to-jaw in a hearing a few years back,
and the old pork chop's been taking it out on the company
ever since."

Hugh Whitaker burst through the doorway carrying a stack
of manila folders. His tie was loosened and his collar unbuttoned. Even before the archeologist said anything, Gallagher
could tell from his expression and Rita's reaction that the news
wasn't good. Her face was pinched as she tapped the ash of
her cigarette into the ashtray.

Whitaker plopped the folders on the table and said, "Shit
on the proverbial stick." He sat down, brushed back his shaggy
hair, and wiped sweat from his forehead. "I've gone through
all the manifests," he said, his tone apologetic. He nodded to
Gallagher, glanced at Finch, and then looked at Rita. "I went
over *Magdalena*'s twice."

Rita leaned back, her jaw set, and gazed over at the marine
radio. She kept tapping the cigarette even though the ash was
already off.

"The bar's number's just not there," Whitaker said. Rita's
silence seemed to daunt him for a moment. He licked his lips

and glanced again at the lawyer. "The cup's still a heck of a find, Rita. And the hog'll keep the company afloat, keep the investors . . ."

Rita leaned forward, her bright eyes intense. "It's *Magdalena*'s motherlode," she said. "We're onto the motherlode." She gnawed at her lower lip. "We need proof, Hugh. Indisputable goddamned proof. And we need it fast."

The four people around the table grew silent. Whitaker shuffled the file folders, Finch finished his beer, and Rita, without looking at the others, grabbed her cigarettes and lighter and stuck them in her pocket. Finally, glancing at her watch, she said, "I need some air. I'll be on the dock waiting for Tim."

"I've got a dozen calls to make at the office," Finch said, looking from Rita to Whitaker. "I'll catch up with you later."

Whitaker nodded.

Rita reached over and patted Whitaker on the forearm. "Sorry, Hugh," she said to him. "I'm just so damned sure . . ." She pushed back her chair and stood up. "I can feel it." Her voice was low, almost a whisper. "I know we're onto *Magdalena*'s motherlode." She turned and walked out the door, the soles of her sandals slapping the pavement outside.

After watching her leave, Finch shook his head, leaned his bulky frame over the table, and said, "The damned board hearing and Nick's . . . Something's got to give." He took a deep breath, clapped the tabletop, and began to gather up the legal briefs. "Well, gents," he said as he slid the papers into his battered leather briefcase, "it's back to the fields."

15

As Finch lumbered out the door trailing a plume of cigar smoke, Gallagher said to Whitaker, "You look like you need a beer, Hugh."

Whitaker straightened the pile of folders, shook his head, and said, "Actually, I could use something stronger, Jack. I'm always the bearer of bad news. Always the one that has to say 'no.'" He went over, took an ice tray from the freezer, and cracked half a dozen cubes into a glass. "And, you know, it gets pretty goddamned old." He lifted an almost empty bottle of dark rum from the bottom drawer of Rita's desk, held it up to the light, and smiled ironically. "Looks like Rita's been hitting it pretty hard."

"How long've you been with Doubloon?" Gallagher asked.

Whitaker splashed the rum over the ice, replaced the empty bottle, and shut the drawer with his foot. "Almost ten years. Right out of graduate school at the University of Chicago. I'd done some fieldwork, but I'd never held a teaching..." He laughed quietly to himself and sat down at the table. "I thought working for a treasure hunter would give me a lot of experience fast." He slid an ice cube into his mouth and cracked it with his teeth. "And it did. I worked with more treasure in my first year than most archeologists handle in a lifetime." He laughed again. "I also repaired equipment, delivered supplies to the divers, worked on the salvage boats when we were shorthanded, and dove to make pictorial records of the sites."

Gallagher picked up his beer. "You grew up in Chicago?"

"No. Saugatuck. Across the lake, in Michigan."

Gallagher nodded.

"You ever been there?" Whitaker asked.

"No, but I promised a friend that I'd go for the colors this fall."

"You should," Whitaker said. "You're living in Chicago now, right?"

"Yeah. Flying for American. My first year."

"Make sure you get up around Petoskey," Whitaker said. "The Michigan shore is much prettier."

"You lived on the lake?"

"Not exactly. About a half-mile inland." Whitaker rotated his glass so that the ice in it rattled. "But I sailed all my life. Worked summers at the harbor. Practically grew up on boats."

Gallagher took a long draught of beer. "What do you think about the allegations in the paper that the company's been breaking laws and damaging the environment?" he asked.

"In the time I've been working for Doubloon," Whitaker answered, "salvage has changed, gone high-tech. Nick didn't change with the times. His approach was always more hands on. But we still found more treasure than anybody but Mel Fisher and Tommy Thompson." He hesitated for a moment before continuing. "Nick'd do almost anything for an edge, Jack. And I've taken some heat, some real shit, in the profession for working with him. But few archeologists, and none that work for the government, understand treasure." He cracked another ice cube and stared into his glass. "I mean, the rosary you found . . . to touch it straight from the sea . . . Didn't finding it affect you?"

"Yeah, Hugh," Gallagher answered. "I'd be lying if I said it didn't."

Whitaker nodded. "And that's something the profession . . . Most archeologists are so busy writing esoteric academic papers . . ." His voice held anger and disdain. "Hell, they'd even find a way to make that rosary you found boring."

"I think I know what you mean," Gallagher answered. Some of his classmates at Annapolis had wanted to ride desks rather than fly jets. They'd put up with their shipboard tours only as a route to jobs in the Pentagon. He took the doubloon from his pocket and held it in his palm in front of Whitaker.

Color rising in his cheeks, Whitaker leaned forward, stared at it, and stammered, "Where'd you get that?"

Gallagher rolled the coin between his thumb and forefinger. "Rita gave it to me as a bonus for finding the rosary. It was Nick's."

"Oh," Whitaker said. He sat back in his chair and laughed. "I thought you found . . . You couldn't be *that* lucky."

Gallagher held up the doubloon. "Rita told me that there were only three of these," he said.

"That's right," Whitaker answered. "This one." He pointed to the doubloon. "I've got one, and Braxton's is up in Tallahassee with a numismatist." He put on his glasses, took the doubloon from Gallagher, and examined it. "That's what I meant about those academic morons. They've never seen anything exactly like this, so they assume it's got to be a fake."

He pulled his gold pen from his pocket, pointed the tip at the "H" on the doubloon's face, and gazed across the table at Gallagher.

"There was no known mint in Havana," Gallagher answered Whitaker's implied question, "so the experts don't think it's real."

"Exactly." Whitaker fondled the coin for a moment. "As though Nick would take the time and effort to counterfeit anything as beautifully intricate as this."

"So you think it could've been aboard the *Santa María Magdalena*?" Gallagher asked.

"Yeah." Whitaker shrugged. "Or any of the other galleons that sank in 1642 or 1643."

"It wouldn't have been worth it to mint just a few coins. There must be a lot of 'em."

Whitaker smiled. "That's sure as hell what Nick thought."

"And you agree?"

Whitaker tapped the manila folders. "There's no record of any gold coins on any of the galleons' manifests," he said.

"Rita said something about a governor's cargo?"

Whitaker stared at Gallagher for a moment and then nodded. "Yes," he answered. "The term *Gobernadora Carga* was added to the end of *Santa María Magdalena*'s manifest. It had to've been some private cargo registered to Havana's governor." He handed back the doubloon. "And Don Pedro de Aguilar y Guzmán, the governor-general of Cuba, was aboard *Magdalena* when she sank. Don Pedro, Philip IV's cousin, had been banished from Philip's court in 1640—a venal man, even by the Spanish aristocracy's notoriously corrupt standards."

Gallagher pocketed the coin, stood, and stretched. "But the cargo's got to be the doubloons?" he asked.

Whitaker shrugged again. "There's no description of the cargo at all. And it'd be premature to draw any conclusions." He scooped the last ice cubes from his glass and chewed them. "Look, Jack, Nick used to get these wild hunches. While I was in Spain, he even held a goddamned seance, tried to talk to Columbus and Cortés, even *Magdalena*'s captain . . ."

"But you agreed with my father," Gallagher persisted, "that the doubloons must be part of some galleon's motherlode? And it could be *Magdalena*'s?"

"Definitely." Whitaker glanced at the doorway and then took off his glasses again. "Absolutely." He scratched his beard pensively. "Nick and I only disagreed about where out there . . ." He waved his arm. ". . . the motherlode can be found."

Later, as the sun, a colorless disk, slipped beneath the cirrus clouds, Gallagher stood with Rita and Whitaker on the dock. The heat hovered in the high nineties, and the smoke from Rita's cigarette hung for a moment in the humid air around them before dissipating. Whitaker paced back and forth carrying his file folders; the soles of his cordovan loafers squeaked on the planking. Gallagher's shirt clung to him as he sweated out the beer he'd drunk. Gazing at the blue parrotfish in the water, he remembered waiting nearby for Hernández before they had dived at the Western Dry Rocks. When *Sea Rover* rounded the seawall, Rita sighed and tossed her cigarette into the water. One of the parrotfish rose toward the butt for a second before turning away.

Whitaker stopped pacing and whispered, "Oh, shit!"

Gallagher and Rita turned to see Hernández and Vogel heading by the waterfront market. Hernández wore a bright yellow sundress and carried a notebook and tape recorder. Vogel's blue workshirt stretched over his belly above his blue jeans. He spoke boisterously, and Hernández seemed to be hanging on his every word. A thin bearded man with two cameras dangling on straps around his neck and a large leather bag slung over his shoulder followed a couple of steps behind them. Rita looked askance at Gallagher and lit another cigarette.

Tim, who stood in *Sea Rover*'s wheelhouse, gave the ship's horn three short blasts. The salvage boat then reduced speed and swung around so that it could back down against the pier. Tim eased *Sea Rover* into the dock and, while his two divers tied the boat off, waved to his mother and slid down the ladder's railing. Straining, he lifted an oblong gray-black boulder to the level of his chest. Rita clapped, and Gallagher raised his fist in the air. Tim lowered the silver bar to his waist, leaving a dark smudge on his T-shirt. As Whitaker moved toward him, Tim stepped onto the gunwale, teetered there for a second under the weight of the bar, and clomped heavily onto the dock.

Vogel stopped ten feet astern the salvage boat. The photographer came up next to Gallagher and began to snap pictures. As Gallagher turned, Hernández, who was opening her notebook, smiled at him. Rita glanced from Hernández to Gallagher and back to the reporter. The photographer motioned for Rita and Whitaker to get into the next shot. Tim and Whitaker each held an end of the bar, and Rita stood in the middle. Tim beamed for the camera, but both Rita's and Whitaker's smiles were strained. When they laid the bar on the dock, Whitaker crouched to check the serial number.

Hernández came over to Gallagher and said, "Hello there, Wolf."

Gallagher smiled, touched her arm, and said, "Hello, Josie. I was hoping to bump into you today . . ." He glanced at Rita, who was watching Whitaker double-check the bar's serial number against the photocopy of a manifest. ". . . but maybe not here." He nodded toward Vogel. "And definitely not with your buddy."

"Pete glommed onto me in the parking lot, Jack," Hernández said. "He already knew about Tim bringing in treasure." She ran her hand along his forearm. "I told you Key West is a small town—and news travels fast."

Rita leaned over Whitaker. She smiled momentarily and then stared grimly at the silver bar. The photographer stood on a bench to shoot down at the two people inspecting the serial number.

"I've got some work to do," Hernández said to Gallagher. "But I should be finished by nine if you'd like a late dinner."

"I'd like that," he answered. "Name a spot."

"How would you like to eat Cuban?" she asked, her dark eyes shining.

"Sounds good," he answered. "My treat."

Laughing, she said, "We'll wrestle over that later. Come by the office about nine." Notebook open, she strolled over to Rita and Whitaker to ask them questions.

Figuring that he shouldn't be involved in the interview, Gallagher headed toward *Sea Rover*'s stern. Dive gear and lines were scattered on the boat's deck. Two battered red elbow-shaped steel tubes, similar to those on *Intrepid*, were tilted over the stern.

Sidling over toward Gallagher, Vogel said, "Can't stay away from treasure, huh, flyboy?" He reeked of bourbon and sour sweat.

Gallagher didn't answer.

"I got a right to parta that hog," Vogel said to Gallagher. He scraped his diamond-studded crucifix with his stumps, and his voice became even lower. "I'm owed a piece a . . ."

Vogel stopped speaking. Tim stood on *Sea Rover*'s deck with a partially crushed gold goblet in his hand. The exterior of the goblet's bent rim was incised with images of lions and dolphins and fire-breathing dragons. The stem had a twined floral design. Rita and Finch stared at the cup; Hernández scribbled notes. The divers gawked over Tim's shoulders, and the photographer forgot for a moment to take any pictures.

"My God," Whitaker mumbled. He closed his manila folder, took the gold cup, and turned it so that he could look inside it.

Tim shouted, "Jack, ya gotta see this."

As Gallagher approached, Whitaker lifted the cup. Its interior held a ring of empty settings and a small, twisted cage at its base.

"This," Whitaker said, "is a poison cup, a great find, an important find. The cage in the bottom is for a bezoar stone, which, the alchemists thought, absorbed arsenic. The nobility trusted nobody, not even friends and family . . ." He smiled ironically. ". . . Especially not friends and family." He ran his forefinger over the ring of empty settings along the rim. "It was studded with precious stones, probably emeralds. Had to've belonged to somebody important, somebody of high rank."

Gallagher instinctively reached for the cup. Before he could touch it, a gnarled hand lunged past his. As Whitaker jerked the cup back, Gallagher swung around and bumped into Vogel.

"That fuckin' treasure's mine," Vogel muttered.

"Get your ass out of here, Pete," Rita hissed.

The photographer frantically switched rolls of film as Gallagher stepped between Vogel and the others. Vogel squared his shoulders; a snakelike vein pulsed above the scar on his forehead.

"Stay outa this, flyboy," Vogel rasped. He pushed Gallagher's chest with his good hand.

Gallagher set his feet.

Vogel clenched his fists. "You got no fuckin' idea what you're getting into, boy," he said, his voice a hoarse whisper. "No fuckin' idea."

Gallagher snapped his hand forward, grabbed Vogel's wrist, and twisted it downward. Vogel winced, stumbled forward, and glared up at Gallagher. They stood there for a moment, each measuring the other. Gallagher wrenched the wrist harder until Vogel relaxed his shoulders and leaned back. Vogel pulled himself free, tapped Gallagher lightly on the chest with his maimed hand, grinned, and said, "You'll fuckin' regret this, boy." He spat into the water, glowered at Tim and Rita, turned, and stomped away. The photographer, who had taken an entire roll of film on auto-advance, lowered his camera. Hernández held her pen against the notebook, but she hadn't written a word.

16

At ten forty-five that night, Gallagher entered La Habana Café, a Cuban restaurant three blocks from the din of Duval Street. Low, syncopated Latin music emanated from the small dimly lit bar to his right. Two dozen framed photographs lined the wall on his left. Straight ahead, a hallway led to the dining room. Hernández, who had called his hotel to tell him she was running late and would meet him at the restaurant instead of her office, was nowhere in sight. As he glanced at the autographed photos of Cuban athletes and entertainers, he was approached by the dapper, older man he had shared the pew with at the funeral and later seen on the Sea Ray surveying the piers at the Bight.

"Señor Gallagher," the man said, extending his right hand. His starched white shirt and dark silk tie were impeccable; his matching gold tie clasp and cuff links gleamed.

Gallagher shook the man's hand.

"I am Enrique Cardona, proprietor of La Habana," the man said. His tone was cordial, his English stilted. He looked at Gallagher through thick, black-rimmed glasses. "María José phoned. She has been detained yet a little longer at the newspaper." He smiled. "Do not worry, however. I will keep the kitchen open."

"Thanks," Gallagher said, glancing again at the photographs. Those that were not promotional portraits showed Cardona standing with or shaking the hand of each celebrity.

"Your father, Nicholas Gallagher," Cardona said, "dined with us regularly in the old days . . ." He raised his arm and gestured toward the dining room. ". . . when La Habana Café was only a storefront restaurant. I was an admirer of your father, of his quest for Spanish treasure." He gripped Gallagher's elbow. "Come. Look at this." He led Gallagher down the hallway toward the dining room and stopped at the end of the line of photographs. Above an autographed picture of Adolpho Luque in a New York Yankees uniform was a shot of Cardona standing in front of the restaurant's door with Nick and Rita and Tim. Nick Gallagher, an arm around Rita's waist and a hand on Tim's shoulder, was grinning. Rita gazed directly at the camera, and Tim, who appeared to be about five years old, cocked his head to the left. Cardona stood stiffly to the right of the family. The inscription, scrawled boldly in black ink, read, "*Mi amigo, Maestro Enrique!*—Nick Gallagher, Treasure Hunter."

Staring at the photograph of Nick with his second wife and second son, Gallagher was struck by his father's grin, which seemed to encompass everyone. He felt again the emptiness he had experienced at the funeral. His father's overt happiness, separate and distinct from the man's earlier life in Iowa, caused pangs of sadness, almost melancholy, in Gallagher. He felt no resentment, but a deep sense of loss washed over him.

"Señor Gallagher," Cardona said, interrupting his

thoughts, "let me seat you. You can enjoy a cocktail while you wait for María José."

The dining room was almost empty, but a few patrons sat at tables drinking coffee from white demitasse cups, smoking cigarettes, and chatting energetically in Spanish. The priest who had said Nick Gallagher's funeral mass sat by himself at a small table, seemingly oblivious to the noise around him, reading from a black leather-bound breviary. Cardona pointed to a table near the back under a large woodcut of a galleon hanging on the wall among finely engraved silver plates set in glass cases.

When Gallagher paused to look more closely at a plate depicting a Spanish caravel under full sail, Cardona said, "That was your father's favorite, too."

Gallagher gazed at the other plates. "They're beautiful," he said. "Where did you get them?"

"I made them," Cardona answered. "How do you say? An avocation from the old days." When Gallagher was seated, he asked, "May I offer you something from the bar?"

"A beer," Gallagher said. "Dark, if you have it. Anything Cuban?"

Cardona scowled. "No. Never. I would not give the *communistas* a peso for their watery *cerveza*." He smiled. "But German dark—yes. It tastes like beer."

Just as Cardona returned with a Beck's Dark, Hernández came into the dining room. Smelling of lilacs, she hugged Gallagher as he stood to greet her. "Sorry," she said almost breathlessly. She then turned to Cardona, who had just set the glass of beer on the white linen tablecloth, and said, "Maestro, it's good to see you. Are we too late to eat?"

Cardona slid the empty tray onto the table. "María José," he said, "you are never too late." Her eyes sparkled as he kissed her hand. He pulled her chair out for her, unfolded her cloth napkin with a flourish, set it on her lap, and then picked up the tray and returned to the bar to get her a glass of pinot grigio.

Gallagher let Hernández order for both of them. A muscular young Hispanic waiter in a spotless white shirt and a black bow tie served them an appetizer of fresh shrimp with garlic and sherry butter. They ate at a leisurely pace, allowing the conversation to meander. When he asked her about the Marine Antiquities Board, she begged off answering, telling him that she definitely needed to let the reporter in her rest for a change. By the time their dinners arrived, all the restaurant's patrons had left except for one elderly couple and the priest. Sipping his third beer, Gallagher felt disoriented, as though he had stepped out of the touristy world of Key West back into a different, more sensible time.

Gallagher and Hernández shared two dinners, one of grilled snapper and the other of shredded pork with onions. Gallagher liked everything except the yucca, which, though laced with garlic, still reminded him of the boiled potatoes he had eaten too often in the navy. Hernández ate heartily, surprising him with the amount of black beans and rice she consumed. After the waiter took their plates, Cardona approached the table carrying an old 35mm Canon with a flash attachment. He pressed his glasses against the bridge of his nose and asked if everything had been satisfactory.

Hernández smiled at him and said, *"Sí, excelente. Gracias."*

"I am glad," Cardona answered in English. "And you enjoyed it, too?" he asked, turning to Gallagher.

"Very much," Gallagher answered, "especially the shrimp."

"Ah, excellent," Cardona said. "The shrimp are caught daily. We have our own boat, and the shrimp and fish are brought directly here to the restaurant." He turned to Hernández and, his tone more grave, asked, "Any news on the late wires tonight from Havana?"

Hernández shook her head. "Only more rumors about Castro's failing health. He wasn't seen or heard from again today."

Cardona nodded, tilted his head, and looked at Gallagher. "Well," he said, smiling again, "I would like to have my photograph taken with the two of you, if you don't mind." He held up the camera and gestured to the waiter who stood at attention by the kitchen door.

Shortly after one-thirty, Gallagher and Hernández strolled down Duval Street toward the ocean. Each of the antiquated black and white steel clocks on the lampposts displayed a different incorrect time. Three scraggly, long-haired men sharing a cigarette panhandled them halfheartedly. The souvenir shops and restaurants were closed, but the metallic throb of the rock 'n' roll band at Sloppy Joe's still pulsed along the street. The bar's three wide French doors were open, and Gallagher glanced in at the numerous photographs of Ernest Hemingway and the mammoth sailfish hanging on the wall.

They turned on Greene Street, Hernández steering him away from Duval's blare and twang, and continued walking until they reached the Maritime Museum, housed in the old red-brick city hall. The sweet odor of hibiscus wavered in the warm breeze, and Gallagher felt drowsy and serene. As they gazed at the astrolabe, pieces of eight, and chunk of old timber in the window display, Hernández said, "In their own way, the Conchs take their piracy pretty seriously." She let go of his arm. "The whole town was built on wrecking and salvaging."

"So you admit," Gallagher said, "that pillaging the sea didn't start with Nick Gallagher."

She hooked her arm around his and sighed. "Yes," she answered, "but there's a difference. The wreckers had immense respect for the sea—just not for the captains who sailed it." She smiled. "And definitely not for any flotsam and jetsam that could be hauled ashore and sold."

As they walked along the deserted street, he said, "But you've already told me that you thought my father had respect for the ocean."

"Yeah, he did," she answered. She paused for a moment, looking up at the tops of the palms near the trailer park. The moon was a pale crescent behind sparse clouds. "And even I will admit that sewage—the garbage we all dump every day—is a far greater threat to the reefs than any salvor."

"What about Pete Vogel?"

"Definitely a pirate—and a menace," she said.

"But that's twice I've seen you talking with him, today and at the cemetery."

"What's that supposed to mean?" She squeezed his arm. "I've got to talk to him, Jack. It's my job. And the old sot makes good copy—just like Nick did."

Gallagher stopped walking and looked directly at her. "But he's not like my father."

"Not when he's drinking, anyway." Her tone became more somber. "He stayed dry all through the admiralty hearing and the appeals. But he's fallen off the wagon again—*hard*. And, yeah, Jack, he's not only insanely greedy, but he's got a mean streak that Nick never had. And volatile—he can be a violent s.o.b."

"I caught a bit of that today," he said as they began to stroll again.

She shook her head. "No, you didn't. He'll never try to take you in a fair fight. That was obvious this afternoon. But he won't forget what happened." She paused. "Watch yourself, Wolf. When he's bingeing, he's got a screw loose."

He nodded. "Yeah, I've looked through the clippings. Seems like somebody else usually got the worst of it."

"Guys have been cut."

"One guy was shot."

She shrugged. "That happened before I came to town. And as with most things involving Pete, the story's different depending on who you talk to. Apparently, there were no witnesses, and no gun was found."

They stood by a rusted steel tower that had on it a small red hand-painted sign saying Key West Triffel Tower. "The sites my father . . . the ones the judge cut Vogel out of, are those the sites Tim and Ozzie are working now?" he asked.

"You bet. The Havana Bank, the site where Nick found the three doubloons—all the western sites." She smiled and poked him in the ribs. "Not a bad guess, Wolf. Maybe we can make a reporter of you yet."

He laughed. "There's a depressing thought," he said. "You think Vogel's still holding a grudge?"

She leaned up against him. "Yeah, Wolf," she said. "Pete's harboring a boatload of bitterness, and a lot of it's focused on Nick."

They headed around the corner by the Doubloon office. "Enough to kill my father, to have him killed?" he asked. The parking lot was poorly lit, and scant light filtered from the sky.

She paused for a moment. "I don't know," she said. "I don't think Pete would've been subtle enough to sink the boat like that. Blow it up, maybe. . . ."

The sound of glass shattering and the sudden flash, like a bulb popping, startled them. As Gallagher glanced over her shoulder, he saw the Doubloon office door slightly ajar. "What the . . . ?" he said.

Her gaze followed his. He jogged toward the door, and she trailed warily after him. The molding had been splintered near the dead bolt. He slowly nudged the door open, squinted into the darkness, and took a half-step forward.

Suddenly, the shaft of the rapier that had been hanging on the wall streaked out of the darkness. As Gallagher lunged to his left, the rapier's blade slashed his right arm just below his shoulder. He fell onto the cement and rolled over on his side as the rapier rattled to the ground next to him.

"*Carajo*," Hernández yelled.

A lanky man holding a brown plastic bag in his gloved right hand burst past Gallagher and flung Hernández aside. She fell hard, the side of her head striking the pavement. The man scurried across the parking lot, his long, greasy black hair flopping like a mane as he ran.

Gallagher sprang to his feet, stared for a moment at the rapier, and crouched next to Hernández. Even in the low light, blood shone darkly in her hair and trickled along her ear. As her glazed eyes began to focus on him, he scanned the parking lot, but the man had already disappeared.

When Gallagher cupped her head with his hand, she reached up to him and said, "Jack, I think I'm . . ." She turned away and vomited.

"It'll be okay, Josie," he said, stroking her sweating forehead. "Don't move. I'll get help."

When he raised his right arm to push open the office door, he noticed that his sleeve was drenched with blood and the back of his hand was wet. Only then did he feel the hot, searing pain. The taste of garlic and beans rose in his throat. Tearing away the sleeve, he found a deep three-inch-long gash in his deltoid. He wadded up the ripped sleeve and pressed the material against the wound. "Damn," he mumbled as he stepped into the ransacked office.

He knelt next to Rita's overturned desk, grabbed the phone with his left hand, and punched 911. Next to him, the computer lay on its side on the floor, its keyboard torn away and the conch shoved through its screen. His father's books on Columbus and the Caribbean had been swept from the glass-fronted bookcases. The open drawers of the file cabinets lining the other wall had been rifled, and folders were strewn across the floor among the shattered glass. Blood ran from beneath Gallagher's torn shirt. "Damn," he said again as he pressed the material harder against the wound.

17

At quarter past seven in the morning, Gallagher stood in the mounting humidity outside the Doubloon, Inc., door explaining what he remembered to Louis Escobar, a swarthy police sergeant with a Latino accent. Gallagher's bandaged wound showed only as a lumpy protrusion under the flimsy green surgical shirt he had been given at the hospital's emergency room where his shoulder had been disinfected and stitched. He had been questioned by the police and then told to go home and get some rest, but instead he'd spent the night at Hernández's bedside. The cut in her scalp was superficial, but the concussion was severe—and the doctors were holding her in the hospital for observation. She had wanted to file a story, despite her blinding headache, and her editor had finally been called to the hospital to tell her that she must take at least a twenty-four-hour leave before continuing her work.

Gallagher returned to the office when Hernández fell asleep soon after sunrise. He had refused any painkillers stronger than ibuprofen, and a mixture of burning in his shoulder, anger, and adrenaline was keeping him awake. Sergeant Escobar was particularly interested in the fact that the burglar had not only worn gloves but also bypassed the alarm. And, despite the fact that Gallagher had already given a full description to another police officer at the hospital's emergency room, he'd had to repeat every detail.

Rita stood near an evidence technician who was examining the doorjamb and handle for fibers and other residue. Her eyes were swollen, as though she hadn't slept at all. She ground a cigarette into the pavement, ran her hand through her hair, turned toward Escobar, and asked, "Can I go in now, Sergeant?"

"Yes, Mrs. Gallagher," Escobar said. He scratched his dark mustache. "Remember, I've got to have a list of everything that's missing." He smiled at her. "ASAP, Mrs. Gallagher."

She gnawed at her lip, nodded, and entered the office.

Escobar turned back to Gallagher and asked, "Any identifying marks? Anything at all?"

Gallagher shook his head awkwardly. His shoulder had become stiff, and any movement was painful. "Like I said, tall, skinny, dirty, long hair, wearing jeans and a dark T-shirt."

Smiling ironically, Escobar said, "End-of-the-roader. You've just described half the addicts in town." He pushed up on the brim of his hat. "They keep drifting south until they can't go no further. And then we're stuck with 'em." He scribbled a final note, flipped his notebook shut, and clicked the pen top. "Think you could identify him?"

"Maybe," Gallagher answered. His muscles burned, and the stitched skin under his bandages felt tight and hot. "But I doubt it," he added, shaking his head.

Escobar slipped the pen into his uniform pocket. "Hell," he said. "Any of those dirtballs could've heard about the treasure coming in yesterday and thought you'd be dumb enough to leave it in the office. Trashing the place is just like the sons of bitches." He went over to the office door and called, "Mrs. Gallagher, any idea yet what's missing?"

Gallagher followed Escobar to the door and looked in at the chaos.

Tying a red handkerchief around her head, Rita answered, "No." She shook her head. "Hell, no." Her shoulders slumped as she dropped her arms and rubbed her hands on her jeans.

"Okay," Escobar said. He pointed with his thumb over his shoulder. "The ET's gonna finish up outside. I'll let you know if we turn up anything." He surveyed the office one last time, pulled his cap down tighter, and nodded to Gallagher.

Rita began to gather the scattered papers and pile them on the conference table. With his left hand, Gallagher lifted one of the overturned pressed-back chairs and set it in its place at the table.

Dropping a stack of folders onto the table, Rita said, "Look, Jack, I don't need your help." Her eyes were bleary, and her voice was almost a cough. "Go get some sleep."

He lifted another chair, gazed at her, and said, "That's all right. I'd like to help."

She stooped, picked up three of his father's books about Columbus, brushed the dust off the top one, and, her lips pinched, glared at him. "Really, Jack," she said, "it's not necessary. I'll handle things here."

He slid the chair next to the other one, and then, without answering, reached for a third chair.

She slammed the books on the table. "What the hell . . ." Her voice cracked in anger and frustration. "What the hell were you doing here with Josie?"

Gallagher exhaled slowly. The sharp pain in his shoulder

was turning to a deep ache. Fatigue was finally creeping in on him, and he felt clammy and dirty. "Nothing," he answered. "We had a late dinner, and we went for a walk."

She continued to glower at him. "You've still got a key, right?"

He took a deep breath and waved his left hand. "Rita," he said, "we were out walking. That's it. And, if we hadn't come along, everything probably would've been a lot worse."

She looked away from him at the destruction around her, bit her lip, and scowled. "And I thought you were the god-damned luck." She knelt to pick up a couple more books, slid them on the table, and added, her voice becoming both sad and bitter, "Maybe you should just stay the hell away from the office, Jack. If you want to help out, work on the boats." Her face was already smudged with dirt and sweat, and she wiped her forehead with the back of her hand. "And, frankly, you can sell your goddamned ten percent to the devil himself. I don't care anymore."

"Rita," Gallagher began, "you're not thinking clear . . ."

Hugh Whitaker entered the open doorway, stopped abruptly, and muttered, "Holy shit!" A newspaper in one hand and a tall cup of Starbuck's coffee in the other, he was backlit by the bright morning sunshine. "What the . . . What happened?" he stammered.

Rita laid a wad of receipts on the table and answered, "We were ripped off by some end-of-the-roader. The asshole apparently thought he was going to cash in on Tim's goblet."

Whitaker didn't move. "How'd it . . . ? When?"

"One-thirty," Rita said. "I called you, but there was no answer."

"Jesus, shit." Whitaker brushed his beard with the newspaper. "I'd turned the phone off so I could get some sleep for a change. They didn't . . . Did they get upstairs?"

"Doesn't look like it," Rita said. "Thank God for small favors." She took off the handkerchief and wiped her face. "Jack saw the door open and surprised him," she said.

Whitaker started. He stepped into the office, turned to Gallagher, and asked, "You saw him?"

Too stiff to turn all the way around, Gallagher answered, "Yeah."

"Did you get a good look at . . ." Whitaker paused, gazing at Gallagher's hospital garb. "You're . . . What happened?"

"The bastard cut me with the rapier," Gallagher answered.

Rita fumbled in her pocket for her pack of Marlboros, shook one out, and stared at it without lighting it.

Whitaker slid his cup of coffee onto the table near a stack of vouchers. "Where?" he asked. "How?"

Gallagher didn't feel much like talking. "In the arm," he said.

"You okay?"

"I'll get by."

Whitaker picked up his cup, sipped the coffee, and replaced the cup on the table. "What the heck were you doing down here in the middle of the night?" he asked.

Before Gallagher could answer, Rita said, "Out snooping around with Josie." Both weariness and indignation were in her voice.

"She was here?" Whitaker asked. He put his glasses on and exhaled sharply. "Jesus, shit."

"You got it," Rita said. "And she supposedly got knocked

out by the guy. She's still in the hospital." Her hand shook as she lit her cigarette. "I can't wait to see how she plays this out in the *Trib*."

"Jesus." Whitaker looked over at Gallagher. "Josie's why I came by early today." He unfolded the newspaper and handed it to Rita. "She's been at it again."

The three-column story in the lower right section of the front page was headlined "More Spanish Treasure Found." A photograph showed Whitaker and Tim and Rita with the silver hog propped in front of them on the dock.

"It's not that bad a likeness," Rita said, her crabbed smile suggesting this was the final bit of humor she could muster.

Whitaker took another sip of his coffee. "Read on," he said.

The smoke from her cigarette twirled above Rita as she hunched over the article. Whitaker went over to the open door and gazed out into the sunlight. Gallagher's shoulder throbbed, his eyes burned, and he was becoming too tired to care about Rita's reaction to the article.

Rita kneaded her handkerchief and shook her head slowly but said nothing while she read. When she finished the article, she exhaled, turned the newspaper around so that it faced Gallagher, and asked angrily, "What the . . . ? What do you know about this? What the hell did you tell her?"

Gallagher skimmed the article. The lead and two subsequent paragraphs focused on the discovery of the gold goblet and silver bar. The fourth paragraph, however, pointed out that Whitaker had been unable to identify the bar. Given the impending Antiquities Board hearing, the article went on, questions about the authenticity of the discovery were inevitably going to be raised. Other, more troubling questions about

Nick Gallagher's death persisted. The article concluded with a source close to Doubloon saying, "You have to wonder what's going on with Doubloon, what's going to happen next, and where Doubloon's quest for treasure will ultimately end." As the quotation echoed in his mind, he licked his lips, which tasted metallic. Hernández had written the article before she had met him for dinner, before they had gone for their walk to the waterfront, before he had been slashed by a seventeenth-century sword, and before she had landed in the hospital.

"I don't know anything about this," Gallagher said, his mind sifting through his conversations with Hernández. He'd never made those exact statements, but they'd certainly talked around them. He gazed down at the newspaper, unable to stop himself from questioning his relationship with her. "I didn't say that stuff."

"Yeah, right." Rita coughed hard and frowned at him. "And you were just out for a walk last night."

Gallagher didn't answer. His head ached, and his arm pulsed with pain. With his left hand, he took two ibuprofen from his pants pocket, flipped them into his mouth, and swallowed them dry. He wanted to get away from the office to walk and think, but he wasn't sure he had the energy to do either.

Whitaker returned to the table, picked up his cup of coffee, and sipped it. Finally, he broke the silence, saying, "The rapier, huh? Jesus Christ." He shook his head. "And you got a look at the guy?"

A rotund man in his mid-sixties, wearing a wide-brimmed hat and holding a manila envelope in his hand, appeared in the office doorway. His face was flushed, and his jowls were flaccid; purple veins crisscrossed his nose. He sauntered into the office and said in a high-pitched voice, "My, my. It looks like we've had some trouble here."

Rita folded the newspaper and scowled across the piles of documents at the man just as she had glared across the grave site at him in the cemetery when he'd been talking to Vogel.

"Good morning, Governor," Whitaker said as he backed away from the table.

The man paused, hitched his powder-blue pants as he gazed around the room, and then accosted Gallagher. Extending his pudgy right hand, he said, "Mrs. Gallagher, where are your manners?" His tone was overly polite, and he smelled of Old Spice. "I am Robert Lee Beecham, the former lieutenant governor and current director of antiquities of this fine state. And you, sir, must be Jack Gallagher."

Gallagher wiped his right hand on his pants, raised it, shook Beecham's hand, and, although Beecham's grip was limp, winced from the pain. "I've heard a lot about you, Mr. Beecham," he said, his voice wry.

Beecham looked confused for a moment and then turned toward Rita and said, "What, may I ask, has happened here in paradise?"

Rita exhaled smoke through her nose and answered, her tone cold, "Break-in last night."

"Yes, indeed," Beecham said, his voice still cordial. "Yes, indeed."

Watching those around the table, Whitaker moved toward the door.

"What's your business here, Mr. Beecham?" Rita asked as she jammed out her cigarette.

"Ah, yes," he said. He surveyed the office again. "I'm afraid, given the situation here, this will not come as glad tidings." He unfastened the envelope's clips and daintily slipped out a sheet of paper. "Other business brings me to Key West this morning, but as long as I'm here, I thought I would personally deliver this prior to attending to my other duties." He turned the sheet of paper so that Rita could see it and said, his tone again highly formal, "Here, Mrs. Gallagher, is a list of documents that the Office of Antiquities needs in order to determine a final recommendation to the board on the disposition of the Doubloon, Inc., salvage sites."

Rita glowered at the list and said nothing.

Beecham slid the sheet back into the envelope, clipped it, and handed the envelope to her.

Tossing the envelope onto a pile of folders, she asked, "Why wasn't this stuff submitted directly to Braxton Finch?"

Beecham smiled broadly. "I thought it might save time if I gave it to you personally."

Whitaker stepped forward and cleared his throat. "When, uh, do you need this information, Governor?"

Continuing to smile, Beecham pulled a white monogrammed handkerchief from his back pocket, took off his hat, and wiped his forehead. "My intention," he said more to Rita than to Whitaker, "was to seek compliance today. But . . ." He glanced at the heaps of documents on the conference table. ". . . that would seem to be an inconvenience." His voice became officious. "Still, the Office of Antiquities needs to make a recommendation this week. And any delay in submitting the documentation will only serve to further debilitate Doubloon's already tenuous case." He smiled at Rita, who looked away at the shattered computer monitor.

Feeling dizzy, Gallagher pressed his left hand on the table-top for a moment, took a deep breath, turned, and said, "Mr. Beecham, it's time for you to leave."

Beecham inhaled, puffing out his chest. He glanced from Gallagher to Rita and back. "My conversation," he said, "is with Mrs. Gallagher." His voice held an edge for the first time.

"And I'm telling you that your conversation is over," Gallagher answered. Sweat ran down his neck and back. He stared at Beecham, who didn't look directly back.

Seeming to have noticed the bandages under Gallagher's shirt for the first time, Beecham gazed at Rita and Whitaker, hesitated, and then said, "Yes." The smile returned to his face and the cordiality to his voice. "I've finished my business here." He folded the handkerchief and put it in his pocket. As he fingered the brim of his hat, he said, "I see that the apple has not fallen far from the tree." He waved the hat at the envelope, looked again at Rita, and added, "Those documents are absolutely essential. The Office of Antiquities expects full compliance. Be certain to expedite their delivery." Ignoring Gallagher, he nodded to the others, put on his hat, and strolled from the office.

18

Late that afternoon, Gallagher walked over to Hernández, who sat at a small wooden table in an open courtyard bar around the corner from his hotel. An awning cast an ellipse of shade for the table's two chairs. The air was muggy, the breeze slack; only a few tufts of clouds hung in the hazy sky. The Rolling Stones' "Sympathy for the Devil" played on the sound system. As Gallagher slid into the chair across from Hernández, the waitress, a tan young woman in a black mini-skirt and white halter, set a basket of conch fritters, a Dixie, and a seltzer with a slice of lime on the table.

Released from the hospital only an hour earlier, Hernández wore a floppy sun hat to cover her bandages. Her eyes were bloodshot, but she showed no other sign of the concussion. "Hi, Wolf," she said. "I ordered you a beer. Hope that's okay."

"Thanks, Josie," Gallagher said. "Beer's fine." His arm was inflamed and his shoulder stiff, but he'd become used to the pain. He had slept fitfully for five hours after leaving the Doubloon office. He'd then bathed sitting in a tub and shaved left-handed. He'd learned from a call to Finch that Rita had determined that a few silver coins, "chump change" the lawyer had called them, and a couple of computer disks were the only things missing from the office after the break-in. Rita had al-

ready used the gold goblet and silver bar as collateral on a loan
for new equipment.

Hernández sipped the seltzer. "Well, Wolf," she said, "dining with you may be good for me. Not only did I get to meet
a number of handsome young doctors, but my editor's going
to increase my insurance." She put down her glass, lifted a
brown, deep-fried conch fritter from the basket, and dipped
the fritter into the boat of hot sauce. "Of course, he does think
I have some kind of death wish for hanging out with you at
night down by the docks." She popped the whole conch fritter
into her mouth.

He didn't answer at first. When he'd called to ask her to
meet him, he'd barely been able to keep the anger out of his
voice. Given her concussion, he didn't want to swoop down
on her, guns blazing, but he couldn't merely disengage either.
He took a drink of his beer and then began to scrape the label
with his thumbnail. "I'm heading out on *Intrepid* in the morning," he said.

She coughed, chewed on the fritter, and said, "What?"

He shook his head. "I keep thinking the answer to my
father's death lies out there somewhere."

"I don't know, Wolf," she said, rubbing her eye. "You're
even starting to sound like Nick." She took another sip of the
seltzer. "What about your arm?"

"I can at least help out with the light work."

She squinted at him. "What's really going on, Wolf?"

He shrugged. "Rita doesn't want me around the office anymore."

"Why not?"

"Because she's losing it. She's spinning her wheels. Has no clue what she really wants."

"And because I was at the office with you last night?"

"Yeah," he said. "That, and your piece in the *Trib*." He continued to scrape the bottle's label.

"What about the piece?"

He picked at the section of his sleeve that was sticking to the bandage. "That stuff about the bar not being authentic. And that quote at the end. She assumed that I . . ." He looked at the shredded label. "You backed me into a goddamned corner, Josie."

"I was just doing my job, Jack. I write the truth, and if Rita doesn't . . ." She took a pair of sunglasses from her purse, cleaned the lenses with a paper napkin, and put on the glasses. "Nobody would attribute that quote to you."

"She did." He leaned forward, his right arm limp in his lap and his left resting on the table. "And I . . . You're using me to get at my father's killer. To get the goddamned story."

She took off her sunglasses. "I am not," she said, a dark glint replacing the bleariness in her eyes. "No more than you've been using me." She picked up a conch fritter, held it above the sauce, and then dropped it back in the basket. She wiped her hands and leaned forward so that their faces were close and their arms were touching. When she spoke again, her voice was barely audible over the music. "You're right about one thing though, Jack. I think somebody killed Nick. But I don't know who, and . . ."

"Who's your source?" he interrupted. As she began to lean back, he held her arm. "Who the hell is your source?"

She stared at his hand and then looked fiercely into his eyes. When he let go of her arm, she sat back in her chair. "No," she said, shaking her head. "Uh-uh, Jack."

Raising his left hand in exasperation, he said, "But your source is the key to this whole damned thing, Josie."

She didn't answer him immediately. When she did speak, her tone was warmer. "That's right," she said. "My source could be the key. That's something I've been thinking about. And it's something I'm going to have to live with." She stared at her glass, lifted it, and swirled the ice. "I like you, Jack," she whispered. She put down the glass, scratched her eyebrow, and then traced a "j" in the condensation on the glass. Looking first at the lump under his shirt and then into his eyes, she added, "I'm sorry you're caught in the middle. I really am. And whatever the hell is going on with Doubloon and those damned salvage sites, I think . . . I hope we—you and I—are going to end up on the same side."

He shook his head slowly, unsure what to believe. "Stop playing games with me, Josie," he said.

"I'm *not* . . ." She sucked in her breath and pushed back her chair. "Fine, if that's the way . . . if that's what you think I've . . ."

"I'm worried that you . . ."

"Don't worry about me, Jack," she snapped. "Take care of yourself." She stood up, snatched her purse from the table, and looked down again at her glass, where the "j" was dripping into some indecipherable rune. "I'm honestly not sure what's going on yet. And I know that until I figure it out, I can't tell anybody—not even you—the name of my source. It's too bad, Jack. It really is. But that's the way it works." She put on her sunglasses and pulled down her hat. As she walked around the table past him, she brushed her hand gently along his wounded shoulder.

Just before dawn, as Gallagher approached *Intrepid*'s mooring, Millan, Thibodeaux, and the two divers who had previously been working with Tim were loading twelve-gallon ice chests onto the salvage boat's stern. The temperature was already in the high eighties, and only a freshening breeze from the ocean kept the air from being oppressive. A fat, barefoot old man in blue jeans and a blue and white striped shirt sat against a piling having a vociferous argument with himself. The tip of his cigarette traced glowing figures in the half-light as he waved his hand to reinforce some point. The divers, working silently, ignored the man. Gallagher laid his sports bag on the dock and nodded to Millan.

"I got your message, amigo," Millan said. "And having an extra hand'll be just fine. How're you feeling?"

Gallagher smiled. "Not too bad." He raised his right arm almost to the level of his head before wincing. "Pretty good."

Millan reached out, pointed to Gallagher's sports bag, and said, "Come on aboard, amigo. You and me, we've got some war stories to tell."

Gallagher handed his bag to Millan and hopped aboard *Intrepid*. Millan carried the bag through the hatchway, and Thibodeaux, sauntering over from the stern, said, "Hey, Jack, where y'at?" His long hair hung in clumps, and sweat dripped from his face. "You and Josie broke up dat fuckin' burglary, huh? Stopped de bastard from gettin' at de treasure upstairs."

The mention of Hernández's name froze Gallagher for a second. The night before, he had almost called her. He'd wanted to talk with her in order to clear the air, but he'd also realized that they both needed sleep and that it was too soon to risk another verbal dogfight. "Mornin', Dewey," he said, nodding. "We just sort of tripped onto it."

"You and Josie, huh. Dat's somet'ing else, I'm tellin' ya." Thibodeaux pulled up his New Orleans Saints T-shirt and wiped the sweat from his face. "And ya got your wing clipped for de trouble?"

"It'll be fine," Gallagher answered. He glanced up as Millan returned though the hatchway and climbed to the wheelhouse. The two divers sat on the ice chests drinking water from plastic bottles. "I left that dive gear you lent me in the Doubloon office," he said to Thibodeaux.

"Yeah, I got it okay. Rita gave me de bag when we got in last night."

Gallagher looked into Thibodeaux's eyes. "The regulator was faulty," he said simply.

Thibodeaux shook his head. "I checked out dat gear, I'm tellin' ya."

Gallagher didn't answer. He gazed up at the wheelhouse where Millan was starting the tug's engines.

"What're ya tryin' ta tell me, podna?" Thibodeaux asked.

"The regulator froze open at about fifty feet. I would've been in deep shit if Hernández hadn't been there."

Thibodeaux pulled at his earring. "How de fuck could I of checked it at fifty feet?"

Gallagher again didn't answer. Turning, he saw Rita and

Whitaker walking along the dock toward the salvage boat. Rita held a pack of Marlboros and her lighter; Whitaker carried a rolled chart.

"I'm tellin' ya," Thibodeaux said, "dat gear was workin' good."

When Rita and Whitaker reached the gunwale, Gallagher said, "Mornin'."

"How are you, Jack?" Whitaker said.

Rita barely nodded.

Thibodeaux stared at Gallagher for a moment before turning to the others. "We're pretty much shipshape, I'm tellin' ya," he said to Rita. "Ready ta rock 'n' roll."

She nodded, lit a cigarette, raised her head, and exhaled blue smoke into first light. Gallagher stepped back and leaned his good shoulder against the bulkhead.

Whitaker peered at the jabbering fat man before saying to Thibodeaux, "I've got the spot marked." He then gazed at Rita, but her pinched expression didn't change.

"Don't look at me," she said, smoke escaping from her nostrils. "Dewey's the mapper."

Whitaker passed the chart to Thibodeaux, who unrolled it, scanned it quickly, and then glanced from Whitaker to Rita and back to Whitaker. "Dis is pretty far easta where we been workin', ya know dat," he said.

"That's right," Whitaker answered. "I've been going over the data from all the old magnetometer hits."

"We've only got four days to find something definitive," Rita said, "something that conclusively labels the artifact path as *Magdalena*'s. It's our best shot."

Whitaker ran his fingers through his beard. "I'll be radioing Tim to make the magnetometer runs this morning. By the time you get there, he'll have the buoys set."

Thibodeaux stared at Rita. "Tim, he ain't gonna like dis," he said.

Rita squeezed the filter of her cigarette. "Hugh's got the data," she answered. As she shrugged, she bit the corner of her lip and shook her head. "We've got to go with the data." She dropped the cigarette butt on the dock and ground it with her heel. "We've got no other choice."

19

When *Intrepid* arrived at the dive site that afternoon, a series of orange buoys was set in a loose grid, but *Sea Rover* was nowhere in sight. The sky was clear except for sparse cirrus clouds trailing wispy tails; a light chop of less than a foot rocked the boat. When Millan idled the engines, Thibodeaux and the two divers set four anchors, two off the bow and two off the stern.

Gallagher climbed to the wheelhouse, where Millan stood by the polished wooden wheel trying to raise Tim on the marine radio. In front of the captain, below the expanse of windows, a black compass was mounted on a binnacle. The engines' double throttles stood on either side of a black bank of gauges. *Intrepid*'s red, leatherbound logbook and the radio with its handheld microphone rested on a shelf to the right of the starboard throttle. The wheelhouse smelled of saltwater and sea air.

Millan held the radio's microphone close to his mouth and said into it, "*Sea Rover, Sea Rover, Sea Rover*, this is *Intrepid*, KTA 1811. Over." He then glanced up above the middle window at the clock and the barometer in the electronic console between the depthfinder's screen and the sub-bottom profiler.

"Any luck?" Gallagher asked.

"*Nada, amigo*," Millan answered. "But he's out there." He waved his thick arm in an arc. "And with all these buoys set, he can't be gone long."

Gallagher smiled. "And each one's marking treasure."

Millan nodded. "Could be, amigo." He laughed aloud. "You never know. You drag the magnetometer back and forth over the area. Whenever the mag registers something metal, it pings. You drop a buoy to mark the spot. Then, you dive on it." He laughed again, his gold tooth gleaming. "You could find treasure. Or an old train wheel . . . or an unexploded bomb." He paused, gazing out the windows at the wide expanse of water. "Finding treasure out here is like finding a needle in a haystack. People think it's impossible. But if you look hard enough and long enough, you might just find that needle." He turned and pointed out the back window at the buoy off the boat's port side. "And the magnetometer and sub-bottom profiler, they make it easier."

Gallagher glanced at the leather gun case lying across two mahogany brackets set in the bulkhead above the back windows. He then watched as Thibodeaux and the two divers lowered the two large rusted red tubes, bent at right angles, down over the boat's stern.

"The afterburners, they were Nick's idea, amigo," Millan said. "They may not be pretty, but they do the job real good."

Thinking about Hernández's comment about the damage they did, Gallagher asked, "Why do you call them afterburners?"

"Tim named them that when he was a kid." Millan shrugged. "I guess he thought they looked like jet engines. And they *blast* the propwash straight down. Blows the sand away and gives the divers more visibility."

Thibodeaux worked the electric winch as the stocky diver with the tattoos held a guyline tied to the top of the steel tubing. The lanky diver stood nearby holding a heavy pipe wrench.

"The anchors," Millan said, "keep the stream of clear water steady even when we're blowin' full throttle."

Remembering what he'd come to the wheelhouse to talk with Millan about, Gallagher nodded. "Why was Dewey so sure that Tim wouldn't go for Hugh's plan?" he asked.

Millan glanced again at the clock and turned toward Gallagher. "Deep water or shallow. It was causing trouble even before Nick died. Everybody but Nick thought *Magdalena* must've already been breaking apart as she hit the shoals—*el Banco de Habana.*"

Gallagher leaned against the bulkhead, nodded, and asked, "Everybody?" The sweat made the bandage on his arm soggy, and the wound itched.

"Pretty much everybody," Millan answered, "Tim, Hugh, Braxton, Rita, Dewey, me." He scratched his belly for a moment. "The artifact trail," he continued, "fades out in the deeper water west of *el Banco.* So *Magdalena*'s treasure must be near here somewhere." He placed his left hand on the wheel's top spoke, which was notched, and looked out at a buoy bobbing in the low chop. "But Nick had this hunch that the motherlode was farther west." He pointed with his thumb over his shoulder. "Out there in deeper water."

"What made him think so?"

"Nick had lots of ideas, amigo. Nobody, not even Rita, knew where he got some of 'em." Millan shrugged. "What made him think anything?"

Aware he didn't know the answer to that question, Gallagher shook his head.

"It was like Nick—he could sometimes get into the minds of those galleon captains," Millan went on. "Like he could walk the decks in their boots. At that last meeting, people were arguing with Nick, and he just kept saying, 'That's not what *Magdalena*'s captain did. . . . He headed for the open sea.' Like it was a *fact. Comprénde?*"

"I'm not sure," Gallagher muttered. In some ways, he felt, the more he learned about his father, the less he knew the man. Certainly there was more to him than the Iowa farmer yearning for adventure at sea or even the treasure hunter affecting a pirate image. "What'd you think?" he asked.

"Me?" Millan smiled broadly and licked his gold tooth. "I been around Nick a long time, Jack," he answered. "It makes more sense if *Magdalena* lies over this way. But I never bet against Nick. Never."

The radio crackled, "*Intrepid, Intrepid*. This is *Sea Rover*. MLM 2241. Over."

Nodding to Gallagher, Millan held up the microphone and said, "*Sea Rover*, this is *Intrepid*. Switch to channel sixty-eight. Over."

"Roger, *Intrepid*. Switching to sixty-eight. Over." Tim's voice sounded deeper and older over the radio.

As Millan reached past Gallagher to switch the radio's frequency, he said, "Coast guard and every other mother's son monitors the distress and calling frequency so we got to get off it."

The radio crackled again. "*Intrepid*, this is *Sea Rover*. Over."

"*Hola, amigo*," Millan answered. "What's your heading? Over."

"Headin' for treasure, Oz. Going deep," Tim answered. "Today's our day, amigo."

Millan shook his head and grinned again at Gallagher. "Looks like you left us some dives back here," he said into the microphone.

Gallagher looked back at the boat's stern, where the divers had set a tarp over the afterburners' brace to provide some shade.

"How many buoys did you set?" Millan asked.

"Twenty-two," Tim answered. "Two double pings, one in the middle of the quadrant and the other near the northwest corner."

Millan raised his finger from the microphone's call button and said to Gallagher, "Double pings are the big hits. Something really sets off the mag." He pressed the call button and asked, "You didn't stay for the party, amigo?"

Laughter rang over the radio. "Couldn't," Tim answered. "Like I said, we're headin' for treasure. Going deep."

Millan rolled his eyes at Gallagher. "*Sí, amigo*," he said into the microphone. "I read you. We'll talk again at 2130. Okay?"

"Roger," Tim replied. "2130. This is *Sea Rover*. MLM 2241. Over and out."

As Millan switched the radio back to the calling frequency, Gallagher asked, "Where is he?"

"You heard him, amigo. Somewhere to the west. He's heading back to deep water."

"Why? I thought you said Tim was for shallow water."

Millan rubbed his hand along the wheel's polished wood. "*Sí*," he answered. "I did. But after Nick died, it's been like Tim has to finish what Nick . . ."

A loud banging on the mailbox caused both men to turn and look out the back window. The two divers stood in full gear by the dive ladder. Thibodeaux held the pipe wrench in his left hand and had his right thumb pointed up. Millan waved, turned around, switched on *Intrepid*'s engines, and adjusted the throttles. As its engines revved, *Intrepid* pulled back and forth at its anchor lines before settling into a stable position. A moment later, bubbles erupted all around the salvage boat's stern. The odor of exhaust momentarily overrode the smell of sea salt. Thibodeaux clapped each of the divers on the back, and they scissors-stepped into the water.

As Gallagher watched the bubbles churning around the stern, he said, "You started to tell me about Tim."

"*Sí*," Millan answered. He gazed out the front windshield for a moment and then said, "It's like Tim . . . Rita and him both . . . have got Nick's . . ."

"Obsession?"

"*Sí*, obsession. Tim's got to finish Nick's work out there. He's got to do it. And nobody's going to tell him nothing." He pointed out at the roiling water off the stern. "That's why we've got Tim's divers. He was starting to burn 'em out, pushing 'em into too many deep dives. Not giving 'em enough time between dives to decompress. So we switched crews for a couple of days. He's like Nick that way."

Gallagher thought about what Beecham had said in Doubloon's office about apples not falling far from the tree. "So Rita favors deep water now, too?" he asked.

"No, not really. But enough to let Tim go ahead and dive out there," Millan answered, patting the notch in the wheel's top spoke. "Between us and the sea, amigo, you can bet it's tearing her up." He glanced out the back window as Thibodeaux attached the butt of the air hose to the compressor. "She *thinks* we should be diving here. But she *feels* the motherlode's out there somewhere." He shook his head; his dark eyes were sad. "And we're running out of time fast, amigo."

20

During the first afternoon, *Intrepid*'s divers checked six of the sites marked by the buoys, but they found only an oil drum and a rusted World War One generator among the lesser jetsam strewn across the shallow ocean floor. As the divers discovered more junk, Gallagher began to picture the ocean as a vast tract where men had been dumping their garbage for thousands of years—and Hernández's concerns about Florida's coral reefs seemed all the more justified.

That night, after eating dinner, placing a call to Tim that provided no new information, and listening to Thibodeaux's guitar playing and singing of Cajun songs in a ragoût of French and English slang, Gallagher took his air mattress up to the deck outside the bridge. The deck was cooler than the forward cabin, and, still mindful of his father's death, he wanted to be somewhere out in the open. The stars glimmered in the haze— as though a sequined shroud covered the sky. The light, intermittent breeze barely rocked the boat. Just before dawn, as he lay half-awake still lost in a dream of the sky flying open and enemy fighters, bogies everywhere, hurtling at him from out of the sun, the wind died completely.

Working in the leaden heat and humidity all that day, the crew labored through the arduous cycle of moving to the next buoy, setting the anchors, lowering the afterburners, blasting the sandy bottom with *Intrepid*'s propwash, diving on the site, and raising the anchors again. For the most part, the water was shallow enough to enable Thibodeaux and the two divers to do jump dives—quick repetitive dives that required no decompression. Gallagher's shoulder, although still sore, was less stiff, and he was able, using his left arm, to help with the raising and lowering of the anchors and the afterburners. Thibodeaux spoke to Gallagher only when necessary, and the divers tended to ignore him during the salvage routine.

While the divers were down, Gallagher talked with Millan in the wheelhouse or sat in the stern under the tarp and watched the sand and water shoot out of the suction hose and through the screen mesh off the starboard gunwale. The screen caught seashells and small rocks but no coins or other treasure. The noise from the engines and the compressor, although at first numbing, gradually slid into the back of his mind, and he began to slip into a slow sea-time governed more by the dives and the sun's path than by a clock. Neither the tension he had felt in the Doubloon office nor the deep, rising anger he had experienced with Vogel, the end-of-the-roader, and Beecham disappeared entirely, but both the stress and the anger receded before the persistent roll of the water. Still, though there was now no opportunity, he found himself needing to talk with Hernández.

By the third morning, the wind was slack and the sun barely shone in the thick haze. That afternoon cumulus clouds, billowing like smoke, blotted out the eastern horizon. As Thibodeaux and the divers readied their gear for the first dive after lunch, Millan called Gallagher to the wheelhouse. *Intrepid*'s captain wore faded jeans and a loose T-shirt. Two flannel rags cut from an old work shirt and a can of gun oil with an orange and red bull's-eye logo stood on the counter above the radio. Millan pointed to the screen of the sub-bottom profiler set in the bulkhead console above the front windows. "One of Tim's double pings, amigo," he said.

Gallagher stared at the gray-green screen for a moment and then tapped an elongated white image near the bottom of the screen.

Millan nodded. "Something big is buried there in eight foot of sand," he said. "Something very big."

The pale image, shaped like a capital "T," seemed to waver against the darker background of the screen. As Gallagher continued to stare at the image, he rubbed his right arm with his fingers.

Millan adjusted the port throttle, checked the barometer, gazed out the window at the cloud bank building in the distance, turned, and said, "*La tormenta, mi amigo*, she is looking bad."

Glancing at the hourly barometric pressure readings in the log, Gallagher said, "Heading our way, huh."

"*Sí*. We will get in only one dive before she hits us," Millan said. He reached up beyond Gallagher for the gun case on the rack. As he unzipped the cracked leather case, he asked, "How does your arm feel, amigo?"

"Okay. Pretty good," Gallagher answered. "I don't know if I could do push-ups, but it's better."

Millan slid the shotgun from the case's thick lamb's wool liner, squirted gun oil onto one of the flannel rags, and began to carefully wipe the gun's double barrel. "Rita told me you got a good look at the hombre that cut you," he said as he stopped rubbing the barrel and inspected it for signs of rust.

"I got a glimpse of him. A drifter, probably strung out."

Millan slid the rag over the shotgun's stock and then put the rag on top of the other piece of flannel. "He was wearing gloves?" he asked.

"The cops thought that was strange, too." Gallagher scratched his ear. "And he knew enough to bypass the alarm."

Millan broke open the shotgun's action and peered through the barrels. "Maybe, amigo," he said, "you will meet the hombre again." He snapped the action shut.

Although he was not sure what Millan meant, Gallagher nodded. "That's one fine weapon you've got there, Ozzie," he said.

Millan gazed fondly for a moment at the shotgun before handing it to Gallagher. "*Italiano,*" he said. "A gift from Nick."

The gun was so well balanced that it felt light in Gallagher's hands. He inhaled the odor of gun oil as he brushed his fingers along the intricate bouquet engraving on the frame's metalwork.

"The rapier," Millan said, "its blade cut your shoulder?"

Gallagher cradled the shotgun in his left arm. "The deltoid," he answered. "Sliced pretty deeply into the muscle, but missed the bone and artery."

Millan smiled. "You are lucky. *Afortunado.* The hombre did not know how to use the rapier. You will be fine." He patted his belly. "Guns sometimes do not make such clean wounds."

"I noticed the scar before," Gallagher said.

Millan pulled up his shirt. "The bullet," he said, touching

the four-inch blotch on his distended stomach, "came out here." Still holding up the shirt, he turned so that Gallagher could see the smaller, more circular scar on his back below the rib cage. "But I, too, was lucky." He dropped his shirt. "I lost only my spleen."

As Gallagher handed him the shotgun, he asked, "What happened?"

Millan looked at him a moment and then turned away. "Nick saved my life," he said to the ocean.

"How?" Gallagher asked. "When?"

Millan slid the shotgun back into its case and rezipped it. "*Mi padre*," he said, "was the best fisherman in Baracoa. A maestro. Rich people came from la Habana and the States to fish with us. We fished only for marlin." He reached up and placed the shotgun back on the rack. "During the revolution, some of these people who had fished with my father wanted to leave . . . to get their families out of Cuba. Batista . . ." He wiped the back of his hand across his mouth. ". . . *Hijo de puta*. But these people were amigos." He turned to face the ocean again. "Over the years, some of them wanted to get things to people inside Cuba. *Mi padre* and me, being fisher-men . . ." He looked back into Gallagher's eyes. ". . . and black. We could come and go from Baracoa where other people could not."

Gallagher met Millan's gaze. "You wouldn't draw much attention."

Millan held his gaze. "*Sí, amigo. Sí.*" He turned and looked away again. "One night, it went bad. A government patrol ambushed us." He shook his head. "The bribes did not reach the right officials. Or we were betrayed." He rubbed the spot where the gnarled scar protruded under his shirt. "I was wounded, but I escaped. *Mi padre* was taken." He adjusted the starboard engine's throttle. "They killed him. Stood him against a tree and shot him." He squeezed the port engine's throttle, looked out at the water, and exhaled slowly. "They murdered him. I made it to our boat and set a northward course. Sometime during the night, I must've shut down the engine and passed out. I do not remember." He rubbed his belly again. "At dawn, Nick found me adrift in the Straits." He slid his tongue over his gold tooth. "In those days Nick did the mag runs himself in a converted cabin cruiser."

Gallagher glanced at the wavering "T" on the sub-bottom profiler's screen, gazed out at the ocean, and then looked into Millan's eyes.

"I was loco with pain and fever," Millan said. "Nick was smart enough not to call the coast guard. He took me to the only *cubanos* he knew in Key West." He put the flannel rags and the can of gun oil in the cupboard below the radio, turned, and with his index finger lightly tapped Gallagher on the chest. "He saved my life, Jack. I owe your *padre* my life."

21

Shouts from the stern interrupted Millan. Gallagher turned to see Thibodeaux hanging from the dive ladder waving wildly. As Gallagher and Millan raced to the deck, Thibodeaux pulled off his mask and shouted, "Anchor. Ozzie, we found . . ." The building waves sloshed around him. He shook the water from his face and hair. ". . . one big fuckin' anchor. Ring and shank are huge, I'm tellin' ya."

"A galleon's?" Millan asked, grinning and lightly clapping Gallagher on the left shoulder.

"Looks like it, podna!"

The tarp flapped in the rising wind.

"*Magdalena*'s?" Gallagher asked.

Thibodeaux wiped mucus from his nose and mouth. "No way to tell yet," he answered. He tilted his head sideways and tapped the heel of his palm against his temple. "But maybe, yeah. It's old. And bigger dan any fuckin' anchor I ever saw." He glanced at the darkening sky and then looked over at Millan. "Give us five more minutes here, and den move about fifteen feet sout'east and blast a hole." He pulled his mask onto his head. "And we're gonna need de Nikon. We gotta get pics for Hugh."

"Ready for a dive, amigo?" Millan said to Gallagher.

"I can handle things topside if you want to see the anchor," Gallagher answered.

"It don't matter who it is," Thibodeaux said as he lowered his shoulder and scooped his arm to retrieve his regulator's mouthpiece, "just as long as we get de shots before de fuckin' storm hits."

Millan touched his ear with his thick forefinger. "I don't dive anymore," he said to Gallagher. "Wrecked my eardrum a couple years back. And the dive might do you good, amigo."

Fifteen minutes later, after Gallagher had helped Millan reset *Intrepid*'s anchors, he donned a weight belt, harness, tank, regulator, fins, and a mask. The gusting wind buffeted him as he scissors-stepped into the water. He readjusted his mask, turned, and grabbed the dive ladder's top rung.

Millan knelt, handed him the orange and black underwater camera and strobe, made a circle of his thumb and forefinger, and said, "The anchor is *Magdalena*'s, amigo." He tapped his chest with his fingers. "I can feel it."

Gallagher descended the dive line through the bubbling propwash. The saltwater stung his wound, and the harness dug into his sore shoulder until, once he reached the sandy bottom, his natural buoyancy relieved much of the pressure. He equalized, took several slow breaths, let the relative quiet engulf him, and scanned the site. One of the anchor's giant flukes jutted out of the sand like the tip of a massive arrow. As Thibodeaux swam over to him, the other two divers worked the suction hose around the anchor's partially buried crown. The divers' slow movements in the filtered light made them look like rhythmic, dancing shadows.

Thibodeaux took the camera from Gallagher and pointed

to the anchor's huge ring. Trying to estimate the anchor's length, Gallagher glanced from its ring to its crown and back. Then he followed Thibodeaux over toward the ring, which was more than half his height and almost a foot thick. Thibodeaux had him hover next to the ring to provide perspective while he shot photographs. The strobe flashed in Gallagher's eyes like lightning, and the propwash looked like shafts of silver rain. The stinging in his stitched arm lessened to an itching that almost felt good.

When the lanky diver tapped on his air tank with the haft of his dive knife, both Thibodeaux and Gallagher turned to see that the divers had uncovered the spot where the anchor's shank and crown met. The stocky diver, who had been introduced to Gallagher only as Matt, held the suction hose in one hand and waved his other arm at them. All four men gathered close around the anchor's crown staring at the well-preserved double-dolphin foundry mark and the Roman numerals MDCXXXIX. Gallagher did the arithmetic, and then, the date ringing in his head, grabbed Thibodeaux's shoulder, nodded vigorously, and gave the divers the thumbs-up sign.

The divers, confused by Gallagher's exuberance, glanced at each other. Thibodeaux held up the camera, and the other three men backed off for a moment so that he could take photographs of the foundry mark and numerals. As the two divers again began to work the suction hose around the edge of the crown, Gallagher watched closely to see if they uncovered any other markings.

A deep metallic thumping suddenly reverberated through the water—Millan's hammering on the hull to signal the divers to surface. By the time they reached the dive ladder, bulging cumulonimbus clouds scudded above them, turning day into night. *Intrepid* yanked erratically at its anchors. As the divers hustled out of their gear, they were pelted with large, warm drops of rain. While Thibodeaux and the two divers raised the dive ladder and then pulled in and coiled the suction hose, Gallagher stowed the camera and dive gear. Thibodeaux and Gallagher lashed the compressor to a cleat on the starboard gunwale as the two divers pulled down and rolled the tarp before it tore away. All four men raised the afterburners and lashed them to the brace. They then raised the stern anchors but left the bow anchors in place.

After changing the soaked bandage on his arm, putting on a dry shirt and jeans, and taking a maroon rain slicker from the hold, Gallagher clambered up to the wheelhouse. The lights of the electronic screens cast the wheelhouse in a pale hue; the wipers beat back and forth across the windshield. Millan, who was on the radio telling Tim about the anchor and the imminent storm, scowled at the darkness. As Millan signed off on the call, Gallagher stared over the churning sea at the slashing bolts of lightning.

"The anchor," Gallagher said to Millan over the rolling thunder, "was set in 1639."

Millan, seemingly unmoved by the news, continued to squint out the window. "*Sí, amigo,*" he answered, "and now *la mar* will show us her temper." He smiled unhappily. "I hope you did not eat too much for lunch."

Gallagher laughed, but *Intrepid*'s rolling was already making him queasy. "How bad'll it get?" he asked as he grabbed the binnacle for support. He glanced out the back window where the stocky diver, looking like a troll in his yellow rain suit, was rummaging through the cooler next to the compressor.

Millan pointed to the wind indicator, whose needle was fluctuating between twenty-five and thirty-five knots. "*Muy mal*," he said. "The waves will be walls. *La mar*, she is angry with us for finding the anchor."

"What?" Gallagher stared at the captain to see if he was kidding.

Lightning arced across *Intrepid*'s bow, and thunder clapped an instant later.

Without smiling, Millan said, "*La mar* never gives up her treasure without a price. Nick understood that, Jack. She's always a mystery. Always. No matter how . . ."

Suddenly the wheelhouse began to glow.

Light shone in Millan's dark eyes. "*Cristo*," he murmured.

Gallagher spun around, looking about at the gleaming instruments. A crackling like a brush fire rose from the salvage boat. Out the wheelhouse's back window the afterburners' brace glowed red. Framed by coruscating light, the stocky diver stood transfixed on the deck, the pipe wrench in his left hand aglow. The air crackled and buzzed.

"Matt, he is . . . it's . . . ," Millan whispered. Making the sign of the cross, he added, "*Santa Elmo. Santa Elmo.*"

Gallagher, who had seen Saint Elmo's fire only at a distance, watched as a red gleaming ball seemed to roll across the afterdeck and pop against the compressor.

Matt turned, dropped the wrench, raised his arms, and gazed into the wheelhouse. His foul-weather suit flapped in the driving rain. His expression was stupefied, his eyes glazed.

Thibodeaux got to Matt just before Millan and Gallagher reached the deck. The glow faded, and the buzzing subsided. As they led Matt into the galley, he turned slowly in circles gazing at his hands. Urine and water dripping from his rain suit formed a puddle on the deck. The dishes and supplies in the galley's cabinets rattled as the boat rolled. Matt smiled at the others, but his eyes remained glazed. He didn't respond to Gallagher's questions. Calmly, almost gently, Millan helped him take off the rain suit; Thibodeaux gave him dry shorts and a T-shirt. The lanky diver led him into the forward cabin where he lay on the port bunk and examined his hands as though they still gleamed.

By nightfall the wind bellowed at more than forty knots; spindrift flew from the foaming fifteen-foot waves. The anchor lines chafed, and water from the crashing waves ran into the hold. Although the bilge pump throbbed, Thibodeaux, Gallagher, and the lanky diver also had to take turns manning the hand pump to keep the engine room dry. When the starboard anchor line snapped, *Intrepid* swung broadside to the wind and began to yaw. The large coolers slid about like toy boxes. Each of the men working the pumps became seasick.

During his fifth turn at the pump, Gallagher worked with his left arm until he was too sick to stand. Sweating and gasping for air, he slumped against the bulkhead. The odor of fuel oil permeated the hold. He knew he had been in worse storms while aboard aircraft carriers, but he was also aware, even in his semiconscious stupor, that he had never been out in a small boat in weather this heavy. When Millan, the only one not seasick, switched on *Intrepid*'s engines in an attempt to turn the boat's bow back into the storm, the fumes swirled through the engine room and the hold. Gallagher retched until he was too weak to move. Vomit and saltwater sloshed around him as he lay on the deck sliding back and forth with the reeling boat.

22

Gallagher was not sure how he passed the night. At one point, Thibodeaux was hunched near him on the deck vomiting, moaning, and cursing in Creole. At another point, something heavy crashed on the afterdeck above him, but he was lost so deeply in a fog of nausea that he did not care what had broken loose. Just before dawn the rain stopped and the wind slackened, but the sea continued to batter *Intrepid*. At first light, Millan raised the anchor and headed the salvage boat into the waves. He nursed the wheel and throttles so that he could adjust *Intrepid*'s speed and angle to the steepness of each incoming wave.

The going was sloppy, but Gallagher dragged himself up onto the deck and lay there, his cheek against the wet steel, gulping the fresh air. As the spindrift soaked him, he shivered despite the morning's humidity. The rapier's wound ached, and the bandage was soggy with sweat and saltwater. The sun broke through the clouds intermittently, causing the spray to sparkle around Gallagher on the deck. Still, nearly an hour passed before he could climb the ship's ladder to the shower and, slouching against the bulkhead, douse himself with fresh water. He let the water run through his hair, over his face, and into his mouth. His arm was swollen, and, when he peeled away the bandage, he saw that the wound had turned purple.

Hunched over and carrying his clothes, Gallagher made his way back down to the afterdeck, where Thibodeaux, who had recovered more quickly, was cutting away the jagged section of railing that had smashed when the compressor and ice chest had torn loose and hurtled overboard. Having showered earlier, he had a red bandana tied around his head to keep his long, damp hair out of his face as he worked. Matt, who remembered nothing of the storm, chattered at Thibodeaux.

By the time *Intrepid* approached Key West, the sky had cleared and the sun was shining. Gallagher slouched against the bulkhead, his head low, staring at the decking. The wind had died suddenly, and the strange, oppressive humidity after the storm made him feel as though he were breathing swamp water. Millan turned the salvage boat, set a zigzag course for the Bight, and ran through the entrance on a following sea. Still able to think of nothing but getting off the water, Gallagher kept his focus on the deck until the salvage boat was moored. As Gallagher stood up and looked at the Waterfront Market, which seemed the color of bile, three short, sharp blasts of a ship's horn startled him. With the noise echoing in his aching head, he glanced irritably across the finger piers, past *Maestro III*, at a sleek fifty-five-foot metallic blue dive boat. A bright red ROV—a remotely operated vehicle used for underwater exploration—rested like a bug-eyed, Day-Glo crab in a cradle on the lower deck aft of the flying bridge.

After three additional mind-rattling blasts from the ship's horn, Pete Vogel appeared shirtless on the dive boat's bridge. Even at a distance of forty yards, his diamond-studded crucifix glinted in the light. He grinned at *Intrepid*'s crew, raised a glass filled with ice and dark liquid, and waved with his free hand.

"What de fuck?" Thibodeaux muttered as he secured a bumper's line to a cleat.

"Come on aboard," Vogel shouted across the water. "Have a couple of cold ones on me."

Gallagher, who wanted nothing more than to be on solid ground, looked at Thibodeaux, smiled ironically, and mumbled, "Yeah, right."

Still staring at the dive boat, Thibodeaux repeated, "What de fuckin' fuck?"

Gallagher leaned against the railing and gazed across the water. He was so preoccupied with Vogel's boat that he didn't notice Rita and Whitaker approaching *Intrepid* until they were near the bow. Whitaker pushed his glasses higher on his nose and looked over at Vogel on the dive boat's bridge.

"Came in yesterday afternoon just before the storm," Rita said. "And he's been acting like he's the goddamn Salvage King of South Florida. Like he's already cashed in on *Magdalena*'s treasure."

Millan climbed down from the bridge; the two divers, who'd been coiling lines and storing equipment when the ship's horn had sounded, stood gaping at the dive boat.

"Whenever he sees one of us, he invites us aboard," Whitaker said. Rita nodded toward the ROV at the boat's stern. "The son of a bitch says he wants us to meet Dirk, who's going to find the motherlode."

Millan whistled a long, low note. "Where in hell did the hombre get the money?" he asked.

Rita shook her head.

Thibodeaux pulled at his earring. "He's pissed away every fuckin' cent he ever made, ya know dat," he said.

Whitaker said, "Rumor has it he's being backed by some high rollers out of Miami."

Rita seemed to notice the condition of *Intrepid* and its crew for the first time. "Looks like the storm beat on you pretty good," she said to Millan.

"*La mar*, she was furious at us," Millan answered. "And Jack got a taste of her anger."

Gallagher smiled wanly, glanced again at Vogel's boat, and climbed over the gunwale onto the dock.

Rita's smile was tight. "That storm's just a preview of what's coming." she said.

"Brenda's a *huracán*?" Millan asked.

"Glad you, at least, have been monitoring the weather," she answered. "She's still a tropical storm. But the new projections show she's gonna be big. And they've got her heading right for Cuba."

Millan nodded but didn't say anything.

Glancing at the two divers who had begun to bring the bagged garbage and empty ice chests out onto the deck, Rita asked, "What about Matt?" She pulled a Marlboro from her pack and tapped the cigarette against the back of her wrist. "How's he doing?"

"He wasn't too bright to start wit'," Thibodeaux answered.

Rita shook her head, turned, and stared out beyond Vogel's boat at the power plant. Gallagher, who felt as though the pier was slowly undulating, glanced toward the sidewalk running along the waterfront.

Thibodeaux took a roll of film from the pocket of his

cutoffs and tossed it to Whitaker saying, "Here's de shots a de anchor."

Whitaker bobbled the film for a moment before catching it. "Thanks," he said. "This could be just what we need." As he spoke, his voice rose with excitement. "I've already checked the records, and *Magdalena*'s anchors were all struck at Seville in 1639." He flipped the roll a few inches into the air and caught it again. "I've faxed a note to the Archive of the Indies asking if any other anchors were struck that year. If not, we've finally got the evidence Braxton needs." He turned to Rita and said, "I'll get the film to Quick Prints right away. We should know something definite this afternoon . . . or tomorrow at the latest."

Rita stared at the unlit cigarette, broke it in half, and threw the ends into the water. "It's *Magdalena*'s anchor, all right," she murmured.

Whitaker gazed at Rita for a moment, nodded, and said, "You bet." He slipped the film into the pocket of his khakis and then, turning to leave, added, "Good work, Dewey." Already walking away, he nodded over his shoulder. "Ozzie, Jack, nice going. This could be it."

Gallagher leaned against the corner of the bookcase nearest the stairwell in the Doubloon office. Though uninvited, he'd followed Millan into the meeting. The glass in all of the bookcases had been replaced, and the office showed no signs of the break-in except that the rapier no longer hung on the wall and the conch no longer lay on Rita's desk. A more powerful computer stood on Rita's desk, a new radio transmitter

and receiver rested on the counter to the right of the air conditioner, and an upgraded fax machine lay on a wheeled
wooden cart by the counter. Thibodeaux sat across the table
from Rita. Seated to his right, Millan scanned the front page
of that morning's *Key West Tribune*, which lay on a heap of
file folders on the table. The newspaper headlined rumors of
Fidel Castro's death and the reactions of Cuban-American
groups in Miami and Washington, D.C. Gallagher was relieved that Hernández's byline appeared only above the story
on the Cubans in Miami; the front page carried nothing at all
about Doubloon.

Rita took a pink message slip from the pile of papers
and, reaching out to hand it to Gallagher, said, "Before I forget, Sergeant Escobar called this morning. The cops picked up
an end-of-the-roader last night who had some cobs on him.
They think he might be the guy that trashed the place. Escobar wants you to come to the station and see if you can ID
him."

Gallagher nodded. Just beginning to feel human again, he
sipped from a cold can of ginger ale he'd bought at the market.

Rita pulled a report bound in blue vinyl from beneath the
manila folders and, her hand shaking, flipped it onto the table.
The report slid across the newspaper and came to rest in front
of Thibodeaux and Millan. The cover featured Florida's state
seal and Robert Lee Beecham's name in embossed gold lettering. She gnawed at her lip. "That damn thing," she said, "ac-
cuses us of everything from running rum to black-marketing
babies."

Millan looked up from his reading. "If the report's that

bad," he said, "can't Braxton make it work against Señor Bee-cham?"

Smiling for the first time, Rita nodded. "Yeah, Oz," she answered. "In fact, Jack's friend Josie had an article in yesterday's *Trib* about the report. Called it a crock. Said anyone familiar with any of the local salvage operations would know it was crap."

Gallagher took another sip of ginger ale.

Thibodeaux glanced at the report's cover, rubbed the stubble on his chin, and asked, "So where does dat leave us?"

Rita pursed her lips. "Braxton thinks the goblet and silver bar'll show that the sites are still producing. The anchor's gonna help, too. And the chicken inspector's report is so obviously biased that Braxton can threaten to tie the board up in litigation for the rest of their natural lives." She glanced at the blue report. "And they know he'll do it, swamp them with civil suits, if they terminate our leases." As she slumped back in her chair and shook her head slowly, she added, "But Bobby Lee is so hellbent on screwing us, they won't be able to renew the leases either."

"That hombre won't let go of Nick," Millan said.

Rita leaned forward and shook a Marlboro from her pack. "None of us can," she said. She got the gold lighter to flare on the second try and lit the cigarette.

Millan folded the paper and asked, his voice low, "Tim's not coming in, is he, Rita?"

Rita sat back in her chair and exhaled. "He says he's too close. He can feel it. Feel the treasure. Feel *Magdalena* down there."

"Jesus, shee-it," Thibodeaux muttered. He pulled the bandana from his head, ran his hand through the long white streak in his hair, scratched his scalp, and stuffed the bandana into the pocket of his cutoffs.

"I told him we needed him for the hearing," Rita said almost in a whisper.

Millan pushed back his chair and stood up. His voice was soft, and he spoke to Rita as though they were the only two people in the room. "I raised Tim on the radio on our way in," he said. "The storm beat the *mierda* out of him, too." He laid his hands on the back of the chair. "It's too rough to use the afterburners, and he's pushing my divers to the wheel's edge. They're finding *nada*." He ran his tongue over his gold tooth and nodded. "I told him he had to come in."

Rita stared at the captain for a moment. "He won't," she said slowly and deliberately. "Not even for me."

23

The police station's waiting room smelled of industrial cleanser, mildew, and sweat. A long, scuffed beige counter bisected the room. In front of the counter, orange molded-plastic chairs lined each faded yellow wall. Behind the counter, desks and tables, most overflowing with stacks of files, formed a cluttered grid. After asking for Sergeant Escobar, Gallagher took a seat two chairs from a woman in a tentlike floral housedress. He had showered again and changed into long pants and a sportshirt, but he still hadn't slept. Sweat ran in rivulets down his back, and the room seemed to rock slowly.

A few minutes later, Hernández and Escobar strolled from a doorway at the opposite end of the room. Hernandez carried a brown leather briefcase, and Escobar waved a manila folder as he spoke to her. When Hernández saw Gallagher, she led the policeman toward him.

As Gallagher stood up, the sergeant paused at the counter to talk with a clerk. Hernández continued across the room until, a few feet from Gallagher, she stopped abruptly and said, "God, Jack, you look like you've been through the wringer."

"Yeah, literally," he said. Her head was no longer bandaged, but the cut along her hairline was still visible. "How're you feeling?" he asked.

"The headache's still pretty constant," she answered. "But it's not so bad I can't work."

He nodded. "What're you doing here?"

"Louis hoped I could get a make on Doubloon's nocturnal invader," she said. "But I couldn't pick him out of the lineup." She shook her head. "Louis probably won't even have you bother with it." Gazing into his face, she added, "Got caught in last night's blow, huh?"

The woman seated in the chair stared at them as she fanned herself with a section of newspaper.

"Yeah, got whacked pretty good." He shrugged and looked over at Escobar, who was nodding to the clerk. "I heard you actually wrote something nice about Doubloon."

As she came closer, her dark eyes glinted. "Not pro-Doubloon, Jack," she said. "Antibureaucracy . . . and anti-Beecham."

Gallagher smiled. "It's a start."

Escobar glanced at Hernández and Gallagher, nodded again to the clerk, and crossed the room toward them.

"Could we talk, Jack?" Hernández asked, still gazing at him.

Gallagher reached out with his hand, almost touched her shoulder, and let his hand drop to his side. "Yes," he said. "Good idea. I'd like that."

Approaching Gallagher, Escobar said, "Thanks for coming." As the two men shook hands, he added, "You look a little green around the gills."

"Apparently," Gallagher answered.

"I'll let you two gentlemen go on about your business," Hernández said, smiling at Escobar. "I've got some stuff I need to check on." She brushed her hand along Gallagher's arm. "Call me later," she said to him before turning and heading over to the counter.

As Escobar led Gallagher through the maze of desks toward the far doorway, he said, "We picked up this scumbag last night. Got him for possession. But unless I can make something bigger stick, he'll be back on the street tonight." He pushed open the door, and they headed down a narrow hallway covered with the same flaking yellow paint. "Thought he might be your boy because he had a couple of silver coins on him. Old Spanish coins."

"Couldn't Rita or Hugh Whitaker identify the coins?" Gallagher asked.

Escobar stopped outside another door, nodded, and said, "Whitaker took a look at them. Said they were the right vintage, but they could've come from any number of places." As he turned the door's handle, he added, "And the dude's real unclear about how he got 'em."

A uniformed officer stood by the door as Escobar and Gallagher entered the plain, square, brightly lit room furnished with only a wooden table and three orange plastic chairs. A tall, gaunt man in dirty denims and a Florida State University T-shirt sat hunched in one chair picking a scab on his forearm. His long stringy hair fell across his face. Although his hands were washed, his knuckles were gray. His fingernails, bitten to the nubs, were black around the cuticles. He did not look up when the two men stood across the table from him.

Escobar motioned Gallagher to a chair opposite the man. Then, still standing, the sergeant said, "We got a visitor for you, Patrick. His name's Jack Gallagher. Somebody cut him with a sword last week." He rolled up his sleeves as he spoke. "Coupla inches higher, would've gotten his neck. Maybe killed him."

The man raised his head and looked at Gallagher. His dark brown eyes registered nothing, and he went back to picking the scab. His forearm was pockmarked and bruised, the color of a plum.

Escobar took three silver cobs from his pocket and tossed them onto the table. The man flinched but didn't look up. "Shit, I'd hate to think anybody'd be stupid enough to try to kill a guy for a few lousy silver coins," Escobar said.

The man looked again at Gallagher, but his eyes remained blank. Escobar turned the third chair around, sat down, and slid one of the cobs across the table with his forefinger. As Gallagher studied the man, he felt as though he'd seen him before. Images of that night flashed through his mind—his strolling past the shops and bars with Hernández, the Doubloon door ajar, the rapier streaking out of the darkness, the figure loping away, and the searing pain. The man certainly could have been the burglar, but he could as easily have been one of the end-of-the-roaders Gallagher had passed on Duval or had seen around the dock. Realizing that there was no way he could make a positive identification, he smiled ironically to himself and shook his head.

Escobar leaned close to the man and said, "This guy's office down at the Bight was burglarized, Patrick. Some expensive equipment was destroyed. Is that something you know about?"

The man glanced at the sergeant and then lowered his eyes. "Is it, Patrick?" Escobar repeated.

The man sniffled and then ran the back of his hand across

the base of his nose. "I don't know nothin'," he said to the floor.

Escobar looked first at Gallagher and then at the uniformed guard who still stood by the door. "Yeah, yeah," the sergeant said, tapping the coin nearest him. "You've said that before. But here's the thing. I'm not saying you did it. I just figure that 'cause you got these coins you must know something about it." He leaned back, resting his forearms on the back of the chair. "You talk to me, Patrick, and maybe I can do you a favor. Cut you some slack on the drug bust." He folded his hands. "Think about it, Patrick."

Staring at his hands, the man sniffled loudly, cleared his throat, and swallowed.

Gallagher stood up. The walls were closing in on him, and the air was fetid—but his mind was clearing. As he fingered the edge of the bandage under his shirt, he stared at the coins on the table. A single thought rose like a glittering air bubble toward the surface of his mind. "Patrick," he said, "or whatever the hell your name is, somebody's going to get rich off the stuff you stole from that office." He reached into his pants pocket, took out the doubloon, and flashed it in front of the man's face. The three silver cobs, their lettering corroded and their edges uneven, looked like badly struck lead by comparison.

As the man gaped at the doubloon, Gallagher turned it over twice so that both the shield and the Jerusalem cross shone in the overhead light. Escobar stared at the doubloon, and the guard took two steps from the door to get a better look.

Gallagher held the doubloon near the man's face for another ten seconds and then flipped it, caught it, and slid it back into his pocket. "Yep. Somebody," he repeated, "is sure as hell getting rich off that stuff you stole."

The man glanced up quickly at Gallagher, looked away at the cobs, and wiped his nose with the back of his hand. Gallagher walked over to the door, nodded to the guard who stood there with his mouth agape, opened the door, entered the hall, and slammed the door behind him.

Escobar caught up with Gallagher halfway down the hallway and, grabbing his left shoulder, said, "What the hell was that all about?"

Gallagher turned toward the sergeant and said, "That's him all right. I know it's him, but I couldn't swear to it in court."

Escobar scratched his mustache. "I meant, what was that with the gold coin?"

"You said it yourself," Gallagher answered. "Nobody, at least no burglar smart enough to wear gloves and to deactivate the alarm, is dumb enough to kill somebody over a couple of coins."

"Yeah," Escobar said. "We've been working on the assumption that you and Hernández stumbled onto the guy before he got upstairs, and he just grabbed whatever he could when he bolted."

"I don't think so." Gallagher pulled at his collar and rubbed his neck. "He wasn't after treasure, at least not directly. Whoever sent him wanted the computer disks, not the stuff upstairs. And certainly not the goddamned coins."

"Shit," Escobar said. He began to speak more to himself than to Gallagher. "That must be why Hernández started suddenly asking me for the list Mrs. Gallagher made of what was stolen."

"She did?"

"Yeah, right after the lineup, when I showed her the coins."

Gallagher shook his head, and Escobar turned to go back to the interrogation room.

"Let him go," Gallagher called after the sergeant.

Escobar turned back around. "What?" he asked. "Why?"

"You've got no proof," Gallagher answered. "If you let him go, maybe he'll lead you back to whoever hired him."

Escobar nodded. "So that's why the big deal about somebody getting rich."

Gallagher didn't answer.

Escobar rubbed his mustache. "Yeah, you're right," he said. "He never would've stolen the disks on his own. It wouldn't even occur to him. And there'd be nowhere to fence 'em unless he knew somebody who wanted 'em." His smile was ironic. "Hell, the sword he cut you with would've been worth a lot more than the disks out on the street." He lowered his voice, as though he was thinking aloud. "Somebody sent him for those disks, all right."

24

The next morning, as Gallagher entered the old red-brick maritime courthouse that stood only a hundred yards from the ocean, he was taken by the smell of wood and seawater, which seemed to him to hearken back to the days of clipper ships and windjammers. With its thick walls, high ceilings, and dark walnut paneling, the admiralty courtroom was not, despite the lack of air conditioning, oppressively hot. He had fallen asleep in his hotel room after leaving the police station the previous afternoon, and when he'd finally had a chance to call Hernández, he'd gotten only her voice mail. Later that night, still mulling over who might benefit most from the information on the computer disks, he'd meandered alone through Key West's side streets. As he walked, he went over in his mind everything that had happened since he'd arrived in town for his father's funeral. He knew there had to be some underlying order to it all, but a clear pattern failed to emerge. At one point, he'd stopped near the gate to the cemetery, where the night-blooming cereus glowed like Christmas lights under the hazy sky. Finally, he'd slept badly for a few hours toward dawn, dreaming again of fending off MIGs hurtling at him from blindingly bright sunlight.

Gallagher took a seat on the bench behind Thibodeaux

and Millan in the gallery outside the courtroom's ornate walnut railing. The three members of the antiquity board sat at a long, raised table between the unoccupied judge's bench and the two rectangular tables for the advocates. The chairman of the board, a tall, thin man with sharp facial features and a shock of silver hair, sat at the middle of the table. A handsome fifty-year-old woman with high cheekbones sat to his left. To the chairman's right, a ruddy, muscular man, a year or so older than Gallagher, pulled uncomfortably at the collar of his starched blue shirt.

Rita and Whitaker were already seated with Finch at the left-hand advocates' table. Beecham, resplendent in a light seersucker suit, stood next to the other table speaking intently to a short, plump man. To the far right, near the empty jury box, Hernández sat alone at the reporters' table, her notebook and a tape recorder lying on the polished veneer in front of her. When her eyes met Gallagher's, she nodded, and the slightest hint of an enigmatic smile crossed her face—as though she now understood something he hadn't yet fathomed.

The morning's proceedings moved at a ponderous pace. As the plump man handed Beecham documents, the director of antiquities reviewed the allegations in the report he had previously submitted. Finch, speaking in a deep, resonant voice that reverberated through the courtroom, rebutted each of the report's points. Beecham referred repeatedly to the 1987 Historic Shipwreck Preservation Act, and Finch continually reminded him that a number of the salvage leases predated the law. Both men spoke in formal, deferential tones that belied the accusations they flung at each other. Four large ceiling fans clicked as they twirled, and the mewing of gulls rode the breeze that occasionally alleviated the increasing heaviness in the room. Gallagher started to sweat, and the wound he'd rebandaged began again to itch. After an hour, he noticed Pete Vogel sidle into the back of the gallery and slouch onto a bench.

Just before eleven, Finch sprang the discovery of the anchor on Beecham and the board commissioners. As Whitaker gave Finch the stack of eight-by-ten color blowups of the photographs Thibodeaux had shot at the salvage site, Beecham stood, straightened his suitcoat, and said, "This is highly irregular. Neither the Office of Antiquities nor any other state agency was informed about the discovery of this anchor." His face was pink, but his voice was controlled, even calm.

Finch cleared his throat. "While it is true," he said to the commissioners rather than to Beecham, "that we did not contact the Office of Antiquities, the explanation is simple." He raised the pictures in his hand. "We did not receive the photographic evidence until early evening yesterday. In fact, our staff archeologist worked most of the night to establish the anchor's authenticity." He gazed briefly at each of the commissioners. "Our conclusion is that it is *Santa María Magdalena*'s anchor. And the diver who made the discovery and our archeologist, both of whom are present here today, are prepared to testify before this commission to provide any requisite verification."

"Mr. Finch, it is not necessary for you to call the diver." Beecham bowed slightly in mock deference; his tone was overly pleasant, almost condescending. "If Doubloon, Incorporated, states that an anchor was discovered only yesterday, no one would cast doubt on such an assertion." He waved his chubby hand at the photographs Finch held. "But this anchor could certainly be an anomaly. Who's to say it's not an eighteenth-century artifact? Or even something more recent?"

Thibodeaux, who had on a clean shirt and a bolo with a silver clasp in the shape of an alligator, hooked his elbow over the back of the bench, and whispered loudly to Millan, "Damn. Braxton told me I'd get a chance to take de stand, ya know dat. And I'm tellin' ya, I was ready, podna. Ready ta rock."

Millan nodded but didn't answer.

Finch smiled amiably at Beecham. "Well, sir," he said, "if you or any of your staff from the Office of Antiquities would like, Dr. Whitaker would, I'm sure, be happy to speak to the matter of the anchor's authenticity—either here before this commission or at some later date in your offices."

The chairman glanced at his colleagues, nodded gravely, and said, "This new evidence is certainly an issue of concern to this board. Presenting the testimony at this time is, therefore, appropriate, Mr. Finch."

Whitaker rose to his full height, his shoulders thrown back. His suit, though not new, was well tailored and fastidiously pressed. His hair, combed down, was less unruly, and his beard was even more neatly trimmed. As he sauntered by Finch, he took the photographs from the lawyer. He sat in an oak armchair located midway between the commissioners and Hernández, crossed his legs, and gazed at Beecham.

"Mr. Beecham," the chairman said, "you may proceed."

Finch gestured expansively toward Beecham as if to usher him forward.

Beecham hitched up his trousers and smiled at the commissioners. "Dr. Whitaker," he said, "you are Doubloon, Incorporated's only archeologist, is that true?" His tone was altered, the condescension more overt than it had been with Finch.

"Yes, sir," Whitaker answered.

Beecham licked his lips. "And what other positions, may I ask, have you held in the profession?"

Whitaker looked Beecham in the eye. "This has been my only job, sir," he answered. "But if it's my credentials that are in question here, I have a doctorate in antiquities from the University of Chicago." He began to smile. "I've published twenty-five articles on treasure salvaging, I've lectured extensively, and I've provided expert interviews to the national and international media."

"And was that degree in marine archeology?" Beecham asked.

Whitaker ran his hand through his hair and gazed up for a moment at one of the fans. "Actually," he admitted, "my specialty was classical civilizations. The Mediterranean and the Middle East. But most of the standards and procedures still apply."

"Indeed," Beecham said. He pulled at the cuffs of his suitcoat, glanced at his plump assistant, and nodded as if in thought. "And these articles you mentioned, they've appeared in scholarly journals?"

Whitaker remained smiling. "No, sir," he answered. "Most have been in magazines like *National Geographic* and *Smithsonian*—ones that people actually read."

Beecham walked nearer the chair and gestured at the photographs in Whitaker's lap. "And these pictures, you say, were taken yesterday?" he asked, his tone incredulous.

"Dewey Thibodeaux shot them the day before," Whitaker answered. "We received these prints last night."

"Ah," Beecham said, glancing again at his assistant. "And you've been able to ascertain in less than fifteen hours that the anchor is from the galleon *Santa María Magdalena*?"

"That's the supposition, yes."

"Supposition?" Beecham looked at the board chairman. "We are laboring here, Dr. Whitaker, under the impression that Mr. Finch stated that you would verify the anchor's authenticity."

Finch twisted his bishop's ring as he gazed at Beecham.

Unfazed, Whitaker answered, "We have an overwhelming preponderance of evidence suggesting it's *Magdalena*'s."

"A preponderance?" Beecham scoffed. "And what exactly is this preponderance of evidence?"

Whitaker took his glasses from his suitcoat pocket and, slipping them on, said, "May I explain?"

"Please do, Dr. Whitaker," Beecham answered, his voice sardonic. "This should be enlightening."

Whitaker hunched his shoulders, shuffled the photographs, and raised a close-up showing the Roman numerals on the anchor's crown. "Notice," he said, "that the double dolphin markings are Spanish. And the date the anchor was struck is, as you can see, 1639, both of which obviously indicate that it's from one of the plate fleets, the treasure fleets—not some later period. I have faxed this information to the Archive of the Indies in Seville, Spain." He reached over and passed the picture to the female commissioner, who scanned it before giving it to the chairman. Whitaker then sifted through the photographs and held up a shot of one of the anchor's flukes.

"Furthermore," he went on, "the anchor is similar in all major respects to other galleon anchors recovered from salvage sites of the 1622 and 1715 plate fleets."

Hernández took notes furiously; Rita spun a black pen between her fingers. Thibodeaux thrust his fist in the air, but Millan remained impassive. Gallagher glanced at Vogel, who sat forward, his forearms on his knees and the crucifix dangling between his legs, as he stared at Whitaker. Outside the courtroom's high open windows, gulls crossed the pale sky.

"Finally, and most importantly," Whitaker said as he passed on the second photograph, "the size alone indicates that it's a sheet anchor." He selected a long shot of the divers hovering next to the anchor, waved it at Beecham, and gave it to the woman.

"A sheet anchor?" the chairman asked as he squinted at the picture the woman held.

"Yes, sir," Whitaker answered. "A Spanish ship's captain used a sheet anchor, stored in a galleon's hold, only as a last resort in the most difficult situations. Either the galleon was breaking up on the shoals at that point, or the captain believed his ship was in such danger that he had only that single option left." His eyes brightened as though an idea had just occurred to him. "The former is far more likely. But either way, you can safely assume that a galleon's wreckage lies nearby."

"A galleon," Beecham said, trying to draw the board's attention back to himself, "But not necessarily *Santa María Magdalena*."

"*Magdalena*'s captain, Bartólome de Alcala, was not only the commander of the plate fleet but also one of the Spanish Empire's most experienced and respected seamen. He would have done everything humanly possible to keep his ship from sinking, but in a hurricane . . ." Whitaker shrugged, raised his shoulders, and stared directly into Beecham's eyes. "It has to be *Magdalena*'s," he added as though it were an established fact.

Seeming perplexed for the first time, Beecham sputtered, "You haven't provided any proof whatever. Many galleons must have sunk in the area."

Taking off his glasses, Whitaker said serenely, "In the general vicinity, yes. But in that spot, no." He slid his glasses into his coat pocket, straightened the stack of photographs, and looked again into Beecham's face. "The proof, Governor, is irrefutable."

"You . . .," Beecham stammered. "What about *Neustra Señora de Candelaria*? Or the *Concepción* or the *Consolación*? Or the *Santa Catalina*? Or . . . or any number of sunken galleons?"

"Excuse me, gentlemen . . .," the ruddy commissioner said in a slow drawl. He fiddled with the knot of his tie. "This conversation isn't going to resolve anything." He picked up the first photograph. "Dr. Whitaker, you mentioned earlier that you faxed the foundry markings and date to Spain."

Whitaker nodded. "In fact, I expected a reply already, but we haven't received one yet."

"And the response you get will resolve this issue?" the commissioner asked.

"As I said, yes, it will. Beyond doubt."

"And you expect this response soon?"

Whitaker nodded again. "Yes. I expect to have definitive information within the . . ." He glanced at his gold wristwatch. "It's probably at the office now."

"Good." The ruddy commissioner leaned forward and looked at his colleagues. "Then I suggest we break for lunch and reconvene at, say, one o'clock."

The woman nodded, and the chairman said, "Fine. Excellent idea."

Nodding to himself, Whitaker slipped the remaining photographs onto the commissioners' table. Beecham raised his forefinger and opened his mouth to speak, but then lowered his hand and shook his head. Vogel sat back and wiped his mouth with his stumps. Hernández still jotted notes, but Rita was already standing, gnawing her lip and rubbing the fingers of her right hand together.

25

Outside the courthouse, the humidity was stifling. The breeze had died, and the haziness had deepened. While Rita and Whitaker hurried to the Doubloon office to check for the fax, Millan invited Gallagher along to the Chart House Bar for lunch with Finch and Thibodeaux. Though Gallagher had intended to catch up with Hernández, he welcomed the chance to talk with the others. He was still unable to make sense of who would have stolen the disks and why—and he hoped someone would say something at lunch that would focus his thoughts.

The bar was far more crowded than it had been the other time Gallagher was there, and the four men huddled at the only empty table, in the far corner away from the television. After the waitress, a stumpy young woman with short blond hair, brought their drinks, Thibodeaux raised his bottle of Dixie and said, "Ta Braxton Finch and Hugh Whitaker, for droppin' dat anchor on Beecham's head. Blew de bastard right outa de water." Laughing, he turned toward Gallagher. "Just like a fuckin' smart bomb, huh, Jack?"

Gallagher nodded, although he didn't agree that Beecham had seemed very flustered. He sipped his beer and then asked Finch, "What do you think? Will the anchor do it?"

Finch put down his bloody Mary, wiped his mouth with a cocktail napkin, and answered, "It'll help, Jack. No question about that." He cracked a peanut shell and popped the peanuts into his mouth. "But don't go betting the ranch on the outcome. Not yet, anyway."

Swirling his beer in his half-empty bottle, Thibodeaux said, "Yeah. De fuckin' chicken inspector's gonna have ta do some-t'ing ta save face, I'm tellin' ya."

"True, amigo," Millan said. "And you know he's still got to be holdin' a couple of cards."

Turning back to Finch, Gallagher asked, "Was there anything in the papers this morning about the hearing?"

Finch lifted the celery stalk from his glass and bit off half of it. He shook his head as he chewed.

"*Nada*, Jack," Millan said. "Nothing about the company at all."

Gallagher scratched the side of his nose. "Braxton," he asked, "what . . . ?"

Whitaker burst into the room carrying a rolled chart and a brown manila envelope. He held the envelope high as he dodged among the tables. "I got it," he shouted. Then, aware that the others in the bar were looking at him, he added, "The fax came." His voice, though lower, was still ebullient. Sweating and almost breathless, he placed the rolled chart on the table, brushed back his disheveled hair, and slid two pieces of paper from the envelope. "Dewey, you did it, partner." Waving the paper, he repeated, "You did it."

Finch cleared his throat and said, "Hugh, slow down, boy. You're going to bust a gasket."

Whitaker took a deep breath and handed the pieces of

paper across the table to Finch. As the lawyer perused the papers, Whitaker said to the others, "The fact that it's a sheet anchor. That's the key." He glanced at Finch. "The foundry cast dozens of other anchors in 1639, but only one sheet anchor . . ."

Millan nodded, and Thibodeaux grinned; Finch looked up from the paper.

"*Santa María Magdalena's*," Whitaker said, his voice suddenly almost solemn.

Thibodeaux raised his arm and whooped; Gallagher tapped his bottle against Millan's margarita glass.

Finch smiled, rubbed his chin with the heel of his hand, and said, "Sit down, will ya, Hugh. I don't want this news to hit Miami before we've finished our drinks."

Whitaker pulled over a chair, sat down, and leaned his elbows on the table. "But here's the best part," he said, his voice quaking. "As I told the board, galleons kept sheet anchors stored. And *Magdalena's* crew couldn't have gotten that anchor onto the deck during a hurricane. No way."

"So de hull musta ripped open right around dere," Thibodeaux said.

Whitaker smiled, raised his hands, and shrugged.

"Does Rita know about this?" Millan asked, pointing to the papers that Finch still held.

"Not yet," Whitaker answered. "She only stopped at the office for a second. Said she had to head home for something." He picked up the rolled chart as the waitress slid the plates with cheeseburgers and other sandwiches onto the table. None of the five men looked at the waitress or the food. "The fax arrived just after she left," Whitaker added. He waved the chart and looked directly at Finch. "I was thinking on the way over here. What if we compromise?"

"What de hell?" Thibodeaux stammered.

Whitaker glanced at each of the others as he said, "What if we seek to renew just the eastern sites and the Havana Bank? Offer to give up the western sites?" Sweat beaded on his forehead. "With the anchor, they've almost got to let us hold onto those sites."

Gallagher, who had never much liked compromises, shook his head and gazed up at the television where Muhammad Ali silently pummeled Sonny Liston.

Finch stroked his chin, cocked his head, hesitated, and then said, "I don't know, Hugh. Compromising is kissing your cousin."

Whitaker put on his glasses, looked at each of the others, and then spoke directly to Finch. "Hear me out, will you, Braxton?" he said. "Just give the idea half a chance."

Finch nodded. "Yeah. Okay, Hugh," he answered as he moved his bloody Mary and corned beef sandwich out of the way so that Whitaker could unroll the chart on the table.

Drops of sweat fell on the chart as Whitaker leaned over and traced with his gold pen a line that circumscribed less than half of the area on which Doubloon held leases. He then looked up at the others and said, "We can hold onto the sites around where you found the anchor and the spots like the Havana Bank where we've already recovered artifacts." He picked up a paper napkin and wiped his forehead. Almost as an afterthought, he added, "And we could let go of the sites where the artifact trail peters out." Glancing at Finch, he asked, "What do you think?"

As he idly turned his bishop's ring so that the emerald caught the light, Finch scanned the chart again. "It would reduce both our operating costs and record keeping," he said. "That'd help us with our investors as well as with that bozo, Beecham."

"No way we get in bed wit' dat fuckin' chicken inspector, I'm tellin' ya," Thibodeaux said.

Finch turned to Thibodeaux and said, "You're the one who said Beecham is going to need some way to save his worthless hide from public ridicule."

Thibodeaux nodded. "Yeah. Dat's true," he said. Shaking his head, he sat back in his chair. "I still don't like it, but ya got a point dere, podna."

Still unsure about the idea, Gallagher stared at the chart. The sites the company would give up, he realized, were those farther west, beyond the area where Tim was working. "What about the silver bar and goblet?" he asked.

Whitaker smiled. "Good point, Jack," he said. "I thought of that, too." With the tip of his pen, he pointed at the line he had drawn on the chart. "Tim found them here, at the periphery of these sites. But he's been moving too far afield. Predictably, he's found nothing since he went back out. There's no trail at all." He wadded the napkin he still held in his hand. "And, we're going to have to give up something."

"What about Rita?" Gallagher asked. "What'll she think?"

Everyone looked at Millan.

"Rita won't like it," the boat captain said, shaking his head. "And I don't like it either, amigos." He tapped the chart with his thick index finger. "You're giving away all those sites Nick was planning to work next month."

"Christ, Ozzie, not that again!" Whitaker said, his voice still quivering. "We've all been over that ground before. The sites around the Havana Bank and that anchor are the only critical ones." He waved his hand over the chart. "The other sites don't matter."

"Rita might well accept the compromise," Finch said. "She's as worn out as an old dishrag by all the haggling. And we can't know if we don't approach her with it."

Tugging at his earring, Thibodeaux said, "Half de sites are a helluva lot better dan none. And she knows dat."

Finch looked around the table and then said, "I can broach the concept when the hearing reconvenes this afternoon. See how it flies." He turned back toward Millan and added, "You should probably be the one to talk with Rita."

Millan's gold tooth gleamed as he smiled. "How'd I know that was com'n', Braxton?" he said. Shaking his head again, he turned to Whitaker and asked, "Can I use the chart, amigo, so I can at least show her what we'd be holdin' onto?"

"Absolutely," Whitaker answered. He leaned back in his chair, ran the napkin across his forehead, and smiled. "We won't need it until we find out if the Gov'll buy into the concept."

As Millan rolled the chart, he said as much to himself as to the others, "*Sí*, I'll do it. I'll do it." He pushed back his chair, stood up, and lifted the chart in one hand and his cheeseburger in the other. "See you hombres back at the hearing."

While Finch and Whitaker discussed how they would present Doubloon's compromise offer to the board, Gallagher studied them. Finch's experience seemed to temper Whitaker's enthusiasm, but the two men worked well together. Paying only scant attention to the conversation, Thibodeaux devoured his cheeseburger and ordered another Dixie.

When the four men left the Chart House, heat radiated above the pavement, and even the tourists were slowing into a midday torpor. Gallagher rolled his neck and, glancing across the street, glimpsed the end-of-the-roader he'd seen in the police station's interrogation room the previous afternoon. The man leaned against a black lightpost glaring at Gallagher and the three others who were still talking about the compromise. When Gallagher stopped abruptly and stared across the street, the man turned, slinked away into the crowd of tourists, and headed toward the corner.

"What's the matter, Jack?" Whitaker asked when he noticed that Gallagher had halted.

"It's him," Gallagher said, stepping off the curb into the street, "the dirtball that broke into the office."

Finch grabbed Gallagher's left arm. "Whoa, Jack," he said, "we don't need you going off half-cocked."

Gallagher paused, and Finch let go of his arm as a thin, extremely tan brunette woman on a fat-tired bicycle swerved to avoid them. Laughing, she glanced back over her shoulder at Gallagher as she rode away.

"You mean de dude dat cut ya?" Thibodeaux asked.

Gallagher stepped back onto the sidewalk. "Yeah," he answered. "Sergeant Escobar must've released him." He looked again across the street, but the man was nowhere in sight.

"You identified him?" Whitaker asked.

"Yeah," Gallagher said, turning back to the others. "I mean, no." He shrugged. "I knew it was him, but I couldn't have sworn to it in court."

"It's not important right now," Finch said as he began to walk toward the courthouse. "Let's get going, gentlemen. We've got a deal to cut."

26

When the chairman of the Antiquities Board reconvened the hearing, neither Rita nor Millan was present. Hernández, seeming to know something had changed, caught Gallagher's eye as he sat near Thibodeaux in the front of the gallery. Near the back of the gallery, Enrique Cardona sat quietly with his hands folded in his lap. Pete Vogel leaned against the wall. As soon as the chairman set down his gavel, Finch took the fax that Whitaker handed him, rose, strolled around to the front of the table, held up the fax, and said, "I have here conclusive evidence from the Archive of the Indies in Seville, Spain, that the anchor we described this morning is *Santa María Magdalena*'s." He turned pointedly toward Beecham. "And I would like to offer anyone, and especially the esteemed director of antiquities of the State of Florida, the opportunity to inspect the anchor at the site to verify its authenticity."

As Beecham was about to respond, Rita and Millan entered the room. While Rita carried the chart to the advocates' table, Millan slipped into the empty seat between Gallagher and Thibodeaux, leaned over, and whispered, "*Mierda*, that's what she thinks of it. But she'll let Braxton see if it'll fly."

Finch returned to the advocates' table, put his hand on

Rita's shoulder, tilted his head, spoke softly to her, and nod-ded. Her eyes fierce, she whispered back to him. He shook his head.

Whitaker sat in his chair silently shuffling documents.

Finch faced the commissioners and began to speak again in a deep voice. "Doubloon, Incorporated," he said, "has an indisputable legal right to retain all of the sites licensed to it. However . . ." He paused, turned, and looked at Beecham. ". . . in the interest of simplifying the proceedings and pre-cluding subsequent litigation, the company might be willing to compromise . . ." He turned back toward the board mem-bers. ". . . if it meant that Doubloon would receive guarantees of free and clear access to certain selected sites."

As Finch spoke about the reduced record keeping and the smaller area to oversee, Beecham leaned back in his chair, crossed his legs, and stared at him. The chairman, seemingly enrapt, nodded repeatedly, and the ruddy commissioner began to sift through the documents in front of him.

When Finch finished, Beecham stood up slowly, placed the palms of his hands on the table, cocked his head, and cleared his throat. "This concept," he announced, "is the first sensible, indeed, the first responsible idea Doubloon has offered." He stood up straight and raised his hands. "Perhaps," he went on, "fewer sites would be managed with the sort of competence and integrity that marine salvage truly requires." He glanced at Rita. "I would have to consider the specific points of the proposal—and I would demand that all work on the sites be curtailed until the compromise agreement is reached." He smiled magnanimously at Finch. "But this idea definitely has merit."

Finch and Beecham remained standing across from each other. The chairman nodded vigorously and then looked at the woman on his left, who fingered her gold necklace for a moment before nodding also. The ruddy commissioner pulled a newspaper clipping from among the documents in front of him and said, "I don't much like it. I'm new to this board, so I don't know exactly how this business usually works." He pulled at his collar. "But compromising is just plain wrong." His drawl became more pronounced. "This hearing is supposed to enable us to reach a final decision. Compromising does nothing."

Beecham's neck reddened. "Sometimes, sir," he said directly to the man, "compromise is the best course of action." His voice was laced with condescension. "Why, our nation was built on compromise."

The commissioner stared back at Beecham for a moment. "With all due respect, Mr. Beecham," he said, "compromise is crap."

His face florid, Beecham said nothing. His cheek below his left eye twitched as he set his jaw. Hernández scribbled in her notepad; Rita dropped her pen on the table and smiled for the first time. Whitaker's eyes grew larger behind the lenses of his glasses, and the sheet of paper he held quivered. Thibodeaux elbowed Millan in the ribs and said, "A commissioner wit' de balls ta stand up ta de chicken inspector. Dis could get good, I'm tellin' ya."

"The hombre's got *cohones*," Millan whispered.

The ruddy commissioner looked over at the chairman and said, "What we're supposed to be doing today is deciding if Doubloon's track record merits lease renewals. Renewing some leases and not others sends a contradictory message to everybody." He turned toward Beecham. "If your report is true, Governor, then compromise would let every salvor in the state think they could trash whatever they want as long as they're willing to bargain later." He waved the newspaper clipping. "And if the report's not true, then what we've been doing today is just some bogus witch-hunt."

Beecham stiffened; a vein in his temple pulsed. "My report," he sputtered, his voice barely controlled, "is . . . I've served this state since you were . . . You . . ."

The plump man in the blue and pink tie reached across the table and grabbed Beecham's sleeve.

Ignoring Beecham, the ruddy man held up the newspaper article, turned to the other two commissioners, and said, "This makes me wonder what the hell's been going on down here." He passed the clipping to the chairman. "I mean, here's what I take as an objective view of the situation. And, frankly, it sounds like the truth's being trampled by the politics of the whole thing."

As the plump man pulled Beecham back toward the table, the chairman scanned the article, looked over at Hernández, and said, "The reporter is here, I believe." He glanced at both Finch and Beecham and then turned back toward the ruddy man. "Perhaps you'd like to ask her some questions directly?"

Hernández stopped writing. Almost involuntarily, she looked from the commissioners past the advocates' table toward Gallagher. Her eyes were bright and steady.

"This is an outrage," Beecham bristled as he freed himself from the plump man's grip. "Ms. Hernández isn't objective about that pack of pirates. That article hasn't a shred of truth. Not one god-blasted iota!"

Finch turned to the commission's chairman and, his tone sarcastic, said, "Pirates? A pack of pirates? There's an objective . . ."

"You old fart," Whitaker yelled. He leapt to his feet, pulled off his glasses, and waved them at Beecham. "You wouldn't know the truth if you stepped in it."

The chairman banged his gavel, stood, and shouted, "Wait. Wait just one . . ."

"What?" Beecham blubbered. "What are you . . . ?" Saliva sprayed from his mouth.

Finch put his hand on Whitaker's shoulder, but the archeologist broke away, shoved a stack of papers onto the floor, and charged around the table toward Beecham.

Millan sprang from his seat, hurdled the railing, raced forward, and threw a bear hug around Whitaker's arms and chest. Beecham, who had instinctively backed away, tripped on a chair leg and flopped backward onto the table. Whitaker struggled for a moment, and then, seeming to become suddenly aware of where he was and what he was doing, sagged in Millan's grip.

While the chairman repeatedly struck the table with his gavel, Finch ran his hands through his thick hair and gazed at Rita, who gnawed her lower lip. Hernández smiled ironically at Gallagher as he stood clutching the railing, blood pounding in his ears. Thibodeaux whooped loudly, and Vogel leaned against the wall and whistled. Millan let go of Whitaker, who gaped for a moment at the papers he'd strewn across the floor, pulled on his glasses, and looked over at the advocates' table.

Rita turned and stalked away. When Gallagher caught up with her at the door and took hold of her forearm, she stopped. Her eyes glistened, but she fought back the tears. "Idiots," she hissed. "Men are such goddamned idiots." She pulled herself from him and stomped out the door. A moment later, Cardona brushed by Gallagher without a word and strode from the courtroom.

As Whitaker surveyed the mayhem he'd caused, Millan shook his head slowly. Beecham righted himself, brushed off his suit, and plodded over to the board chairman. Finch angrily stuffed files back into his battered leather briefcase, and Vogel, grinning, sidled over to Thibodeaux. Hernández approached the ruddy commissioner, shook his hand, introduced herself, and spoke quietly to him. The man glanced at his watch and nodded.

When Gallagher reached Finch, the lawyer snapped his briefcase shut and muttered, "Doubloon is a circus, Jack. Three full rings and a goddamned geek show." He picked up the briefcase and, without saying anything to Millan or Whitaker, turned from the table.

The chairman banged the gavel once again. His face flushed and his hair disheveled as though he himself had been in a scuffle, he said, "All the Doubloon leases will be evaluated together as one group." His voice quavered, and his Adam's apple protruded. "This board's final decision will be rendered in five days. In the meantime, no one, not Doubloon . . ." He looked over at the advocates' table. ". . . or anyone else, is to work those sites." He slammed the gavel one final time. "Any artifacts recovered in the interim will be confiscated by the state." He let the gavel slip from his hand and sat down heavily.

Finch, who had stopped while the chairman spoke, lumbered out of the room.

Hernández came over to Gallagher and said, "Sorry I missed you last night, Jack."

"Seems like Doubloon is providing you with some more hot copy," he said, rubbing the back of his neck.

"Looks that way," she answered. "An archeologist trying to punch out a politician. This could make the wires."

"Yeah," Gallagher said. "It's something you don't see every day." He rolled his neck. "It's all kind of crazy."

She took his arm and leaned close to him. "No, Wolf," she whispered. "It makes sense." She stepped back and gazed into his eyes. "Think about it, Jack. It all makes perfect sense."

He stared back into her bright, dark eyes until she let go of him.

"I've got an interview to do," she said, "and an article to write. But we still need to talk. More than ever."

"Yeah," he said. "Absolutely."

"Dinner at the maestro's at nine-thirty?" she asked, brushing her fingertips across her necklace. "He's been asking about you."

He nodded.

She again leaned close to him and, as she squeezed his forearm, whispered, "Think about what happened here, Jack. And then we'll talk." She held onto his arm for a moment before turning and heading back over to the table where the members of the Antiquities Board still clustered.

27

When Gallagher returned to the gallery where Thibodeaux and Vogel still stood by the railing, Vogel nudged the diver and said in his raspy voice, "The flyboy sure has a taste for sweet poison, don't he?"

Thibodeaux nodded and then, turning to Gallagher, said, "Pete, here, wants ya ta see his new boat."

"What?" Gallagher asked. He looked from Thibodeaux to Vogel.

Vogel smelled as though he'd washed with scented soap. There was no odor of alcohol at all, and his smile was almost friendly. He had unfastened the top three buttons of his shirt, and the crucifix hung above his paunch. "C'mon," he said, "see what me and my partners got on board. Flyin' the ROV makes afterburners and suction hoses look like fuckin' bi-planes." He waved his hand with the stumpy index and little fingers. "Have a margarita or four and see how salvage's really done. It'll do ya good after all this shit."

"Partners?" Gallagher asked.

"Silent partners, expatriates." Vogel's smile turned hostile. "And like any good partners, they're lettin' me run the show. I call the shots."

Gallagher scratched his eyebrow, shook his head, and exhaled. Turning to Thibodeaux, he asked, "And you're going with him?"

Hesitating, Thibodeaux yanked at his earring. "Yeah, podna," he said finally. "We can't do not'in' here, I'm tellin' ya. And anyways, I t'ought it'd be cool ta check out all dat gadgetry on de dive boat." Looking away from Gallagher, he flicked the earring with his middle finger. "See de future, ya know what I mean?"

"What . . . What about Rita?" Gallagher asked.

"She's goin' ta want ta be alone for a while," Thibodeaux answered. "Trust me on dis one, Jack. She don't want ta see you or nobody else right now."

Gallagher glanced at the advocates' table where Millan was helping Whitaker gather up the papers the archeologist had flung onto the floor when he lunged at Beecham. "No, thanks," Gallagher said. "I need to walk for a while, clear my head." He turned to Vogel. "Not today, Pete. Not ever."

Vogel grinned. "Suit yourself, flyboy," he said as he turned to leave, "but Nick's wild-ass dreams are done, and that Doubloon stock you got ain't worth turtle shit anymore."

The afternoon was sultry. Pale clouds veiled the sun as Gallagher, sweating heavily, walked again through Key West. Sticking to side streets, he avoided Duval and its crowds of shoppers and tourists. Everything—the narrow streets with their motley vehicles, the clinging bushes with their fragrant falling blossoms, and the Conch Cottages with their sagging porches—seemed different from the night before. They seemed not more vibrant in the daylight but rather more deteriorated, the cars dilapidated, the shrubbery atrophied, the houses ramshackle. At one point, he stopped by a weather-beaten cottage, little more than a shack, with bare silver-green siding shining in the haze. In the front yard in the shade of an Australian pine, a lone fighting cock strutted along its fenced run pecking at the dirt.

A thick, rich odor, like that of dry rot, pervaded the Bight when, after more than an hour, Gallagher circled back to the Doubloon office, which was dark and closed. His key didn't work in the new lock, so he bought a liter bottle of water at the market and settled on a wood and steel park bench on a patch of burned-out grass near the tin-roofed sheds of the turtle kraals. All around him withered red and pink hibiscus smelled of sweet decay. Behind him the rusted tower, where lookouts had scanned the horizon for returning turtle boats, rose into the blistering sky. Half of the powerboats usually moored at the Bight were gone, their owners, fearful of the approaching storm, having taken them north to safer harbors. He glanced across the finger piers at Cardona's express cruiser. Two piers beyond *Maestro III*, Vogel's metallic blue dive boat, *Vengeance* stenciled in silver-black letters on its stern, glimmered like an apparition. "Cute name," he said aloud.

Gallagher drank a third of the water and set the bottle beside him on the bench. As he thought more about Doubloon, he realized that in some way Vogel had been right. The whole salvage operation seemed inevitably doomed after the afternoon's hearing. Despite Rita's fierce will, the company and her dreams and those of his father were foundering. And Vogel and his anonymous new partners were ready to pounce on whatever flotsam and jetsam was left of the company. Gallagher took the doubloon from his pocket and made it dance across his knuckles, a trick he'd learned using quarters during the slow hours aboard ship. As he manipulated the coin back and forth, he began again to sift through the events since Thibodeaux had discovered *Magdalena*'s anchor—the storm that had nearly wrecked *Intrepid*, Tim's refusal to come in from the sites, the conversation with Sergeant Escobar, the fax from Seville, the empty-eyed end-of-the-roader staring at him, Finch's offer of compromise and Beecham's reaction to it, Whitaker's mindless outburst, Rita's exasperation, and Hernández's comment to him. Her statement that what had happened made sense seemed itself nonsensical.

Wondering what possible order was embedded in the chaos of Doubloon's dealings, he thought again about the computer disks. They held the key to the break-in at the office—and perhaps to everything else that had happened. The harbor lights blinked in the burgeoning haze, and the water stretched like a flat, emerald sheet. A swarthy, bare-chested young man with tattooed arms swabbed *Vengeance*'s deck. Enrique Cardona, walking stiffly and deliberately, crossed the wharf and headed along the finger pier to his boat. Even in the shade, Gallagher continued to sweat profusely. He finished the water and tossed the bottle into a nearby trash can. A coast guard cutter docked at the wharf, and a sailor trotted into the market and returned a few minutes later with two grocery bags. After a time, Thibodeaux, carrying a manila envelope, left *Vengeance* and weaved along the sidewalk toward the Doubloon office. A sleek red thirty-three-foot powerboat, rigged for fishing but far faster than a trawler, entered the Bight and stood off *Maestro III* while a stout, bald man in a clean white T-shirt conferred across the railings with Cardona. A few minutes after the powerboat pulled away, a wiry young man left *Maestro III* in a hurry.

As the sweltering afternoon slipped toward early evening, a deep stillness descended around Gallagher; the occasional breaths of air did not even cause the leaves of the trees near him to tremble. Two frigate birds wheeled around each other in the sky. His mind settled, and he knew, though he wasn't sure how, that he'd missed the meaning of the stolen computer disks, gotten everything wrong, entirely backward. It wasn't that someone could glean vital information from the disks but rather that the information there had to be concealed—from everyone.

He sat on the bench, no longer aware of the comings and goings around him, his mind sorting, darting, the world slowing, dawdling, finally receding altogether. Brushing the face of the doubloon with his thumb, he went back through everything that had occurred since he'd first arrived in Key West. He stared at the coin, held it up to the light, turned it slowly, noted again its condition, its near perfection. And then, still gazing at the coin, he thought about his father—the man's obsession with finding Spanish treasure, the deals made, and the corners cut.

Toward sunset, thunderheads rose like fists in the southwestern sky. Lightning flashed periodically and dark veils passed over the water in the distance, but no rain fell on the island. Gallagher's shirt was damp with sweat, the bandage soggy and heavy. He rubbed his shoulder and rolled his neck. Hernández had been right: all of it, perhaps even his father's death, began to make sense. He needed to see her, to speak with her about what he'd concluded. He knew who her source must be—knew, too, that she'd be willing to confirm his assumptions. He glanced across the water at *Maestro III*, where Cardona stood on the bridge gazing out to sea. With a lot of time remaining before he and Hernández were to meet, he would first confront the Maestro.

28

As Gallagher strode along the finger pier, there was still no wind, and the heaviness blanketed the Bight. He stared across at *Vengeance*, but no one was on deck. When he reached *Maestro III*, Cardona turned, his hands resting on the ship's wheel, and looked down at him. Cardona's eyes blinked rapidly behind his thick black-rimmed glasses. Soft Latin jazz welled from the speakers built into the fiberglass molding on either side of the wheel.

"For just one second, Jack Gallagher," Cardona said, his voice solemn, "I thought you were your father, and we were young men again."

Taken aback by Cardona's statement, Gallagher paused for a moment before saying, "Permission to come aboard, sir?"

"*Sí*, of course." Cardona gestured toward the short gangway.

Gallagher climbed into the aft cockpit below the bridge, and Cardona met him by the U-shaped white vinyl bench surrounding an adjustable table. They shook hands almost formally, and Cardona said, "The antiquities hearing today, it did not go as Señora Gallagher had hoped."

A call on the marine radio interrupted the music.

"No," Gallagher answered. He smiled enigmatically and

stared into the man's eyes. "But most of it went, I suspect, pretty much as others had planned."

Cardona met his gaze. "Perhaps," he said, shrugging. His starched white shirt, open at the collar, looked crisp despite the humidity, and his gold cuff links gleamed. "María José informed me you were coming to La Habana for dinner, but I did not expect to see you here."

"Probably not," Gallagher said. "And I would've expected you to have already gone to the restaurant."

"I was in need of some time alone." Cardona shrugged again. "Well, may I get you something cold to drink? A Heineken?"

Gallagher mopped his forehead with his sleeve. "Something soft," he answered. "Water would be fine." He followed Cardona down into the air-conditioned cabin. The posh galley and salon, all immaculate white fiberglass and vinyl, dazzled in sharp contrast to *Intrepid*'s drab cabin. The jazz wafted from four speakers, and the TV/VCR above the refrigerator was tuned, without sound, to CNN. He took a long, slow breath as he gazed at the engraved platter hanging above the curved sofa that ran along the salon's starboard bulkhead. Even larger and more elaborate than the plates in the restaurant, it showed an intricately rendered scene of a horse-drawn carriage passing *La Fuerza*, the massive stone fortress that had served for centuries as the hub of Havana's colonial life.

Cardona scooped ice from the electric ice-maker into a tall glass, pressed the glass to the automatic spigot on the refrigerator door, and handed the glass to Gallagher. As Cardona pulled a half-filled bottle of sauvignon blanc from the refrigerator, Gallagher held the cold glass to his temples for a moment. "Mr. Cardona," he asked, "why does Ms. Hernández call you 'Maestro'?"

Cardona paused as he was about to pour the wine. "María José?" He blinked at Gallagher and smiled sadly. "It is just an expression, a sign of respect. A term used especially for a man of an older generation."

"Yes," Gallagher said, "I understand that. But it also refers to your work in Cuba, doesn't it?" He tilted the rim of the glass toward the engraved plate. "You were the mint master, weren't you?"

Cardona poured the wine into a short-stemmed glass, cleared his throat, gazed for a moment at the engraving, and then stared at Gallagher. "No, Jack," he said finally. "My father was the mint master. I was simply his apprentice and heir. He was my age now during the insurrection. And he refused to leave even when Che Guevara was victorious at Santa Clara." His eyes were drawn back to the engraving. "Let's return to the deck. The air conditioning keeps away the mildew, but after all these years I still prefer the fresh air. Even in weather like this."

They sat on the U-shaped bench aft of the bridge. The heat pressed in on them, but Cardona seemed not to notice. Gallagher placed his glass on the table and took out the doubloon. He danced the coin back and forth across his knuckles three times and then looked into Cardona's eyes. "There is no motherlode, no treasure, is there?" he asked.

Cardona slid his glass onto the table. "I would have no way of knowing that, Jack," he answered.

"No way, Maestro?" Gallagher persisted. "Really?"

Cardona leaned forward, his elbows on the table, and made

a steeple of his fingers. "Jack, I believe, just as your father did, that there is treasure. And that he was very close." He played his fingertips to the jazz. "That he needed only a little more time."

Gallagher flicked the coin with his finger so that it spun brightly on the smooth white surface of the table. "But there are no doubloons? Whatever the *Gobernadora Carga* is, it's not doubloons."

Cardona studied his hands, once again a steeple, for almost a minute as the doubloon slowed, wobbled, and stopped. Then he met Gallagher's gaze and said, "No. There are only the three."

Gallagher snapped the doubloon from the table and gazed first at the lions facing each other at the base of the castle and then at the "H" to the left of the shield. He stood, slipped the doubloon into his pocket, and looked out at the mouth of the Bight. As the setting sun, haloed by haze, dipped below the layer of clouds, it spread soft pink light across the water. "The three," he said more to himself than to Cardona, "that my father had you counterfeit."

Cardona raised his glass, sipped the sauvignon blanc, and sat back against the cushioned bulkhead.

Gallagher turned and stared down at him. "Who knew?"

"No one."

"Not Rita or Tim or Hugh or Braxton?" He picked up his glass, finished the water, and cracked an ice cube with his teeth. "What about Ozzie?"

"No one," Cardona answered. "It was entirely private, a personal arrangement between your father and me."

Gallagher shook his head. "Just like your other arrange-

ments with my father." Glancing out across the darkening water, he noticed a tug with rusted afterburners passing between
the harbor lights. Thinking at first that Millan had taken
Intrepid out, he gazed at the boat. Then, realizing it wasn't
Intrepid, he looked over at *Vengeance* and murmured, "What
the . . . ?"

The marine radio crackled, ". . . Doubloon Base, this is *Sea
Rover*, MLM 2241. Over." Tim's voice sounded both urgent
and excited.

Gallagher spun, scurried to the bridge, and grabbed the
radio microphone to the right of the wheel. Cardona pulled
himself up on the bench so that he, too, could see the incoming boat. Ignoring protocol, Gallagher pressed the microphone's call button and answered, "Tim, switch to sixty-eight.
Switch to sixty-eight." Sweat swirling down his chest and back,
he punched the radio's setting for channel sixty-eight.

"Doubloon base," Gallagher heard. "This is *Sea Rover . . .*"
Tim's voice cracked with enthusiasm.

"Tim," Gallagher shouted. "Don't dock."

"What . . . ? Who's this?" Tim asked.

"It's Jack," Gallagher shouted into the microphone.

"Huh? Jack? What the . . . Where the hell is everybody?"
Tim sounded bewildered. "I called in hours ago, but nobody
answered."

Cardona climbed to the bridge, switched off the stereo
speakers, and scanned the Raytheon electronic equipment.

Gallagher placed his left hand on the wheel, glanced over
at *Vengeance*, and shook his head as he spoke. "At the hearing,"
he answered. "At the Antiquities Board." Drops of sweat fell
onto the instrument console.

"Shit." Tim paused. Then, exhilaration again in his voice, he said, "Jack, we found . . ."

"Tim, don't say anything," Gallagher yelled, cutting him off. "And don't dock, goddamn it."

There was a longer pause. Gallagher cleared his throat and wiped the sweat from his forehead. He gazed out across the water where *Sea Rover* had slowed enough that it produced no wake.

"We're low on gas," Tim answered. "We got to dock."

"Not here," Gallagher said. "Not now."

"Why?"

"Just don't do it! I'll meet you somewhere. And, I'll explain then."

"Yeah. Okay," Tim said. "I'll be at the gas pump the other side of Mallory Dock. Where all that sunset shit happens. I gotta show ya . . ."

"Tim!" Gallagher's tone was sharp. "Not on the goddamned radio. Over and out." Holding the microphone close to his mouth, he waited until he was sure that Tim would say nothing more. *Sea Rover* came almost to a full stop before beginning to wheel to starboard. He switched the radio back to channel sixteen, slipped the microphone into its cradle, and ran his wrist across his mouth. When he turned to leave the bridge, Cardona stood in his way.

"Jack Gallagher," Cardona said, "you are the only one Nicholas trusted to handle this."

"What?" Gallagher asked, aware that he sounded as perplexed as Tim had in their conversation on the radio.

Cardona pushed his glasses up on the bridge of his nose and gazed at Gallagher. "Whatever you think you may know," he said, "you do not have the whole picture, Jack. Yet your father believed that you could determine what needed to be done. And now you must act."

"Right," Gallagher answered. Time was critical, and he didn't like the fact that the Cuban was starting to sound like an oracle. "Fine. I've got to get going."

"Exactly," Cardona said, stepping aside.

29

Gallagher's shoes clapped on the pavement as he sprinted along the wharf; a young couple exiting the market stared at him. He slowed, running at a steady pace that carried him back along Front Street. Although it was still light, the sun had set, and the glut of tourists dispersing from the festivities on Mallory Dock jabbered in a polyglot of English, German, Spanish, and Japanese. Ice-cream vendors on fat-wheeled bicycles with portable coolers rang their bells, working the crowd. Street peddlers hawked pink conchs, hand-carved figurines, and woven palm hats. And, as Gallagher serpentined through the throng, he caught snatches of a guitar somewhere nearby playing "Son of a Son of a Sailor." By the time he reached the aquarium, he was aware that some of the tourists were snapping pictures of him. As he crossed a vacant parking lot near Truman Annex, he glimpsed *Sea Rover* at the gas dock in the southwest corner of the harbor.

A skinny, hunched old man wearing a Miami Hurricanes cap was pumping gas; Tim paced, head down, along the dock. The old man started when he saw Gallagher jogging toward him. Tim turned and looked up. His hair was matted, and his scraggly red beard hadn't been shaved in days. His face was sunburned and peeling; his eyes were bloodshot, and purple-gray rings puffed under his eyes.

Gallagher didn't stop running until he reached Tim.

"Jack!" Tim exclaimed. "What the f . . ."

Gallagher grabbed Tim by the arm, turned him around, and walked him away from the boat.

Tim pulled himself from Gallagher's grip and faced him squarely. "What the fuck's goin' down?" he asked. "Where is everybody?"

Catching his breath, Gallagher waved his hand in front of Tim's face. "Hold on a second, Tim," he said. He wiped sweat from his eyes with his forearm.

The old man stared at them with the glazed eyes of a habitual drinker.

"Jack," Tim said, "I got ta show ya . . ."

Gallagher put his arm around Tim's shoulder and walked him still farther from the boat. The old man went back to gazing at the fuel line's nozzle.

His arm still around Tim's shoulder, Gallagher asked, "Where are your divers?"

"I sent 'em into town for champagne—bubbly and brewskis and lots of grub," Tim answered, grinning. "We're gonna party 'til sunup Sunday, Jack!"

Gallagher grimaced at the thought of the news the divers might already be spreading. "Show me," he whispered. "Show me what you found, but act like it's no big deal."

Tim led Gallagher onto *Sea Rover*'s deck. As they passed through the galley, Gallagher took a plastic bottle of fresh water from the refrigerator. The stale air in the forward cabin reminded him of the storm, and he drank deeply from the water bottle. On the port bunk, a dirty denim work shirt covered an object two feet high and just over two feet wide. Tim waited until Gallagher was standing next to him and then pulled the shirt away.

"Oh, God!" Gallagher gasped. "Oh, my God." He dropped the plastic bottle onto the decking, water splashing around their feet.

In front of him on the dingy bunk stood an exquisite gold statue of a veiled woman washing the feet of a bearded man in robes. The woman was kneeling, bent forward in reverence and supplication; the man leaned over, his hand touching her shoulder. Wiped clean, the statue glittered in the light of the cabin's two bare bulbs.

His hand shaking, Gallagher reached out and touched the head of the woman. He tried to lift the statue with one hand, but it was too heavy. He crouched in front of the bunk and looked closely at the figures. Although rusted iron bolts protruded from the holes in the four corners of the statue's base, three and a half centuries buried underwater had not damaged the statue itself. Running the tips of his fingers over the head of the man and along the back of the woman, he found himself almost unwilling to let go of the statue. And then he was standing again, and he and Tim were hugging and laughing and shouting. Tears streamed from Tim's bloodshot eyes.

Gallagher let go of Tim, looked again at the gleaming statue, shook his head, and said, "We've got to do something fast with Ms. Magdalene."

"What?"

"The commission shut down all of the lease sites this afternoon. The government'll impound any treasure that comes in. We've got to get her out of town until the legal mess is straightened out."

Wiping his eyes, Tim started to speak but then stopped and gazed at the statue next to him. His hand reached out for the figures. "Why?" he asked. "Why'd they fuck us over like that?"

"Later," Gallagher answered. "I'll explain later."

Tim shook his head and looked up at Gallagher. "But I found the statue this morning, Jack. Around ten. It belongs to m . . . , to Doubloon."

Gallagher nodded. "How long ago did the divers leave?" he asked.

"Five minutes before you showed up. Maybe less."

Gallagher glanced down at the statue. "Do the divers know where the site is?"

Tim picked at the skin peeling from his nose. "Yeah. Not exactly. Only that we were about four miles west of the Havana Bank. In deeper water, about sixty feet. I logged the coordinates, but they're half a minute off each way." He smiled sadly. "It's a trick Dad taught me—minus a half latitude, and plus a half longitude. It gets somebody into the area but doesn't give away where the treasure is."

Gallagher nodded again. "What about the artifact trail?" he asked. "Could it lead somebody to the site?"

Tim stared up at him. "Uh, no," he said. "Probably not. We got nothing before yesterday afternoon, but I just kept following a line northwest into deeper water, like Dad wanted." He looked again at the statue. "Then Sam found a musket after lunch. Suddenly there was lots of debris, spikes and stuff. We followed the trail until sundown, blasting and

diving. We were all past our limits on the fuckin' dive wheel."
He caressed the statue. "And then this morning I found this—
out there near where Dad said it'd be." He reached up and
grabbed Gallagher's forearm. "We've got to be right on it,
Jack . . ." His voice broke, and his eyes welled again. ". . . I
mean, the motherlode. The whole goddamn treasure's got to
be right there . . ."

"Yeah, Tim," Gallagher answered. The look in Tim's eyes
told him he didn't have to add, *But it may not be ours.* He
picked up the plastic bottle and said, "Come on. Let's get out
of here."

Before they left the cabin, Tim replaced the dirty shirt as
though it was a shroud for the statue.

30

When the two men reached *Sea Rover*'s deck, the night was close, the air barely fresher than it had been in the boat's cabin. Fishing through his pockets to make sure he had enough change, Gallagher said, "I'll pay the man and give Rita a call. You get the boat ready to cast off."

"What about Sam and Rick?" Tim asked.

"The divers?" Gallagher scratched his nose. "If they get back fast, we'll take them. If not, we leave 'em." He took a gold Visa card from his wallet and waved the card toward the boat's bow. "The important thing is to get Mary Magdalene the hell out of Key West."

When the old man in the Miami Hurricanes cap hobbled to the stern of the boat, Gallagher asked him where the nearest pay phone was.

The man pointed to a white wood and cinder-block shack twenty yards away along the wharf and said, "Other side a the office." He'd lost most of his teeth, and the words were more hissed than spoken.

While the old man entered the shack with the charge card, Gallagher went over to the phone. He put in two quarters, waited for the electronic message to remind him that he wouldn't receive any change, and hurriedly punched the number of Rita's house. On the fourth ring, he got her voice mail. As he listened to the message, he gazed at half a dozen speckled moths fluttering in the arc of the floodlight attached to the shack's roof. After the signal, he began to speak, thought better of it, and hung up the phone.

The old man came out of the shack with a charge receipt clipped to a plastic board. One of the moths flew too close to the floodlight and, in a burst of smoke like a stricken fighter, spiraled to the pavement, where it twitched and smoldered. While Gallagher signed the receipt and took his card, the old man fidgeted with one of the frayed belt loops of his baggy jeans. When he noticed the moth, he stomped it with his high-top sneaker.

As the old man gave Gallagher his copy of the receipt, he asked, "You Nick's boy?"

Gallagher nodded.

"How 'bout that," the old man said as he extended his wizened hand. "Name's Jimmy. Nice meetin' ya."

Gallagher shook his hand. Needing to make another call, he said, "Good to meet you, Jimmy." He then pulled all the change other than the doubloon from his pocket and shook the coins in his hand.

"Met Nick when he first come to town," the old man said. He pointed with the clipboard toward *Sea Rover*. "Know'd it was Tim, but I did'n recanize you."

Gallagher glanced at the salvage tug where Tim stood in the wheelhouse looking over at them talking. "Well, Jimmy, I've got to make a call."

"Sure. Course," the man answered. "Course." Shaking his head, he limped back into the shack.

Gallagher dialed the *Key West Tribune*, asked for Hernández, and was put on hold for almost two minutes. The moths continued to weave beneath the light, and the canned laughter of a television sitcom came from the shack. When Hernández answered, he said, "Josie, it's Jack. I need your help."

"Jack?" she said. "What's the matter?"

"Your interview, the interview you said you had, was with the new Antiquities Board commissioner, right?"

"Yeah. Right."

"Is he legit?" Gallagher gazed over at *Sea Rover*, where Tim was still silhouetted on the bridge.

"What?" Her voice became stronger, her tone more direct. "What's going on, Jack?"

"Josie," he answered. "I trust your judgment. The man knows Beecham's full of shit. But is the guy in anybody's pocket?"

"No. Definitely not. But . . ."

"Find out," Gallagher cut her off, "if there's proof, irrevocable proof that Doubloon's onto *Magdalena*'s motherlode, whether he'll make sure the leases are renewed. Given, of course, whatever environmental stipulations he needs to impose."

"You mean the sheet anchor? What . . . ?"

"Josie," he interrupted her again, "stop being a goddamned reporter for a second. I need your help."

There was silence on the line for a moment. "I'll find out, Jack," she said finally.

"Josie . . ." He took a deep breath and exhaled slowly. "There's one other thing. I need you to call Rita. Tell her that Tim's okay." He ran his hand through his hair. "But don't leave a message. Speak only to her. Nobody else."

"She's not one of my biggest fans, Jack," Hernández answered. "You know that."

Gallagher nodded at the phone. "Yeah, but tell her I said so. She'll listen to you."

"Yeah, okay."

Tim flashed *Sea Rover*'s running lights off and on.

"And Josie," Gallagher said, "There's going to be lots of rumors flying around town by morning." His voice became lower, almost a whisper. "Please don't publish them."

"Jack, I can't promise . . ."

"Josie, you were right," he said slowly. "It all makes sense. Everything, even my father's death. We both had the burglary backward, huh?"

"Yeah, Jack," she answered. "The disks are the key. I didn't see it at first, either."

They were silent for a moment. A recording told them that three minutes had passed and additional charges would be assessed.

"What about dinner?" she asked.

"I'll try to get there," he said. Then, aware he couldn't lie to her, he added, "Josie, I'm not going to make it. I can't explain now, but I'll tell . . ."

"Jack," she interrupted him.

"Josie?"

"Take care, Jack," she said.

"Thanks," he answered. "Thanks, Josie." He looked out over the water into the darkness beyond the harbor. "You be careful, too. You may already know too much . . ." His voice trailed off.

After she hung up, he shoved another quarter into the phone, turned, and began to jog back to the boat. He stopped abruptly by the shack door and looked into the single bare room. Jimmy sat on a wooden chair sipping from a Coke can and watching a black-and-white television. His feet were propped on a crate, and an empty pint-bottle of rum lay on its side on the concrete floor.

"How far to Miami, Jimmy?" Gallagher shouted.

The old man drew his gaze from the TV. " 'Bout a hun'red-fifty miles," he said with a toothless smile.

"Good," Gallagher said. "We can make it by morning." He waved at the man, turned, and crossed the gas dock.

"What took so long?" Tim called from the door of the wheelhouse.

"Couldn't locate Rita," Gallagher answered as he untied the stern line. "Any sign of your divers?"

"Nope."

"I'll get the lines. Head east, as though we're going to Miami."

Tim stared quizzically down at him for a moment before nodding.

As *Sea Rover* cleared the breakwater, Gallagher climbed to the wheelhouse. It was similar to *Intrepid*'s, but more cramped and less organized. The wheel was unpolished, the throttles and gauges grimy. The logbook lay on top of the radio receiver, and rolled charts angled across the deck in the corner. An old teak and glass barometer hung on the starboard bulkhead.

While Tim set the boat on an east-northeasterly course, he said, "I want to get back to the site. Storm or no fuckin' storm, if we got a boat on it, we'll have a better case later on. The site's got to be working."

Gallagher clapped him on the shoulder. "That's where we're going," he said. "But if people think we're heading up toward Miami, we might buy ourselves some time."

They headed east-northeast for two miles before turning off *Sea Rover*'s running lights and circling back along Hawk Channel just out of sight of land. A shadowy moon rose through a thick haze that extinguished the stars. The muggy air and flat, still water made the night eerie; the boat's engines rumbled across the ocean's strange, quiet darkness. Once they again passed the milky brightness of Key West, they turned southwest and then, as Hawk Channel curved, due west. They talked for a long time about the bedlam at the Antiquities Board hearing, the discovery of the statue, and some, but not all, of Gallagher's conclusions.

Tim showed Gallagher the compass heading, gave the wheel over to him, and curled up on a mattress behind the wheelhouse near the shower. Gallagher nursed a couple of beers while he stood at the wheel alternately gazing out into the darkness and checking the compass, depth finder, and barometer. In the time he'd been aboard, the barometer had already fallen, and he skimmed the log to see how quickly the pressure was dropping. The rumble of the engine and the feel of the vibrating steel under his feet made him drowsy, but he didn't fall asleep.

When Tim relieved him three hours later, Gallagher took off his clothes and lay on the mattress. His left arm bent under his head as a pillow, he tried to think about what he was doing, but the image of the *Magdalena* statue framed by the dingy bunk kept intruding on his thoughts. He had become, he knew, too entangled in Doubloon, in his father's obsession, to turn back. He would have to ride the salvage boat and that obsession wherever they took him. He rolled onto his back. The moon was barely visible in the haze. He searched for the North Star but discovered no stars at all in the vast expanse of shrouded sky.

 allagher awoke when, in the gathering light, the boat slowed almost to an idle. There was no breeze at all; his mouth was dry, and his skin itched from the salt and sweat. His legs and shoulder stiff, he stood and stretched.

Tim leaned out of the wheelhouse, looked down off the starboard bow for a moment, turned, and said, "Morning." His eyes were red and puffy, and his hair stuck up in clumps.

"Morning," Gallagher answered. "Where are we?"

"Almost on the site," Tim said. He pointed toward the gray-brown horizon to the west, licked his lips, and added, "Out near the Dry Tortugas."

Gallagher peered in the direction that Tim had pointed and then scanned the horizon. No land or other boats were in sight.

"Want to make some sandwiches?" Tim asked. "And get some water?"

Gallagher headed down the ship's ladder and ducked through the hatchway. He found a grungy pair of cutoffs and a pair of rubber flip-flops in the forward cabin. As he was about to leave, he pulled the shirt from over the statue. The gold had been beautifully etched and incised, even to the designs of the bracelets on Mary Magdalene's wrists. It took him more than a minute to pull himself away. When he returned to the wheelhouse with the water and a couple of cheese sandwiches, he found that Tim had swung *Sea Rover* around and idled the engines.

"Hold her right here," Tim said. He then slid down the ship's ladder, grabbed a boathook, sidled to the bow, knelt on one knee, leaned over, and snagged an orange life preserver that was floating on the water's surface. Moving with the fluid ease of someone who had grown up around boats, he pulled up the nylon line tied to the life preserver and cleated the line. He then yanked the starboard anchor from its chocks, slipped the anchor overboard, and, using the electric windlass, paid out the anchor line and set the anchor. "Shut 'er down," he shouted to Gallagher.

Working feverishly, Tim set all four anchors and lowered the afterburners over the stern. He and Gallagher slung a tarp from the base of the bridge to the afterburners' brace. Then, before getting on his dive gear, Tim brought a Colt .45 pistol with a ten-shot clip and an M1 semiautomatic rifle with a twenty-round magazine onto the deck.

He handed the rifle to Gallagher and said, "You may need this if anybody comes after us while I'm down."

Gallagher checked the rifle's safety, sighted along its barrel, and nodded. The rifle was heavy, at least two decades old, and not nearly as well maintained as the shotgun aboard *Intrepid*. Tim stowed the pistol behind the cooler, and Gallagher leaned the rifle against the bulkhead under the tarp. Tim's weight belt slid down on his narrow hips until he sucked in his breath and clipped it still tighter around his waist. Before Tim entered the water, Gallagher climbed to the bridge and ran *Sea Rover*'s engines so that a steady wash streamed down toward the site. Tim put on his mask, turned toward the wheelhouse, raised his right thumb in the air, grinned at Gallagher, made a circle of his thumb and forefinger, and scissor-stepped off the deck.

While Tim was diving, Gallagher stayed in the wheelhouse monitoring the engines and the radio. The sky was milky, the morning hot and still and so humid that the instruments' gauges and dials sweated. He periodically checked the barometer, which continued to fall. At twenty-minute intervals he heard calls from Doubloon base; at first, it was Thibodeaux's voice, and later Whitaker's. He answered none of the calls. The world of land, of rules and commissioners, and threats of litigation, became foreign, utterly alien in the rumble of the engines and the roiling wash.

During his first dive Tim found among the debris an encrusted sword, a dagger, and two small silver pitchers, one with an "A" on the handle and the other with a "V." While Tim was back on board decompressing, Gallagher moved the boat a few feet northwest by paying out the bowlines and then resetting first the stern anchors and then the bow anchors. He felt none of the euphoria he'd experienced when he discovered the rosary or when Tim showed him the statue but rather a sense of urgency, almost apprehensiveness.

Tim's second dive produced more treasure, including silver candlesticks, a twisted gold bar, and a gold whistle, but at lunch, Tim only slouched against the bulkhead under the tarp, rubbing his knees and elbows and rolling his shoulders and neck. His long hair dried into thick, unruly clumps, and his face, despite the sunburn, looked ashen in the shade. He drank a lot of water but ate nothing and talked little. When Tim began to fiddle with his dive wheel, a blue and yellow disk attached to a white laminated plastic board, Gallagher asked, "What're you doing?"

Tim turned the wheel, squinted at the small letters and numbers, frowned, and answered, "Checking my bottom time. Seeing how long I got to stay topside." He flipped the plastic board over and looked at a second set of numbers. "I can still get in at least two more dives this afternoon."

Shortly after Gallagher returned to the wheelhouse during Tim's first dive after lunch, he noticed a helicopter passing to the south. Its fuselage tan except for its identifying markings and the Florida state seal, the helicopter circled and hovered directly above *Sea Rover*. As it descended to forty feet above the boat, the helicopter's propwash caused concentric circles of waves to churn in the water. The thwacking of its main rotor blade almost drowned the sound of the tug's engines.

When Gallagher didn't respond to the first call from the helicopter, there was another crackling over the radio. "*Sea Rover, Sea Rover*," a flat voice with a southern accent said, "this dive site's been shut down."

Gallagher glanced over the stern where the white bubbles of *Sea Rover*'s propwash were clearly visible, but he still didn't answer.

"*Sea Rover*," the voice announced after a moment, "you got to head in. The storm in the Caribbean is Force Ten and building. The meteorologists got her wheeling this way."

Gallagher waited until the helicopter arced into the haze before turning off *Sea Rover*'s engines. He then climbed down to the aft deck and hammered on the afterburners with a pipe wrench. A few moments later he could see Tim hovering on the dive line about fifteen feet below the surface. In another three minutes, Tim surfaced. Clinging to the top rung of the dive ladder, he took off his mask, flipped it onto the deck, and wiped mucus from his nose and mouth.

Breathless, Tim shouted, "We're there. I can feel *Magdalena* all around me."

"We had visitors," Gallagher said. "A chopper. State of Florida."

Tim unclipped his harness. "Shit," he said. "We shoulda known that faggot Beecham wouldn't let up."

After Gallagher pulled the tank and regulator onto the deck, Tim leaned down, took off his fins, and lifted them so that Gallagher could take them. Still hanging onto the dive ladder, he raised his arm toward Gallagher and added, "Give me a hand, will ya?"

As Gallagher pulled Tim up onto the deck, he asked, "You okay?"

"Yeah," Tim answered. He slipped into the shade under the tarp and slumped onto the cooler. "Yeah. Just winded. A little dehydrated."

When Gallagher brought him a plastic mug filled with water, Tim was working his dive wheel again. He drank the water quickly, took a deep breath, and said, "I think I can still squeeze in two more dives."

"Tim," Gallagher said, "you don't have to be a hero."

"I'm not being no fuckin' hero," Tim said as he dropped the dive wheel onto the cooler next to him. He looked up at Gallagher with bloodshot eyes that had sharp red lines radiating away from the pupils. "We're just so fuckin' close. We're right on it. I know it, Jack." He shook his head slowly. "I just fuckin' know it."

Gallagher turned and stared out into the haze. The sky was the color of gauze. Wondering how far over the limit on the dive wheel Tim really was, he said, "With those copter jockies spotting us, we'd better at least call Doubloon."

Tim's eyelids drooped. From the darkness under the tarp, he gave Gallagher an exhausted wave. "You do it," he mumbled. "Give 'em a call. I'm just gonna sit here for a while."

When Gallagher reached the Doubloon office on the radio, Millan asked, "What're you doing, Jack? I thought you had some sense, amigo."

"Tim found it, found the *Magdalena* statue," Gallagher answered. "And he's finding more stuff with each dive."

"*Sí, sí,*" Millan said. "But leading people back out to the site is *estúpido*."

Gallagher exhaled; sweat ran down his temples, and his head ached. Even though he knew Millan was right, he protested, "We had to get the statue out of town."

"*Sí,*" Millan said, "but not back to the site. You should've gone to Miami like you told Jimmy. We've got friends there that would've known what to do with the statue. The sharks can already smell that site. They'll be on you like you're chum, amigo."

Gallagher felt as though he were being dressed down by a superior officer. "Okay, okay," he said. He glanced out at the stern but couldn't see Tim under the tarp. "We'll head in immediately."

"No, not right away, amigo," Millan said. "We got to do something about the statue before you reach port. Dewey and Hugh left in the whaler. They should be . . ."

"What?" Gallagher interrupted.

"They're on their way in the whaler."

Gallagher rubbed his face with his hand.

"The whaler's our fastest boat," Millan went on. "They should be there by eighteen hundred, nineteen hundred at the latest. They'll take care of the statue for you. I got to run *Intrepid* up the Keys ahead of the *huracán*, or I'd be out there, too."

"Yeah. Okay," Gallagher answered. Too many possibilities ran through his mind at once.

Millan let out a long, low whistle. "Oh, and Jack," he said, "the hombre that stuck you with the sword, he's dead."

"What the . . ." Gallagher sucked in his breath.

"He was found last night behind a Dumpster off Roosevelt . . . had a needle stuck in his arm and a shiv in his belly." Millan paused before adding, "According to Louis Escobar, time of death's just before some tourists saw you running through town."

Gallagher slammed his hand against the bulkhead. "What the hell does that mean?"

At first, Millan didn't answer. Almost ten seconds passed before he said, "He figures somebody did the hombre. And he wants to talk to you about it. Real bad."

Gallagher let his hand with the microphone fall to his side.

He looked out the wheelhouse's windshield at the sky. The sun was little more than a pale disk in a paler dome.

"Worry about that *mierda* later," Millan said. "I sent you a present with Dewey and Hugh to help you keep the sharks away. Do what you got to do. Then, get back here fast. You'll just beat the *huracán*, amigo. She's going to hit in eight hours, maybe less . . ."

Staring at the barometer, Gallagher was already thinking Millan's final statement.

". . . and *la mar*, she can be very angry, very vengeful."

32

When Gallagher returned to the stern deck, Tim was already diving again. "Shit," Gallagher muttered as he peered down at the the compressed air bubbles rising to the water's surface. "Goddamn it." He picked up the pipe wrench and whacked the afterburners half a dozen times. When, even after five minutes, Tim did not appear at the dive line, Gallagher reset the stern anchor lines Tim had loosened and then went to the wheelhouse to work the engines' throttles. As he gazed out the windshield, he saw a great swirling school of flying fish. They leapt from the water and glided before him like bright coins spilling across the ocean. Even in the haze, their bodies flashed, and their pectoral fins, spread like wings, gleamed.

In less than half an hour, Tim clung again to the dive ladder. By the time Gallagher shut off the engines and reached the deck, Tim had pushed his mask and fins over the gunwale and slid out of his harness. Gallagher lifted the tank and gave Tim a hand. Tim took one step, turned sideways, and slid down onto the deck. Gallagher helped him over to the cooler under the tarp.

"Dizzy," Tim whispered. "Tired." He reached out and took

Gallagher's wrist. "Jack," he said, "there's a fuckin' wall. Move the boat a couple feet."

Squatting next to him, Gallagher said, "I talked to Ozzie. Dewey and Hugh are on their way in the whaler. Should be here by six."

Tim nodded but said only, "It's a fuckin' wall, Jack."

Gallagher stood, went over to the winch, and began to crank the afterburners from the water.

As Gallagher worked, Tim suddenly grabbed his arm from behind. "What're ya doin'?" he asked, his voice cracking.

Gallagher wheeled and faced him. "You're not diving anymore. We're going in as soon as they pick up our lady friend. There's a goddamn hurricane heading this way."

Tim let go of Gallagher's arm and looked up at the wisps of gray clouds in the sky. His shoulders slumped in the leaden air. Then, focusing again on Gallagher, he said, "Just one more dive." He glanced at his dive watch. "In another hour, man. Before they get here." He hobbled over to the gunwale and stared down into the water.

"Tim," Gallagher said, "you're in no shape to dive."

"We're there, Jack," Tim said, looking back at Gallagher. "I double-checked the fuckin' wheel. I'm okay for one more dive."

Gallagher stared into Tim's eyes. His father's compulsion burned there—that quest for treasure that drove the man to his death and spurred both his sons out to sea. Gallagher knew he couldn't let Tim dive again. And he was aware he could stop Tim, drop him right there on the deck, weigh anchor, and run *Sea Rover* for Key West. But he also realized that, whatever happened, he was not going to be the one to douse the light in those eyes. "You can't dive, Tim," he said.

"I got to make the dive, Jack. Got to finish . . ."

"Tim . . ."

Tim limped toward Gallagher. "I gotta do it."

Letting go of the winch handle, Gallagher exhaled slowly. "Tim," he began, "there's no point in . . ."

Tim raised his hand and balled his fist. "I know what I'm doin', Jack." His clenched fist trembled.

"You're not diving anymore, goddamn it," Gallagher said.

"Fuck you, Jack," Tim yelled, his bloodshot eyes flashing with both his mother's fierceness and his father's fixation. "It's my fuckin' boat."

"Yeah, Tim, but . . ."

"I'm the fuckin' captain!"

"Tim!"

Off balance, Tim lunged at Gallagher, swinging wildly.

Gallagher blocked Tim's fist with his forearm, spun him around, and shoved him away. Tim stumbled and then sprawled hard onto the deck. He lay there for a moment stunned, gasping for air as though he'd just been drowning. He then pulled himself up on his scraped elbows. Blood trickled along his right arm.

Gallagher knelt next to him. "Tim," he said, "I'm not telling you that you can't dive. Your body is."

Staring at the patterned steel deck as though it held some message, Tim shook his head slowly.

"The dive'd kill you," Gallagher said. "It's that goddamned simple."

Still panting, Tim squeezed his eyes shut as though he were blocking out Gallagher's words.

Gallagher laid his hand on Tim's shoulder. "I can't let that happen to my only brother," he said.

Tim flinched but didn't move away.

"Not after we've just lost our father," Gallagher said.

Tim opened his eyes but didn't look at Gallagher. "There's a silver wall down there, Jack," he mumbled. "And who the fuck knows what else."

There was little emotion in Tim's voice, and Gallagher didn't at first understand what he meant.

"Hundreds, thousands of doubloons, maybe," Tim went on. "Just where Dad said they'd be. We got to do one more dive. Just one."

"A *silver* wall?" Gallagher asked, standing up and stepping back.

Tim nodded. "And fuckin' more. There's got to be more. That's why I got . . ." He ground the heel of his right hand against his temple, then rose to one knee and turned. "You do it, Jack."

Gallagher looked into Tim's eyes, which still burned with that obsession.

"Move the fuckin' boat," Tim said. "And get your gear on, Jack."

Gallagher propped Tim against the gunwale in the shade near the dive ladder and got him a plastic bottle of water. As Gallagher reset the anchors and switched the engines back on, Tim sipped the water and lethargically rubbed his knees and ankles. Gallagher got a waterproof flashlight and dive gear from the dive locker. When he was about to pull on the harness and tank, Tim handed him his dive watch and his knife in its sheath. "I don't have to dive no more, do I, Jack?" he asked.

"No, Tim," Gallagher said. "You found *Magdalena*'s treasure."

As Gallagher sat by the dive ladder putting on his fins, Tim said, "Head down the line." His breathing was labored, but, though obviously in pain, he smiled. "And when you get down there, don't forget to breathe."

"You sure you're all right?" Gallagher asked.

"I'll be okay," Tim whispered. He reached over and touched Gallagher on the forearm. "And when you come up, stop at fifteen feet for three minutes. Duct tape marks the line." He grimaced. "You won't want to stop, but do it."

Gallagher slipped over the side and descended feetfirst through the propwash. Having trouble equalizing, he had to stop twice to clear his ears. The deeper he went, the less light and color there was. Beyond forty feet, the world around him faded to drab brown and pale green. He had never dived alone, and he found himself gulping air and glancing around. He was only able to regulate his breathing and feel the calmness of the deep when he reached the sandy cavern being created by the force of the water plunging from the afterburners.

He swam in a slow circle around the dive line in the diffused light. Off to the right, where the afterburners had already done their work, there was a dark wall made, it appeared, of huge stones set into the sand. Each end of the wall was still partially buried, but the center of the wall had been cleared by the propwash. Heading over to the pile of slabs almost six feet high, he turned on his dive light and panned across the thirty-five-foot wall.

"*Plata*," he said in Spanish. Despite Tim's warning, he forgot for a moment to breathe. He hovered in front of *Mag-*

dalena's motherlode—hundreds of slabs of silver, tons of silver, a wall of silver, the cornerstone of the Spanish Empire, the prime reason for the Spanish Main, the treasure galleons, the plate fleets, and the conquest of the New World. "Holy shit," he exclaimed, silver bubbles flooding from his regulator.

Hyperventilating, he went over and rubbed his free hand along the sulfide-covered slabs. They felt as though ash and soot had settled on them long ago. He played the light across the wall as he swam its length. The silver wall loomed there, alone and silent, like some arcane monolith. Beyond the wall there was nothing but sand and seawater, a seemingly endless aquatic desert pocked with craters. A shiver ran through him; he turned quickly and arced his light. *Sea Rover*'s hull was a black floating island barely visible in the sea above him.

He slowed his breathing and swam toward the dive line. When he reached the dive line, he looked back at the dark wall. He stared at it until he was once again completely calm. Raising his head, he watched his bubbles rise, expanding and elongating, until they vanished in the descending propwash. He then checked Tim's dive watch. He had left *Sea Rover*'s deck only seven minutes before.

He scanned the area around him with the light. To his left, where the crater was deepening, he noticed something thick and rectangular and green-gold. He swam over to it and fanned the sand with his hand but couldn't find the bottom of it. As the propwash blew away the sand, he saw that the object was a trunk. *A chest*, he thought, *a goddamned treasure chest*. He gulped air again and wildly brushed the sand away. He had assumed that treasure chests were some fiction of pirate lore, but here before him was a sealed chest of finely wrought brass etched with lions standing on their hind legs reaching for the sun.

He dropped his dive light and jerked at the chest's lid with both hands but couldn't open it. He swam over the trunk to its other side but couldn't budge the top there either. He then slipped Tim's knife from its sheath and used the blunt edge of the blade as a pry bar. His breathing grew deeper as he worked the knife's blade under the chest's lid. He next put all of his weight on the knife, using it as a lever, but he floated backward—and the chest remained immobile. Bracing his knees in the sand, he tried yanking the blade upward with all his strength. At first he thought that the lid had shifted, but then he realized he was simply digging his knees deeper into the sand. He worked the blade back and forth until it was free and then used the knife's hard rubber haft as a hammer to pound the chest's encrusted lock. Feeling as though he was working in slow motion, he struck the lock repeatedly.

He was so intent on what he was doing that almost five minutes passed before he noticed that the propwash was un-covering two other chests to his left. One of the chests had fallen on the other—it lay at an angle on its side, and its lid was dented. He reached over and felt under the jagged edge with his fingers. There were almost two inches of space where the seal had broken and the lid had come open. He again fanned the sand furiously with both hands. When he reached the lower end of the tilted chest, he poked the knife into the sand until the blade hit something hard. He then sheathed the knife, retrieved the flashlight, and dug into the sand with his free hand.

There, below the base of the broken chest, gleaming in the

arc of his light, was a five-inch golden amulet of a god with a rotund belly, thick outstretched arms, and an ornate rectangular headdress. Though he had no idea whether it was Aztec or Mayan, he knew it must be Native American. Kneeling for a time in the sand, he stared at the amulet and tried to catch his breath. Leaning forward, he reached out and fanned the sand again. Beneath the amulet was a four-headed golden eagle ornament. The beaks were hooked, and the intricately cast feathers fanned to five points at the base. When he first tried to pick up the artifacts, they fell from his shaking hand like flashes of light. He carefully lifted the amulet and the ornament, each of which weighed more than a pound, and clutched them to his chest. Circling to the dive line, he glanced back at the trunks. He could not imagine how much gold there might be.

In his excitement, he almost missed the mark on the dive line at fifteen feet. He paused for two and a half minutes, hugging the line with his left arm and cradling the artifacts in his right hand. As he surfaced, he slid the amulet and ornament onto *Sea Rover*'s deck. When there was no reaction from Tim, he spat out his regulator, yanked off his mask, and shouted, "Tim. Tim, it's un-fucking-believable!" He swung himself up on the dive ladder. "Chests . . . chests crammed with gold . . . art . . ."

Tim, unconscious and breathing erratically, lay slumped with his face against the deck. His fingers were still twisted around the handle of the overturned water bottle.

33

When Gallagher reached Rita by radio at the Doubloon office, she began immediately, after switching frequencies, to chide him. "How the hell could you take him back out there?" she asked. "He came in, goddamn it, Jack. And you . . . you . . ." Then, abruptly, without his saying a word, she knew something was wrong. "What . . . what is it, Jack?" she asked, her voice quavering. "What's happened?"

"Tim's out. Unconscious." He kept his voice calm and even.

"Oh, God!" she moaned. She took a deep breath and, struggling to control herself, asked, "Symptoms, Jack? What're his symptoms?"

"He was tired, dizzy, dehydrated." He swiped sweat from his eye with the back of his hand. "His breathing was uneven, and he'd been rubbing his knees and ankles."

"Damn . . . goddamn it," she murmured. "How many dives did he make today?"

"Four, an hour each," he answered. He could hear the clicking of a lighter over the radio. "Last one was less, about half an hour. But he was only topside fifteen minutes between the last two dives."

She inhaled and then exhaled slowly. "How deep?"

"Sixty, maybe sixty-five feet."

"Damn," she repeated. "He knows better." Her voice became unnaturally restrained and businesslike, as though she were talking about any diver—not her only son. "We've got to get him to a recompression chamber fast. I'll get a coast guard chopper out there. Cover him up."

"Already have." Worried about Tim going into shock, Gallagher had, before calling Rita, found a blanket under one of the bunks in the forward cabin and, despite the heat and humidity, covered him with it. "The bends?" he asked.

"Nitrogen sickness," she answered, her tone still overly composed. "Nitrogen bubbles in his system . . . in his blood. Maybe in his tissue, his nervous system, too . . . I don't know." She paused. "Jack, lay him on his side with his head lower than his feet. I'll call the coast guard and then get back to you."

Before leaving the wheelhouse, Gallagher switched on *Sea Rover*'s running lights. When he reached the stern deck, he grabbed a bumper, rolled Tim onto his side, and propped his feet on the bumper. Tim's body was warm and sweaty, his pulse weak. He breathed in shallow, erratic gasps. Gallagher covered him with the blanket again and then picked up the gold amulet and ornament he had slid onto the deck.

When Gallagher returned to the bridge, Rita was already calling. "A chopper's on its way," she said. "Have your lights on."

"A-okay," he answered. He set the artifacts on the console above the radio receiver.

"How's Tim doing?" she asked, her voice dispirited.

"The same."

"Any sign of Dewey and Hugh?"

"Not yet."

"They should've been there by now," she said. She exhaled loudly. "You're just like your father—a goddamned loose cannon." Her tone was more crestfallen than angry. "As soon as they get there—and Tim's safely aboard the chopper—get that tub back here fast." She paused, exhaling again. "You do know, don't you, that Brenda's been upgraded to a hurricane?"

Gallagher didn't answer immediately. He gazed at the ornament's four eagle heads. "Rita," he said, "Tim was right." Not wanting to broadcast the discovery of *Magdalena*'s motherlode over the radio, he added simply, "It's not just the lady. Nick was right all along about the deep water."

"Oh, Jesus," she murmured. Her voice was choked, barely audible over the radio. "Oh, Jesus." She cleared her throat. "Stick with Tim, Jack. I can't lose him, too. Not now . . ."

Gallagher carried the artifacts and his street clothes down to the forward cabin. He rolled the amulet and ornament into a towel and put the towel on the port bunk. As he folded his pants, he took the doubloon Rita had given him and slipped it into the pocket of the cutoffs he wore. When he removed the soggy bandage from his arm, red streaks like spider webbing spread from the swollen purple wound across his deltoid. He hadn't noticed any pain, but he assumed it was becoming infected.

Back on deck, he put away his dive gear and then sat down by Tim's side. Tim had turned pale, and his skin had become clammy. Gallagher took the doubloon from his pocket, placed it in Tim's right palm, and closed the young man's fist. Putting his hand on Tim's back where he could feel the shallow, labored breathing, he said, "Hang in there, kid."

Forty-five minutes later when he heard the sound of the helicopter, Gallagher jumped to his feet and scanned the shrouded sky. The coast guard Jayhawk, similar to the navy's Sikorsky search-and-rescue helicopters he knew well, flew by to the south, as though it was slightly off course, and then circled back from the west. It hovered low over *Sea Rover*, as two medics descended in a dual jackseat on a cable lowered from the Jayhawk's starboard hatch.

Both medics wore blue uniforms with radio microphones clipped to their shirts. The taller of the two, a black man with a mustache, knelt over Tim and and took his vital signs. The other medic, a Hispanic with closely cropped black hair, nodded to Gallagher before stooping to open the medical kit he carried. The medic kneeling over Tim provided a running commentary as they worked, but Gallagher couldn't hear much over the rhythmic beating of the helicopter's rotors. He caught the phrase, "secondary shock" and the exclamation, "We got to move quick on this one or we're gonna lose him!" The medic with the kit shouted in a strong Hispanic accent, "Okay, send the basket," and then handed a syringe to the other medic, who injected Tim.

As a stretcher in a steel brace descended from the belly of the helicopter, the medic rolled Tim gingerly onto his back. Tim's palm opened, and the doubloon gleamed like a small round wound. The black medic glanced at Gallagher and then leaned over and closed Tim's fist again.

"Where are you taking him?" Gallagher asked.

"Trumbo Point," the Hispanic medic answered as he put away the used syringe. "Naval hospital recompression chamber." He snapped the medical kit shut. "Best dive doctors south of Norfolk."

The medics slid the basket next to Tim, lowered its brace, and lifted Tim onto the stretcher. They then strapped him in, reset the brace, and stepped back as he was raised from the deck. All three men watched as the basket rose toward the helicopter and disappeared through the hatch.

As the cable was lowered with the jackseat, the Hispanic medic asked Gallagher, "You want to come? We can take you off, too."

"No." Gallagher shook his head. "No thanks. I've got stuff to do."

"Okay," the medic answered. "Your choice. But Brenda's going to make it real messy."

The black medic grinned at Gallagher and said, "We're not gonna want to come back out here, man."

Gallagher nodded. He shook both of their hands and said, "Damn good work. Thanks." When the medics had harnessed themselves into the jackseat, he repeated, "Good work."

"He's got a shot," the black medic shouted as they rose from the deck. "A real shot."

Gallagher stood on the deck until the helicopter's spray and thunder were gone. As he climbed back to the bridge, he felt as though *Sea Rover* was suddenly alone in a vast, silent sea. The stifling heat had not abated at all. The barometer had crashed a quarter-inch in the last hour alone, and the muggy air had become palpable, as though when he moved his hand he could slice it. His entire body itched again from sweat and salt spray, and his saliva was gummy.

Rita answered his radio call immediately. When he told

her that the helicopter was on its way to Trumbo Point Naval Hospital, she sighed and said, "Thank God. I can be there by the time it arrives." She paused and then asked, "What . . . what did the paramedics say?"

"He's got a good shot," Gallagher answered, knowing that wasn't quite what he'd been told.

"Thank God," she repeated, her voice cracking as though she was finally letting herself go.

Gallagher didn't say anything.

"Jack," she went on, her voice choked. "No more. When Dewey and Hugh get there, come in . . . The, uh . . . What you said about Nick being right . . . Tim being right about the deep water and all . . ." She paused for a moment. "It doesn't matter . . . compared to Tim . . ." She sucked in her breath. "Damn it, Jack, don't play chicken with the hurricane. You're too much like your . . . like Nick . . ."

After Gallagher signed off, he went below to the galley. He drank half a bottle of water and then pulled a beer from the refrigerator and headed out to the stern deck. He sat on the cooler with his back against the bulkhead, slid the beer can back and forth across his forehead, and then pressed it against the back of his neck. He wondered what the medics were doing at that moment in an attempt to stabilize Tim—and if Tim really did have a good chance of making it. He pictured Rita racing to the naval hospital, where she would be forced to wait, unable to do anything for her son who, hovering between life and death, would lie in a recompression chamber—an airtight, high-tech womb that would gradually reduce the nitrogen bubbles in his system and eventually, if he was lucky, revitalize him. And then Gallagher thought, too, about Hernández and how she was going to react to this latest bit of Doubloon news.

He rested there in the heavy silence, waiting for Doubloon's whaler. Time played tricks on him in the gathering gloom. Only the evening before he'd been sitting on the bench near the turtle kraals wondering what to make of Doubloon. Ever since, events had been whirling like some tropical storm. Now, the sunset was little more than a gradual fading of light in the thick haze. The sweltering heat intensified with the darkness. With no wind and no chop, the only sound was the intermittent drone of *Sea Rover*'s bilge pump. When he bent to set the beer can, now lukewarm, on the deck, he noticed the Colt and the M1 where they had been stowed that morning.

He stood, stretched, and put a foot up on the gunwale. There was still no breeze, only the dark expanse of sky and water. He felt a deep loneliness that extended across the water and across time to his childhood, his father's playing catch with him, his parents' estrangement, and his own inability to settle down. He realized, too, that, despite the apparent calm at that moment, he was merely in the eye of the storm. The whirling, more furious and perilous, would begin again at any time.

34

Finally, Gallagher heard the distant hum of a large outboard motor. When the motor's pitch changed little, he realized the boat was heading past *Sea Rover* far to the south. He clambered up to the bridge, got the six-battery flashlight stowed next to the logbook, and climbed on top of the wheelhouse. Listening intently, he shined the light in a series of flashes—ten seconds on, five off, ten on.

The light that finally flashed back was more to the southwest than the south. Using Tim's dive watch to keep his signal flashing at regular intervals, he hopped down to the deck of the bridge and then climbed down the ship's ladder to the stern deck. Finally, he saw the sleek white hull of the whaler emerge from the darkness.

As Thibodeaux pulled the whaler alongside *Sea Rover*'s starboard gunwale, he shouted, "T'anks. We were headin' way de fuck by ya." Unlike Hernández's boat, Doubloon's whaler wasn't outfitted for diving. Stripped down, it was little more than a fiberglass shell with two benches, a steering column, and an old Evinrude outboard motor.

Whitaker tossed Gallagher a line and then, hefting a green duffel bag, stepped quickly onto *Sea Rover*'s gunwale and down on the deck. He dropped the duffel, stretched as though his whole body ached, and shook his head. His shirt was wet and his hair disheveled, with damp strands falling across his forehead. His beard was speckled with spray. "I'd forgotten," he said, "how much fun a day in the whaler could be."

Gallagher hitched the line to a cleat on the gunwale near the galley's hatchway.

Thibodeaux laughed, turned to Gallagher, and said, "I'm tellin' ya, Hugh's lost his sea legs. And his sense a humor. Didn't even find it funny when de engine broke down." He set a bumper between the whaler and *Sea Rover*'s hull. "Drifted for more dan two hours. Couldn't even call for help because Hugh's fuckin' cell phone went on de fritz. And de fuckin' runnin' lights still don't work. For a while dere, I t'ought we'd have ta ride out Brenda in de whaler, ya know dat." As he handed a box of shells and Millan's shotgun in its case up to Gallagher, he said, "Dat's from Ozzie. For de fuckin' sharks." He then noticed Gallagher's cutoffs and flip-flops, the sheathed knife strapped to his calf, the dive watch on his wrist, the swollen wound, and his two days' growth of beard. Laughing again, he hopped aboard *Sea Rover* and said, "Hey, podna, you're beginnin' ta look like a Conch." He grinned and clapped Gallagher on the back. "And startin' ta act like a Conch, too, ya' fuckin' renegade."

Gallagher smiled at Thibodeaux but didn't answer. He brushed beads of seawater from the gun case.

Whitaker pushed back his hair, wiped his mouth with the back of his hand, and shook his head again. "Uh, where's Tim?" he asked.

"Trumbo Point Naval Hospital," Gallagher said.

"What?" Whitaker asked.

Thibodeaux's eyes widened.

"Nitrogen sickness," Gallagher answered. "Coast guard chopper picked him up . . ." He paused, trying to reorder time in his mind. ". . . A couple of hours ago. He's in pretty bad shape, but they think he'll make it."

Thibodeaux slammed his right fist against his left palm. "Shee-it," he said, "Tim's got too much savvy, too much fuckin' experience ta do somet'ing like dat."

Gallagher nodded. He looked at each of the men as he said, "It's the treasure, the motherlode. I think he was going to dive 'til he found it or it killed him."

No one said anything for a minute. Whitaker kept brushing his hair back, and Thibodeaux pulled at his earring. Finally, Whitaker asked, "Where's the statue?"

Gallagher put the shotgun and shells on the cooler under the tarp and then led Thibodeaux and Whitaker into the forward cabin. When he pulled the shirt from the statue, Thibodeaux whooped, grinned, and nudged Gallagher with his elbow. "Look at dat, will ya?" he yelled.

Whitaker gasped as he knelt on one knee to get a closer look. Stroking the statue with his hand, he mumbled, "It's amazing . . . the detail . . . priceless . . . absolutely priceless. I've . . . I've never seen anything like it."

While the two men continued to gaze at the statue, Gallagher lifted the towel from the port bunk. As Whitaker stood, Gallagher slowly unfolded the towel and held it up so that the amulet gleamed in the overhead light.

"Holy shee-it!" Thibodeaux whispered.

"My God," Whitaker said. He took the amulet from the towel and inspected it. As he ran his thumb over the figure's belly, he murmured, "Pre-Columbian . . . Aztec . . . gold cast by the lost-wax method . . ." He traced the headdress with his finger. "Where'd you find it?"

"A treasure chest," Gallagher answered as he gave the four-headed eagle to Whitaker.

"A treasure chest?" Whitaker asked, his voice hoarse. He cleared his throat and took a deep breath. "Virtually all of America's pre-Columbian gold artifacts were melted down to pay for the Spanish Empire's wars." His voice became low as he examined the eagle. "That's what would've happened to this if it had reached Seville." He handed the ornament to Thibodeaux.

"What about doubloons, podna?" Thibodeaux asked as he gaped at the eagle. "Did ya find any a dem?"

Gallagher shook his head.

"They're down there," Whitaker said with finality.

"Dewey, Hugh," Gallagher said, "there's a wall of silver. I mean, a wall."

"Hot fuckin' damn," Thibodeaux said.

"Terrific," Whitaker said. "Great." He turned the amulet over and over in his hand. "What about the chest? What'd it look like?"

"*Chests*," Gallagher answered. "Three of them." He shrugged. "Brass. Large."

Whitaker gazed at the amulet in his trembling hand. "The value's incalculable," he said. "Positively incalculable."

"Well," Gallagher said, "I promised Rita I'd let you take me home." He paused for a moment and then added, "We can get the divers out here as soon as Brenda blows through and the government crap's settled."

Thibodeaux shook his head. "Dere ain't no divers, Jack," he said.

"What?" Gallagher asked.

"Vogel bought 'em off," Thibodeaux said. "Offered 'em a grand each up front ta sign on." He shook his head again. "Matt sure as hell ain't gonna be wort' no t'ousand bucks."

Whitaker turned and gazed again at the *Magdalena* statue.

"What the hell?" Gallagher said, although he realized it made sense.

Thibodeaux pulled at his earring. "Tried ta buy me, too, podna," he said. "After de hearin' . . . yesterday . . . on his boat." He scratched his nose as though time was playing tricks on him as well. ". . . Pete offered me t'ree grand up front." He laughed. "Even gave me a fuckin' contract ta sign. I told him I had a percent a whatever Doubloon brought up." He stared at the golden eagle he held. "Pete told me it'd be a percent a not'in' . . . dat I was a dumb shit for staying wit' Rita." He raised the eagle in both hands as though it were an offering. "Jesus," he added as much to himself as to the others, "I'm a fuckin' millionaire, ya know dat."

"We've got to get the government situation straightened out before anybody cashes in on any treasure, Dewey," Whitaker said. "We're going to need documentation, pictures, lots of 'em."

"What about Brenda?" Gallagher asked.

Thibodeaux glanced at his dive watch and shook his head. "We'd be cuttin' it too fuckin' close, I'm tellin' ya," he said.

"As long as we're out of here in half an hour, we'd be okay," Whitaker said.

Looking at Whitaker, Thibodeaux said, "You're de one dat hates a sloppy ride."

"Without the documentation we've got nothing," Whitaker answered. "We won't be able to get back out here for a while. Let's do it."

Thibodeaux turned to Gallagher and said, "What d'ya t'ink, podna?"

Sea Rover rolled in the rising chop. "I think you two've got gold fever," he answered.

Thibodeaux laughed. "Wanna make a night dive and show me de *Magdalena* treasure?" he asked.

"Can't." Gallagher pointed to his ear. "I came up too fast, and I haven't been able to clear."

"Okay," Thibodeaux said. "Dat's all right." He laughed again. "I'll just get us some pics a de site." He glanced at Whitaker. "Maybe bring us up a treasure chest, I'm tellin' ya."

Whitaker nodded and pointed to the statue. "I'll take shots here while you guys get the gear ready." His voice became ebullient. "And after the dive, we'll run like hell for Key West."

As Gallagher climbed to the wheelhouse, a gust of dank wind slapped his face. Despite the suddenly volatile weather, he felt himself entering the zone he'd occasionally experienced flying sorties. The barometer was crashing, but his mind was clearing—and the quick calmness before battle was rising in him. He pulled two hairs from his scalp and set them in a cross on the top of the radio's microphone. He then went down to the dive locker where he found a roll of duct tape, tore off a three-inch piece, ripped a half-inch-wide strip from it, and pressed the strip to his skin under the waistband of his cutoffs. As he climbed back to the stern deck, he felt the deep rocking of the boat in the swells rising to five and six feet. Beneath the overhanging clouds, the night was growing heavier and more unsettled. Thibodeaux sat in the scant light attaching the strobe to the underwater Nikon. Whitaker came out of the cabin, glanced at the two men on the deck, set his camera against the bulkhead next to the Colt pistol, and headed for the ship's ladder to the wheelhouse.

As Whitaker climbed the ladder, Gallagher said, "Why don't you radio Rita? Tell her what we're doing."

Whitaker hesitated for a moment. "Not a bad idea, Jack," he said. "But she'll still be at the hospital. We're not going to reach anybody now." He looked over at Thibodeaux. "And anyway, we'll have plenty of time to call on the way in."

"Yeah," Gallagher said. "Okay. Good point."

While Whitaker was in the wheelhouse, Gallagher went over the dive plan with Thibodeaux. He described the location of the silver wall and explained how the brass chests were piled on top of one another, as though they had been tossed into the sand. As Thibodeaux checked his regulator and slipped on his harness, Gallagher lifted a wrench and struck the port afterburner three times. When Whitaker stepped out of the wheelhouse, Gallagher called up to him, "I'll run the engines, Hugh. You can take a break for a while."

"Ah . . . that's all right, Jack," Whitaker answered. "I don't mind."

"Nah," Gallagher said, "it'll give you more time to check out the statue and the Aztec artifacts."

"Yeah, right," Whitaker said, descending the ladder. "Okay."

Picking up the Nikon, Thibodeaux stared at the two men. Not bothering to remove his earring, he pulled down his mask, checked his regulator, and handed the Nikon to Whitaker. He then looked up at the lowering sky, inserted the regulator's mouthpiece, and scissor-stepped into the water. He turned, made a circle with his thumb and forefinger, and reached for the Nikon. As Whitaker stooped to hand Thibodeaux the camera and strobe, Gallagher climbed to the wheelhouse. He started *Sea Rover*'s engines and then checked the radio's microphone; as he expected, the crossed hairs were gone. He was well into the zone, aware of the world slowing for him as his senses quickened. Squinting into the darkness, he scanned the area without seeing any sign of another boat. Off *Sea Rover*'s stern, the arc of Thibodeaux's dive light faded as the diver descended toward the silver wall and brass chests.

Gallagher yanked the strip of duct tape from under his waistband, picked up the radio's microphone, taped the call button down so that the radio would transmit constantly, replaced the microphone, and slid *Sea Rover*'s logbook in front of it so that the tape wouldn't show. He then raced the engines for a moment and throttled them back so their throbbing was even, set the radio on the distress and calling frequency, turned the radio's volume dial to its maximum setting, and leaned against the wheel to wait. The wind died completely again. He rolled his neck and folded his arms across his chest. Sweating freely, he felt almost light-headed despite the leaden air.

35

Whitaker poked his head in the hatchway and asked, "How's it going?"

Gallagher did not answer. He gazed out the back, where Thibodeaux's light was a translucent gold slick in the dark water.

His shirt hanging loosely over his pants, Whitaker stepped into the wheelhouse. "I may need a hand when Dewey . . . ," he began.

"Hey, Whitaker," Gallagher asked, "what'd you learn in Spain, in Seville?" His voice was calm and clear.

"Huh? What?" Whitaker stammered. He stared at Gallagher for a moment and then glanced out at the stern where the dive light was fading in the depths.

"What'd you find out in Spain?" Gallagher repeated.

Whitaker brushed his hair back with his hand. "What . . . what do you mean?"

Gallagher unfolded his arms and looked at the archeologist for the first time. "You must've found out something," he said, "about the Governor's Cargo or *Magdalena*'s sinking or both. Something in the archives."

"What the . . . I've got no idea what the hell you're talking about."

"I think you do." Gallagher grabbed Whitaker's arm. "My father's dead, Whitaker . . ."

The archeologist pulled himself free. "What the hell's that got to do with me?"

"Everything, Whitaker," Gallagher said. "Everything."

"You're insane," Whitaker said, his voice cracking. Running his hand through his beard, he glanced quickly around the bridge as though he was looking for something. "You've got Conch Fever, Gallagher." His tone became disdainful. "Been out on the water too long."

"Maybe," Gallagher said. "But Sergeant Escobar bought what I told him enough to order a search warrant. Went through your place after you left today . . ." Hoping his bluff was working, he tilted his head and scratched his ear. He pictured the coast guard radio operator who monitored the distress and calling frequency trying frantically to figure out what was happening. And he wondered who else, among those monitoring the channel, might be hearing the conversation. "What do you suppose Escobar found?" he asked Whitaker.

Whitaker glared silently at Gallagher. He ran his hand along the hem of his shirt and then rubbed his thumb and index finger together.

"The disks missing from the Doubloon office?" Gallagher stared into Whitaker's eyes, which twitched behind his glasses. "Documents from Seville?" He scratched the side of his nose. "And the phone records that Escobar's having subpoenaed? What'll they show, Whitaker?"

"Goddamn you," Whitaker hissed. He reached behind his back under his shirt and pulled out the Colt automatic. His hand shook as he pointed the pistol's barrel in Gallagher's face.

Shit, Gallagher thought, *this is working too well.* "Put the gun down, down, Whitaker," he said loudly.

"Fuck you, Gallagher."

Gallagher nodded, smiled ironically at Whitaker, and asked, "What *did* you find in the Seville archives?"

Whitaker sucked in his breath and clenched his teeth. "A letter written by *Magdalena*'s captain. He was the only survivor." He spat the words at Gallagher. "But the letter wasn't in the archives. I was smart enough to trace it through his family, his descendants."

Gallagher nodded again at Whitaker but said nothing. He stared at the Colt's wavering barrel and wondered how to keep Whitaker talking so that the archeologist wouldn't blow his face off. "What'd the letter say?"

Whitaker sneered at him. "It . . . he described how the hurricane ripped away *Magdalena*'s masts. How the crew jettisoned the cannon and the cargo, even the chests of silver coins . . . all the stuff we'd already discovered at the Havana Bank site." He licked his lips. "How they somehow got the sheet anchor on deck before it was washed overboard. How *Magdalena* stayed afloat out into deeper water." His voice became loud, almost a shout. "And he mentioned the chests Cuba's governor brought aboard just before *Magdalena* sailed. He thought the chests were cursed but didn't know what was in 'em. But I did. I knew. We already had the proof."

"Those three doubloons my father found," Gallagher said, "they really got to you, didn't they? Really set you off . . . You can't get them out of . . ."

"They're the first gold coins ever minted in the New World." Whitaker's smile was rancorous. "Invaluable as artifacts alone—*and* pure goddamned gold."

Gallagher inched slowly past the wheel and glanced out toward the stern where the Nikon's strobe lit the depths like distant lightning. "But why'd you murder my father?" Gallagher asked, his voice almost sad. "You had a piece of any treasure found."

"I didn't *murder* Nick," Whitaker said. "And I didn't have a piece of the treasure."

"What?" Gallagher's mind raced.

Anger and frustration showed in Whitaker's eyes. "I secretly sold off my fucking five percent to an investor, a rich *cubano*, two years ago. Just to make ends meet, to keep working for Nick and his goddamn obsession." His breathing was short, and his hand quivered. "I gave up ten years of my life, my standing with my colleagues, everything—for that fucking obsession." The Colt's barrel wavered again. "And I was going to get nothing even though I'm the one that finally figured out where to find *Magdalena*'s treasure."

All the pieces, Gallagher thought, were falling into place. He inched closer to the hatchway. "So you didn't *mean* to kill my father?"

"No, goddamn it. Nick's death . . ." As Whitaker shook his head, a perplexed expression came over his face. "I sank the boat to slow the salvage so the contract would run out. I'd already gotten a verbal commitment from the state for leases on those western sites. And there was no way in hell Nick could've known that the treasure was way out here . . . but he had one of his goddamn hunches."

Gallagher nodded. "And you had that burnout, Patrick, steal the disks and trash the office." He emphasized the dead man's name. "Got rid of the evidence that the silver bar really was *Magdalena*'s and messed up Rita's preparation for the hearing all at the same time."

Whitaker smirked. "You got it. Sticking you with the sword wasn't part of the plan . . ." His smile turned malevolent. ". . . but it would've saved me some trouble if he'd killed you." He switched the Colt to his left hand, wiped his right hand on his pants, and switched the pistol back. Sweat ran down his temples. "He wanted a piece of the action to keep his mouth shut."

Gallagher cocked his head. "So you murdered him, too."

"He killed himself," Whitaker scoffed.

Gallagher inched a bit closer to the hatchway. "When we left the Chart House, it was you, not me, he was after."

"Yeah. He hit me up for cash, but I knew he'd settle for dope." His grin was crooked. "You can't live in the Keys and not know where to cut a deal. All I did was get him some shit that was purer than he thought. He fried his own goddamn brains."

"He had a knife in his gut."

"That wasn't me. One of his buddies must've hit him for the rest of the dope."

"And now the whole thing's blowing up in your face."

"No fucking way." Derision seeped back into Whitaker's voice. "The plan's changed, but I've still got it all worked out."

"You didn't take me into account."

"You've been a fucking nuisance, that's all. Stumbling in and bringing back Nick's goddamn luck with you." Whitaker shook his head. "That goddamn will of Nick's. It's like he somehow knew you'd stick your goddamned nose in Doubloon's business, take his goddamn place."

"So you sabotaged the regulator I was going to use to dive with Josie."

"I thought it might get you to change your mind about staying on." Whitaker bit his lip. "I should've known better. Once you goddamn Gallaghers get something into your fucking heads . . ."

"Jesus," Gallagher said. "You're a piece of work, you greedy bastard."

"Fuck you!" Whitaker shook his head vehemently. "It's not greed." His voice became shrill. "You don't get it. You didn't work for nothing for ten fucking years." His finger twitched on the Colt's trigger. "I'm just getting what's mine, what I deserve."

Gallagher nodded. "Yeah, Whitaker," he said, "at least you got that right."

When Gallagher reached back and began to slide the logbook away from the microphone, Whitaker yelled, "Don't move!" Then, he saw the tape across the radio's call button. "What the . . . ," he stammered. "You . . . asshole."

As Whitaker lunged forward and yanked the microphone and cord from the radio, Gallagher bolted through the hatchway and leapt over the railing. He heard two gunshots and the sound of shattering glass before his right ankle caught the whaler's prow and he pitched headlong into the ocean.

36

As Gallagher twisted around underwater, bullets scored bubbling tracers near him. His lungs burned and pain seared his ankle, but he righted himself, as he had been taught to do during dunkings in his flight training, and swam under *Sea Rover*'s hull. He pulled himself along the hull, cutting his hands on the barnacles. When he reached the water's surface on the port side of the tug near its bow, he gasped for air.

He clung to the bow, out of sight of the deck, and listened for any sound from the tug. Black clouds loomed above him; sudden gusts lifted swells around him. Hearing a scraping in the forward cabin, he swallowed the pain, reached for the port anchor line, and pulled himself hand over hand toward the deck. He hooked his left ankle onto the spillway, rolled onto the deck, and crouched on his left leg near the port anchor's chock. Wanting to come at Whitaker from an unexpected angle, he glanced up at the wheelhouse. He tested his right ankle, but it wouldn't bear any weight. Reaching up, he grabbed the railing's post, swung his left leg up, and hooked his ankle around the stanchion. He then took a deep breath, closed his eyes to the pain, and spun himself up onto *Sea Rover*'s upper deck. He lay prone for a moment before crawling on his belly around the wheelhouse and peering down at the stern deck.

A minute later Whitaker stepped from the galley's hatchway and dragged his duffel bag along the deck. Holding the Colt in his right hand, he glanced warily each way and then stared down at the water. When he saw no sign of anyone, he set the duffel by the starboard gunwale and crossed to the dive ladder. Gallagher snaked across the upper deck by the shower and looked down. The dive light's increased brightness suggested that Thibodeaux had risen to fifteen feet and was hovering at his three-minute decompression stop.

Whitaker crossed back to the starboard gunwale, gazed nervously toward the east, and stuck the Colt into the waistband of his pants. When he lifted the duffel bag with both hands, his shoulders slumped under the weight. Gallagher scuttled across the deck and crouched on his left leg by the wheelhouse's railing. Whitaker dropped the duffel on the deck, stepped up on the gunwale, and hopped down onto the whaler's middle seat. Gallagher gauged the distance from where he was to the whaler's deck. When he tested his ankle again, pain flashed up his leg.

As Whitaker reached back to drag the duffel into the whaler, Gallagher sucked in his breath, clutched the railing with both hands, hurdled it, and dove toward the archeologist. He hit Whitaker's shoulder with such force that the archeologist flipped backward over the seat. Gallagher tumbled sideways, almost careening overboard. While he regained his balance, Whitaker drew the Colt and fired wildly. Then, aiming at Gallagher's forehead, he squeezed the trigger again. The pistol's hammer clicked forward, but no bullet exploded from the barrel.

Whitaker swung the Colt at Gallagher's head, and the barrel slashed Gallagher's ear a second before he could seize Whitaker's forearm. Whitaker's eyes bugged as Gallagher bent his wrist back and struck it repeatedly against the edge of the steering column. Screaming, Whitaker scratched at Gallagher's eyes with the fingers of his free hand. When the Colt finally clattered to the whaler's deck, Gallagher elbowed Whitaker's hand from his face and grabbed the archeologist by the throat. Whitaker again clawed at Gallagher's eyes as Gallagher smashed the archeologist's head against the steering column. Gallagher held Whitaker's throat until the archeologist's hand went limp and slid from Gallagher's face.

Gallagher fell back onto the seat. Aware again of the shooting pain in his ankle, he slumped there until he caught his breath. His face and ear and hands all burned. When he wiped his face, his hand was covered with blood as well as sweat. He reached up and felt the wet, warm gash where the Colt's barrel had ripped his ear. He then scanned the sea below the bank of black clouds and saw the dark shape of a sleek dive boat knifing through the swells toward them. "Shit," he said aloud.

Whitaker rolled over on his side, moaned, and vomited into the bilge. Roiling waves hammered the whaler, and the wind drove it against *Sea Rover*.

"Jack," Thibodeaux shouted, "what de fuck are ya doin'?" He stood on the tug's deck cradling the M1 in the crook of his arm. Water dripped from his long, tangled hair.

"Give me a hand," Gallagher shouted back. He pointed toward the approaching boat.

Thibodeaux leveled the M1's barrel at Gallagher. "What de hell's goin' down, podna?"

Ignoring the rifle, Gallagher pointed at Whitaker. "Hugh sank your boat . . . ," he shouted at Thibodeaux, ". . . killed my father." He glanced over his shoulder at the approaching boat whose blue hull and cockpit were now clearly visible. "And we're about to be in some deep shit." He cupped his hands under Whitaker's arms. "Give me a hand, goddamn it!" he yelled up at Thibodeaux as he lifted the semiconscious archeologist.

Still aiming the rifle at Gallagher, Thibodeaux stood staring at the dive boat for a few seconds more. He then shook his head, leaned the M1 against a cooler, and helped haul Whitaker onto the tug's deck. As Thibodeaux dragged Whitaker under the tarp, Gallagher hopped on his left leg up onto *Sea Rover*'s deck. He leaned against the bulkhead and said, "Move the duffel under there with him."

Thibodeaux unhooked his weight belt and slid it onto the deck. As he pulled the bag under the tarp, he muttered, "Dat dickhead was gonna take off wit' de statue and dose ornaments, I'm tellin' ya." He looked at Whitaker's prone body and then seemed to notice for the first time the scratches on Gallagher's face and the blood dripping down his neck below his ear. Grinning, he said, "Shee-it, Jack. I can't leave you alone for one fuckin' minute." He tugged at his earring. "How de hell did ya know it was Hugh?"

"The theft of the disks. A bunch of little things." He turned on his good leg and looked a third time at the dive boat. "Shut the engines down and turn off the cabin lights. And get any ammo you can find."

As Thibodeaux climbed to the wheelhouse, Gallagher leaned against the bulkhead again and concentrated for a moment on what had to be done next. He then grabbed the gun case, slid the shotgun out, and ran his hand over the engraved metalwork. *Sea Rover*'s engines stopped, and the lights flicked off. He opened the box and pulled out two shells. When the wind abruptly subsided again, a shiver ran through his body. As Thibodeaux returned to the deck, Gallagher broke the shotgun's action, loaded both barrels, and snapped the action shut.

Nodding toward the approaching dive boat, Thibodeaux said, "Dat's Vogel, podna. Dis is gonna get ugly real fast, I'm tellin' ya."

"Yeah," Gallagher answered. "Looks like it."

Vengeance plowed toward *Sea Rover* as though it was going to ram it. Gallagher and Thibodeaux stared at the dive boat until, suddenly, its diesels reversed and it skimmed to a full stop twenty yards away, its bow at an angle to *Sea Rover*'s. As its wake spilled over *Sea Rover*'s gunwale, *Vengeance*'s spotlight panned across *Sea Rover*'s deck. Gallagher shaded his eyes and squinted across at Pete Vogel strutting from *Vengeance*'s flying bridge. A barrel-chested Hispanic and a swarthy younger man with tattooed arms stepped out of the hatchway after him, but Vogel waved them back. He swung an over and under pump-action shotgun in his right hand as he swaggered toward the bow. When he reached the railing above the bowsprit, he aimed the pumpgun at Gallagher and Thibodeaux.

As Thibodeaux raised the M1, Gallagher grabbed his arm and whispered, "Wait."

"I want that statue," Vogel shouted. He braced himself against the railing. "It's mine, goddamn it."

Gallagher rolled his neck, wiped blood and sweat from his eyes, and tightened his grip on the shotgun.

"Hey, flyboy," Vogel rasped, "Nick was right, huh. Fuckin' Nick was right about the deep water!"

"Pete," Thibodeaux shouted, "Hugh took off wit' de statue, ya know dat. Bolted wit' de treasure, I'm tellin' ya."

"In what," Vogel scoffed, "a fuckin' submarine?" He held the pumpgun in his left hand and ran the stumps of his right hand across his face. "Where the fuck is that stuck-up dildo? I heard him make that fuckin' call. And I heard all that shit with the flyboy."

As the wind abruptly blustered, Thibodeaux glanced quizzically at Gallagher and said, "What's dat about?"

Gallagher braced his injured leg against the gunwale. "Pete," he shouted, "the treasure's down there. A wall of silver. But we don't have the divers to bring it up. You made sure of that."

Grinning again, Vogel pointed the pumpgun at Gallagher's face. "I've waited a long time to get my hands on that fuckin' treasure, flyboy. And nobody's gettin' in my way."

Thibodeaux shouted to Vogel, "Hey, Pete, dere's plenty a treasure for everybody. Can't we talk . . ."

"Shut up, shithead," Vogel yelled. "You had your fuckin' chance to talk on my boat. I'm done talkin'." He pumped a shell into the gun's breech. "I ain't leavin' here without that statue. And I don't give a shit who I got to take down." He swung the gun up and fired a round into the scudding clouds.

Thibodeaux cringed, but Gallagher only shook his head, raised the shotgun's barrel, and aimed at Vogel. "Think about it, Pete," he began. "You don't have . . ."

Whitaker crawled out from under the tarp and, as if awakened by the blast of the pumpgun, stood up groggily. Drying vomit caked his beard. Thibodeaux turned the M1 on him just before he toppled over onto his injured wrist and vomited again. Gallagher glanced at the archeologist and then continued to stare across the water.

"Don't make no fuckin' mistake here, flyboy!" Vogel yelled. "I'm takin' what's mine."

Vengeance drifted closer in the swells. A wave slapped against *Sea Rover*'s gunwale, hurling spray. The barrel-chested man left *Vengeance*'s bridge and said something to Vogel, who shook his head vehemently and shoved him away.

Climbing to his feet again, Whitaker muttered, "It's gonna ... The boat's gonna ... I've gotta ... ," and began to stumble toward Gallagher.

"Don't move, ya fuckin' dildo!" Vogel yelled.

As Gallagher shifted the shotgun's stock to ward him off, Whitaker staggered past him toward the hatchway. Vogel raised the pumpgun and fired a second shot into the darkness, freezing Whitaker. Vogel grinned malevolently, lowered the pumpgun, and pointed with his stumps at the archeologist. "You're not goin' nowhere," he yelled. "You figure you and that fat-assed old fag can fuckin' cut me outa what's mine? You'll fuckin' die first!"

Framed by the hatchway, Whitaker turned and stood up straighter; his eyes, despite the glare of the light, seemed to focus for the first time. "Vogel, you asshole," he screamed, "you'll never see any of that gold." Laced once again with disdain, his voice rose. "Not one goddamned doubloon. Ever!" He wiped his beard on his sleeve and sneered into the light. "You don't know shit about what's really going on. But maybe you can understand this, you fucking loser—the deal's done.

And you've been cut out. Completely and fucking absolutely! I've made goddamned sure of it."

Vogel stood stiffly on *Vengeance*'s bow, the veins in his neck pulsing and the gold crucifix gleaming darkly. "God fuckin' damn it," he shouted to the impending storm. He gazed into Gallagher's eyes, rasped, "God fuckin' damn it," more softly, smiled, and let his shoulders slump. Then, suddenly, he swung the gun up and fired.

Whitaker's face disintegrated. He lurched backward, teetered for a moment, and toppled through the hatchway.

Dropping to his right knee, Gallagher took out the spotlight with his first shot and winged Vogel's shoulder with his second. He crouched low behind the gunwale to reload as rounds from the pumpgun thundered into the hull below him and the bulkhead above him. Splintered glass and steel shards rained on him. Thibodeaux raised the M1, but he hesitated, not firing. Waving him back, Gallagher shouted, "Dewey, down. Don't draw his . . ."

Thibodeaux screamed and crumpled under the tarp.

Gallagher snapped the shotgun's action shut on two more rounds, and, squinting through sweat and blood, peered over the gunwale.

Vogel slouched at *Vengeance*'s prow, the empty pumpgun braced on the railing. His shirtsleeve red, he screamed, "Ammunition, fuckhead! I need more fuckin' ammo." The barrel-chested man leaned out of the flying bridge's hatchway but did not approach Vogel, who began to rail at the clouds.

Gallagher wiped his face, glanced over his left shoulder, and then turned to his right. Thibodeaux sprawled in the darkness under the tarp, his bare right foot grinding against the deck. Gallagher propped the shotgun against the gunwale and began to scuff on his good leg toward Thibodeaux.

Suddenly, the world all around Gallagher flashed and roared. *Sea Rover*'s bow heaved abruptly, and the shock wave threw him against the afterburners' brace, knocking the wind out of him. Dry, hot air singed his skin. And then he was tumbling back across the deck. His head and shoulder struck the bulkhead, and he slumped into a heap, dizzy and breathless.

37

Gasping for air, Gallagher could not at first imagine what was happening. *Sea Rover* was aglow. Smoke belched from the hatchway and portholes, stung his eyes, curled around the bridge, and billowed in the wind. His ears rang, and dry heat prickled his skin. And then he was on all fours, aware that he had little time before the fuel tanks or the compressed air cylinders blew. He lowered his head, took a deep breath of the fresher air below the smoke, and scuttled across the deck.

Thibodeaux lay on his back against the port gunwale, his chest heaving. Blood pulsed from a gaping wound in his left thigh. Gallagher pulled off his shirt, took the diver's knife from the sheath, cut a long swatch of cloth, and knotted the tourniquet tightly around Thibodeaux's leg above the wound.

Thibodeaux turned his head, coughed, and said, "What de fuck, Jack?" He bit his lip until it bled.

Glancing again at the wound, Gallagher said, "I guess Whitaker was planning to sink another salvage boat—blow it up with us on it." He looked past the torn tarp at the flames licking the steel casings of the shattered portholes. "I'll get you out of here, partner."

As the heat from the flames poured over them, Gallagher

hooked his arm around Thibodeaux's shoulder and slid backward, dragging the diver across the tilting deck past the duffel bag toward the whaler. Blood from Thibodeaux's wounded leg left a dark trail on the deck. Gallagher scrambled back under the tarp, grabbed the duffel bag, yanked it onto the gunwale, and shoved it overboard into the sea. He then lowered himself into the whaler, which was partially swamped, took a deep breath, and hauled Thibodeaux off *Sea Rover*'s deck. Thibodeaux moaned when his leg hit the saltwater in the whaler's bilge. "It feels like hell, Jack, I'm tellin' ya," he murmured.

Gallagher turned and looked over at *Vengeance*, where Vogel, hunched over and bleeding, was jamming the pumpgun's muzzle into the barrel-chested man's stomach. The man stood his ground, pointed toward *Sea Rover*, and shouted something in Spanish. As Vogel stepped back and swung the pumpgun at him, the man grabbed the barrel, yanked the gun from Vogel, and used its stock to pin him against the bulkhead.

After casting off the whaler's painter, Gallagher pushed away from the salvage boat, clambered past Thibodeaux toward the stern, and muttered, "Shit!" The whaler's steering column was pockmarked, its ignition system shattered. He leaned over the stern, gripped the motor's starter cord, and yanked. The engine coughed but didn't start. "C'mon, you mother!" he grumbled as he pulled the cord again.

Fire raged on *Sea Rover*. Then, three quick explosions shook the tug. A fourth, horrific explosion blew *Sea Rover*'s bridge apart. As the shock wave washed over him, Gallagher swallowed seawater and coughed it back up; Thibodeaux mumbled incomprehensible Creole. Chunks of wood and steel fell on the whaler, and Gallagher had to kick the smoldering shards overboard with his good leg. Listing farther to starboard, *Sea Rover* became a flaming hulk.

When *Vengeance*'s diesels revved, Gallagher glimpsed the barrel-chested man using a fire extinguisher to spread foam on smoking hunks of wood on the foredeck. The pumpgun lay by the hatchway, but Vogel was nowhere in sight. As *Vengeance* turned and veered away from the burning tug, Gallagher shouted across the water. The noise of the dive boat's engines receded as it pounded through the swells, and then the only sound was the eerie murmur of smoke rising in the wind.

When the whaler was two hundred yards astern of *Sea Rover*, the tug turned turtle but did not sink; smoke hung over a gash in the bow of the humpbacked hull. Gallagher yanked the whaler's starter cord a dozen more times, smacked his hand on the housing, sat on the gunwale, and smiled. Gazing at the clouds blustering low overhead, he murmured, "You're in some serious shit, all right, partner." He helped Thibodeaux into the whaler's only life vest and then lashed the diver to the steering column so that if he lost consciousness his head would stay above water. *Vengeance* returned briefly to the smoking hulk, but by then the whaler was too far away for Gallagher's shouts to be heard, and he had nothing with which to signal, even had he been sure that the dive boat was searching for survivors. As though it were some ghost ship partially veiled by smoke, *Vengeance* appeared and disappeared in the distant swells.

Over the next hour, the wind blew in gusts, and the swells increased to eight and nine feet. Thibodeaux hung in a state of semiconsciousness murmuring in Creole. Flashes of blue lightning periodically illuminated a tumultuous world. Feeling he had to do something, Gallagher split his time between checking Thibodeaux and trying to start the whaler's motor. The first squall blew over, beating them with rain. By the time the squall line passed, Gallagher felt at once chilled and over-heated. Rain and salt spray blurred his vision; he lost all sense of direction. The whaler rode a swell and slid into a trough and rode another swell. Whipping spray and blowing foam turned the world white below the black sky.

Gallagher returned to the stern, braced himself, and yanked the starter cord at fifteen-second intervals. After a few minutes, as he paused to catch his breath, a ten-foot wave bashed the whaler, flinging him over the motor and into the sea. He tumbled below the surface. Water shot up his nose and choked him as the surge towed him down. Clawing the water, he stroked against the surge. As he thrashed upward, his lungs burned. When he broke the surface, his arms flailed at the water. He gulped the air, gasping uncontrollably. Hyperventilating, he treaded water, shook his head, and looked around. The whaler had vanished.

He caught his breath, but each time a swell rolled over him, he swallowed more water. His back stiffened. Although the water was in the mid-eighties and the air still in the low nineties, he shivered from the strain of staying afloat. A rumbling like thunder rose through the roar of the storm. He tasted vomit in his throat but forced it down. As he reached the crest of a swell, lightning struck and he glimpsed in the blue light a low, flat hull riding the crest of the wave ahead of him. When he reached the crest of the next swell, he blinked the spray from his eyes, waited for the inevitable arc of blue light, and looked again for the whaler. Swamped, it was almost fully submerged except for its steering column and motor,

which rose from the water like dorsal and caudal fins. Seeming
to ride the bucking beast backward, Thibodeaux swayed in the
lines, his head tilting first forward and then back against the
steering column.

Gallagher stroked with the surge. Fighting the ocean's immense power exhausted him, but he kept paddling, almost
mechanically, aware only of each swell. Coughing salt spray
and bile, he felt the whaler torpedoing back down the trough
before he saw it coming. He instinctively hunched forward so
that the hull only clipped his shoulder. Gagging on saltwater,
he groped for the motor, but his fingers slipped on the wet
casing. Adrenaline pounded in his temples as he pulled himself
toward the boat. The whaler remained just out of his reach
until, at the base of the next trough, the boat suddenly surged
backward again. He hooked his left elbow around the motor's
shaft just above the whaler's gunwale and let the boat drag him
as he tried again to catch his breath.

He worked his grip along the gunwale until he was parallel
to the steering column. With his remaining strength, he flung
himself sideways and grabbed for the column. His hand
slipped down the column but caught the line tied near its base.
Clutching the line, he heaved himself onto the whaler's hull.
He looped his arm under the line, twisted his wrist around it,
and held it fast. Unable to calm his breathing, he choked on
water and spray. His voice cracked when he shouted,
"Dewey . . ." Still clutching the line, he turned. Breathing in
short, erratic gasps, Thibodeaux was unconscious, his head
against the column. His hair was tangled, and his white streak
twisted; his earring lay like a wound on his neck. ". . . Hold
on," Gallagher shouted. "Hold on, goddamn it!"

———

The storm became their universe. Spindrift ripped from the swells. The next squall enervated Gallagher, and the one after it almost tore him again from the whaler. Only his arm, tangled in the line, kept him anchored to the boat. The air filled with foam as swells pushed the whaler to the west. They rode the cliffs of water, precipice upon precipice. Another squall line battered them; foam blew around them in dense streaks. The shrieking wind tore away every thought Gallagher had. Losing all sense of time and place in the pandemonium, he abandoned himself to the sea.

He gradually became aware of a roar above the blast of the wind, though he was too battered by the storm to realize what the sound meant. His mind reeled between memories of his childhood and the reality of the hurricane. The breakers tossed the whaler over the reef into shallow water, but the skidding and scraping only registered when a wave broke over him and slammed him against the seat. The whaler filled with sand and salt spray.

The next wave threw the whaler farther up the beach; the backwash butted the boat toward the sea. Choking, Gallagher looked up just as another breaker pummeled the boat. Knocked against the gunwale, he lay there until the ensuing wave broadsided him. He sat up and turned toward Thibodeaux. The diver's breathing was even more erratic, and the color had drained from his skin. "Dewey," Gallagher yelled over the din of the storm. "Dewey!" He shook Thibodeaux's shoulder until the diver's eyes opened. "Land, Dewey!" he shouted.

As another wave broke over them, Thibodeaux coughed, "Hey, podna, dat silver wall's gonna make us rich!"

Oh, shit, Gallagher thought.

"We're gonna have us one helluva time, I'm tellin' ya," Thibodeaux mumbled in his delirium.

Gallagher untied the line and rolled Thibodeaux out of the whaler. Another wave dashed them against the beach; shivering, Thibodeaux squeezed the sand between his fingers. Gallagher hooked Thibodeaux's shoulder, fell when he tried to put weight on his injured ankle, and, pulling Thibodeaux with him, crabbed his way to higher ground. When he tried to stand, he collapsed again. The rain pelted them, and the wind beat them. They crawled into the sea grass and saltwort, where Gallagher knelt, his head bowed, until yet another wave from the rising storm surge washed around them. Crawling with Thibodeaux past thick clumps of clubwort toward high ground, Gallagher was barely conscious of the pine and palm trees bending above him. He no longer heard the cacophonous wind and surf at all.

On a knoll well away from the beach, they collapsed a third time near an uprooted Australian pine. Gallagher pushed Thibodeaux into the hollow under the base of the trunk and the thick, gnarled roots. When he crawled in after him, Thibodeaux was again murmuring in Creole. With his back to the diver, Gallagher dug himself into the decaying pine needles and sand. Slowly, his shivering abated and his breathing calmed. He lapsed into a weary, storm-battered state, neither fully asleep nor fully awake, in which there was no locus, no clarity, no certainty—only a whirling gyre without center or still point. Nothing, not even the storm, held him.

38

The hurricane raged. The wind gusted, and the storm surge, scouring everything in its path, inundated the area except for the knoll on which Gallagher and Thibodeaux huddled. Sometime later, Gallagher became aware of the weird quiet of the hurricane's eye. At first he didn't remember where he was. A periodic flashing further disconcerted him. Then, the memory of the chaos and death flooded his mind. It seemed as though a lifetime, not sixty hours, had passed since the Marine Antiquities Board hearing.

Gallagher's whole body ached; his knees and shoulders throbbed with pain. His back and neck were so stiff that it was difficult for him to raise his head. His mouth was dry, his lips chafed, and his skin tight from the sand and salt. He touched his ear, which was caked with dried blood and sand, and felt his ankle, which had swollen to the size of a grapefruit. When he turned over, he saw that Thibodeaux was unconscious and breathing spasmodically.

Gallagher crawled out of the hollow into a vast darkness lit by stars spread among gray clouds. The repetitive flashing continued. The wind was fluky, and only the deep black walls of clouds all around told him that he knelt in the eye of the storm. He found a broken branch and, using it as a brace, wobbled to his feet. Leaning on the branch, he hobbled past the whaler, which had been carried inland by the surge and jammed like a lean-to between two Australian pines. When he reached a clearing, he looked out at the frothing ocean and the waves that pounded the island. He guessed that they were stranded on one of the Dry Tortugas, but the intermittent flashing had vanished and he could not see any other islands below the hurricane's approaching wall clouds.

As he made his way back to the pine tree on the knoll, he swallowed any water he found puddled on leaves and fronds. Near a palm tree he collected an armful of windblown coconuts and stowed them in the hollow. When the wind and rain began to buffet him again, he didn't crawl immediately back into the shelter. Bracing himself against the leeward side of the pine tree's trunk, he cupped his hands to his chin and raised his head so that the rain poured into his mouth. When he was finally sated, he slipped back into the hollow.

Gallagher poked a hole in one of the coconuts with the diver's knife, cupped his hand behind Thibodeaux's neck, and poured the milk into his mouth. Thibodeaux sputtered and swallowed. His eyes opened but remained unfocused and feverish. Looking up at Gallagher, he muttered, "I ain't takin' no more a dat fuckin' medicine, I'm tellin' ya."

Gallagher could only get a few more mouthfuls of the milk into him before Thibodeaux lapsed again into unconsciousness. Although he was himself exhausted, he couldn't fall asleep. The wind tore at the trees above him; the rain streamed around him. The force of the storm seemed almost to suck the air away. An Australian pine toppled over, jarring the ground nearby. Finally, with a series of disturbing images of fire and water jangling his mind, he fell into a tempestuous sleep.

When Gallagher awoke, light filtered through the fronds near him. The wind had slackened, but the rain still fell. Thibodeaux's leg below the tourniquet had turned gray. Pus oozed from the black wound, encircled by jagged red lines. *Shit*, Gallagher thought, *I've got to get help fast*. He crawled, light-headed and feverish, out of the hollow into a world of splintered branches and shattered trunks. The air smelled of uprooted earth, dampness, and death. Glancing at Tim's dive watch, he was surprised that it was already nine forty-five in the morning. The steady rain felt good, and, kneeling in the sand, he wiped his face and licked the water from his cracked lips. He ran his hands through his grimy hair and rubbed the back of his neck. As he stretched, the sun flashed for a moment between the clouds, and the water dripping from the fronds sparkled briefly. Above him, a single black frigate bird, its hooked wings spread to seven feet, soared in a wide arc beneath the clouds.

He found another branch to use as a crutch and made his way toward the beach. The storm surge had receded, but the surf still churned. A few yards from the breakers, he stopped as twenty small sea turtles dug themselves out of the sand and padded past dozens of dead terns toward the ocean. In the distance, the top of the red-brick walls of a fort, totally incongruous in the Gulf of Mexico, seemed to float on the roiling waves—and he wondered for a moment if he was hallucinating. But on another island farther away, a black brick and steel lighthouse jutted above the trees. He estimated the distance across the water as little more than a mile.

He hobbled closer to the water, where spray from the breakers whipped his face. Rain spattered on the broken-winged bodies of the terns in the sand around him. Bracing himself with the stick, he turned a full circle in the wet sand. The beach curled away in either direction. If there had been people on the island, they might well have been evacuated before the storm. Anyone searching for *Sea Rover* would likely pass by the island entirely. Swimming through the tumbling surf would be impossible. Scratching his scalp, he looked across the water at the mute, monolithic red-brick fort. He raised his head again, letting the drizzle wash his prickling face and run down his throat, and then limped back up the knoll. When he crawled back into the hollow, Thibodeaux was conscious, more lucid, but shivering uncontrollably.

"Jack," Thibodeaux coughed, "de leg's on fire. My whole body's burnin' up. I'm fuckin' burnin' alive." The pus had stopped oozing, but the leg was a deep gray-green.

Gallagher sliced more coconuts, and Thibodeaux's hands shook as he drank.

"T'anks, Jack," Thibodeaux murmured, staring down at his leg. "But I don't t'ink none a dis is gonna do a lot a fuckin' good."

"I'll get help," Gallagher answered, "but I'm going to have to move you somewhere people'll find you."

"I feel like I'm floatin' away, podna," Thibodeaux said. "Like I'm fuckin' smoke or somet'ing."

Thibodeaux was too weak even to crawl, so Gallagher dragged him to the trees where the whaler was wedged and slid him under the hull so that he was out of the drizzle. Gallagher sliced more coconuts and set them just outside the whaler so that Thibodeaux could reach them after they filled with water. "Keep drinking," he said to Thibodeaux.

The diver's smile was lopsided. "For a coupla millionaires," he choked, "we're in some pretty deep shit. Ya know what I mean, podna?"

"Yeah, partner," Gallagher answered. He looked around through the drizzle at the torn palm fronds and uprooted trees. "It doesn't feel much like paradise, right now."

"I ain't gonna make it, I'm tellin' ya," Thibodeaux said. He grabbed Gallagher's wrist. "T'anks, Jack . . . for getting me off dat tub."

"I'll get help," Gallagher repeated.

"Jack," Thibodeaux murmured, "I . . ." He let go of Gallagher's wrist. "I heard Nick . . . When *Sea Devil* turned turtle . . . he called my name." He gnawed at his cracked and swollen lip. "I heard him t'rough de hull. But I fuckin' panicked. I couldn't breat'e, ya know dat." His face was wan, and his eyes clouded over as he looked away. "Once I made it onta dat hull, I was paralyzed. I just couldn't fuckin' move."

Holding a coconut for Thibodeaux to drink from, Gallagher exhaled slowly. "There's nothing you could've done, Dewey," he said.

Thibodeaux turned his head and sipped the watery coconut milk. When he tried to swallow, he coughed up red-brown bile. "I t'ink about it every fuckin' day, Jack." He looked away again, as though he was hearing something Gallagher couldn't.

"It's okay," Gallagher said as he reached for his makeshift

crutch. Bracing himself, he hobbled to his feet. "Hang in there, partner."

Thibodeaux's eyes, still unfocused, seemed to gaze into a place, distant in time and space, that Gallagher couldn't share.

Gallagher looked down at Thibodeaux for almost a minute, turned, and headed back along the beach. When he had gone less than two hundred yards, he discovered a white rubber boat bumper that had washed ashore. Eighty yards farther on, he passed a charred plank. The rain stopped sporadically, but the sun did not reappear. The air was sultry, and his going was slowed by the crutch's sinking into the wet sand. He still felt flushed, but his aching muscles gradually loosened with the activity, and he began to breathe more deeply. He gazed out periodically at the inaccessible fort that loomed across the water.

When the beach ended at the edge of an impenetrable mangrove thicket, he turned inland. Egrets with wet and matted plumage stood staring at him from the tidal shallows. When he began to skirt the thicket, mosquitoes and flies attacked him. The mangroves were sodden, the bark more brown than red, their few remaining oblong leaves drooping. The odor of the yellow blossoms strewn about by the storm was heavy, the crushed berrylike fruit putrid. His crutch kept sticking in the ooze around the aerial roots descending from the trees' branches; muck covered his legs and slowed him even more. His throat burned, and his eyes stung. Branches lashed his face and arms, causing cuts like cross-hatched tattoos. After half an hour, he admitted the wisdom of the survival training maxim about always staying at a crash site, but he still could not leave their rescue to chance.

The mangrove thicket gave way to a low, swampy meadow of sea grass ringed with bowed trees. Although the rain had stopped again, clouds obscured the sun, and the air was suffocating. His thirst was maddening, but he dared not drink the water. His breathing again became quick and shallow as he plodded on. He began almost to welcome the pain in his ankle, ear, and infected arm; they kept him focused on limping along through the rushes. He would circumnavigate the island if it came to that, but he refused to stop moving. He had not survived a hurricane to die in some noisome marsh. He thought about Hernández and then about his years in the navy, the ships and the sorties and the far-flung ports, and then about growing up an only child on a farm. And finally, he thought about nothing.

The park ranger, a young woman with a long, braided blond ponytail hanging out over the top of her brown poncho, screamed when she saw Gallagher stumbling through the rushes where she was checking the damage done to the sea turtles' habitat. Mud smeared his legs and arms; blood ran from the cuts crisscrossing his face and neck. His grizzled beard and hair were filthy, and his lips were cracked and bleeding. At first only a croaking sound came from his mouth as he leaned on his crutch and raised his free arm toward her. She led him to a stump and sat him down. Her eyes were bright, and freckles dotted her nose. Kneeling next to him, she gave him fresh water from her canteen and then asked him softly if he had been aboard a ship during the hurricane.

"Buddy," he said, "injured buddy." His arm wavered as

he pointed back toward the other side of the island. "The whaler . . . on the beach." When she only smiled and nodded, he grabbed her poncho's hood. "Get help," he coughed. "The whaler on the beach. He's dying."

At first she recoiled from his grasp, but then she looked into his eyes. "We'll find him," she said as she pulled a walkie-talkie from under her poncho. She spoke to someone for a moment, told Gallagher that help was on the way, and then took a red bandana from her pocket and wiped the streaked blood and grime from his face. He wanted to thank her, but he was suddenly too exhausted to move or even speak. By the time another ranger with a first aid kit arrived, he had lapsed into a blue-gray fog.

The next hour produced a blur of people asking him questions and moving him to a bench near the marine research compound's hurricane shelter. Later, while he lay on a stretcher at a helicopter pad, the blond ranger leaned over him and said, "We've found your buddy." Her braid fell across his chest. "He's in pretty bad shape, but he was still alive when they air-vacced him."

A paramedic placed an IV in his arm just before two coast guard crewmen loaded him into a Jayhawk. He slipped in and out of consciousness during the ride back to Key West. The lights of the machinery inside the helicopter and the noise of the rotor blades seemed distant, almost alien. When he was conscious, he felt as though he were underwater looking up through a marsh at the paramedic hovering over him. When he lost consciousness, he entered an aquatic world in which he was trapped inside a cell made of silver slabs. When he began to yell and yank the IV needle from his arm, the paramedic had to sedate him.

39

Gallagher woke slowly, the softly glowing half-moon gradually taking the shape of a wall lamp and the gray twilight forming the contours of a room. The overhead light was turned off, and the pale green walls and the other, empty bed were shadowy. The thin, spectral figure by the window was Rita, brushing her hand along the ledge and gazing out into the darkness at the rain.

Before speaking, he lay still for a moment taking stock. His skin itched everywhere. His throat was parched, and his saliva was gummy with an odd metallic taste. Bandages covered his left ear and parts of both his hands where the barnacles had sliced his skin. Two IV tubes dripped solutions into the vein in the back of his left hand. The palm of his right hand was burned where he had clutched the line in the whaler, and another rope burn arced across his forearm. He shifted his arms first and then his legs. His limbs were stiff, and a soft cast encased his right ankle. Because he felt no pain beyond a dull headache, he wondered what sort of medication he had been given. He then went over in his mind everything that had happened. He knew it wasn't finished, and he began to think about what he still had to do.

When Rita noticed him stirring, she walked over to the

bed. Her face seemed thinner, even more drawn, and her eyes, swollen with fatigue, were watery. She touched him lightly on the shoulder and said, "Oh, Jack, I thought you were . . . I never expected to see . . ." She began to gnaw at her lower lip.

"Where am I?" he asked, his voice cracking with the dryness in his throat.

"Trumbo Point Naval Hospital." She rubbed her thumb and forefinger together.

"What about Dewey?" he asked.

Frowning, she shook her head. "They lost him in the chopper coming in."

He stared at the trails of rain snaking down the window. Not only was it not yet over—it might never be over. "Tim?" he asked. "What about Tim?"

"He's still in the recompression chamber, but he's gonna be okay. Probably no permanent . . . no brain damage and all." She leaned against the bed and smiled. "He's in the other wing. Those navy doctors have done a good job. Taken good care of him." She raised her hand and crossed her fingers. "If everything goes okay, he'll be out in a couple of days."

Gallagher did not say anything.

She shook her head. "It was crazy of him to keep diving. He knew he was over his limit, already sick."

Gallagher reached up with his free hand and wiped his forehead. "He's Nick's kid."

She pressed gently on his forearm. "And so are you," she said. She began to cough, took a tissue from her pocket, and wiped her mouth.

Neither of them spoke for a moment.

"Got a damage report for me?" he asked finally.

Exhaling slowly, she balled up the tissue. "You've got a sprained ankle—a hairline crack or something—but no break." She gazed at the side of his head. "Your ear's gonna need plastic surgery, but the doc doesn't think you'll have any hearing loss or anything. It's infected though. So's your shoulder . . ." She forced a smile. "Lots of cuts and bug bites, too."

He turned his head and looked out the window again.

"That stunt with the radio," she said after a moment. "Doing your own *War of the Worlds* broadcast like that . . . The coast guard, cops, half the Conchs and charter captains between here and Islamorada heard it. The coasties were more than pissed, but it's all down on tape."

"Good," he said. He pointed to the Thermos on the table. "Can I have some water?"

She filled a glass, handed it to him, and slouched against the bed. "We're gonna miss Dewey," she said. "He's . . . What the hell went on out there?"

The cold water made his eyes and forehead ache. "I'll tell you, Rita," he said. "But I want Escobar here. I only want to tell it once."

"I saw him . . . He was in the hall earlier . . ." She played with her hands. "The hurricane sank *Sea Rover*?"

He shook his head. "Hugh blew a hole in the hull."

"Hugh? Oh, Jesus!" She stepped back from the bed as though she had been pushed. "Any chance he made it?"

"No."

"I still can't believe that he would . . . ," she mumbled. "I mean, we were like family to him. Nick would've given him another share, for Chris'sake. Me and Nick were never in it just for the money." She pursed her lips, turned, and squinted out the window. Deep crow's-feet ran from her eyes to her temples. When she turned back toward him, she said, "The cops searched his apartment. The disks from the office were there and a pile of documents locked in a file cabinet. He'd put together a salvage deal with some high rollers from Miami."

"What about Beecham?" he asked.

Shaking her head, she bit her lip. "There's not a goddamned thing to link him. Not directly, anyway. There's no record of bribes or anything like that. Hell, the vindictive bastard hated Nick so much Hugh wouldn't even have had to bribe him." Coughing a second time into the tissue, she grimaced. "And they won't pin anything on him. You watch—some judge'll kill any subpoena of his records. No probable cause, or some crap like that. The old fart's like goddamned Teflon."

He ran his finger along the condensation forming on the glass and then drank the rest of the water. His throat constricted and, almost choking, he could taste the saltwater again. He gazed at the empty glass, cleared his throat, and asked, "Where's *Vengeance*?"

"Huh?" She rubbed her eye. "Was Pete out where you were—at the dive site?"

"What?" he asked. "Isn't *Vengeance* back?"

"No . . . At least I don't think so . . . Somebody . . . Braxton, maybe . . . told me the coasties got some sort of call from *Vengeance* just as Brenda started to blow through. I don't know if it was an SOS . . . and I haven't heard anything since." She squeezed the tissue in her hand. "Was it Pete that shot Dewey?"

"Yeah . . . and Hugh."

"Jesus," she murmured. "I knew he was a friggin' nutcase, but . . ."

Gallagher needed to get out of that bed and that room. "Where's Ozzie?" he asked as he stared at the shunt in the back of his hand.

She glanced at her watch. "Should be back at the dock . . . any time now. He took *Intrepid* up the inland waterway ahead of Brenda. He was gonna reprovision and head out sometime later today or tomorrow." Wracked with coughing a third time, she took a minute to catch her breath. "But with *Sea Rover* sunk . . . I'm not sure . . . We gotta have a boat on the site, though. And I need him to bring in the *Magdalena* statue as soon as possible."

"Let me talk to him before he leaves," he said. "There's stuff he needs to know."

Nodding, she reached into the pocket of her jeans and pulled out a gold coin. "Tim had this in his hand when he was brought in, but he has no idea where he got it."

He put the empty glass on the rolling tray-table beside the bed and then smiled at her. "That's the doubloon you gave me. Nick's talisman."

Tears running down her face, she stared at the coin for a minute. "And there's hundreds more just like it—right?"

Louis Escobar entered the room carrying a black and chrome tape recorder. He was unshaven; his uniform was rumpled, his collar unbuttoned, and his tie loose. "Morning—or, almost," he said, nodding to Rita and then glancing at Gallagher. "And I thought you looked like hell last time I saw you. You up to making a statement?"

"Yeah," Gallagher answered. "Just give us a minute, okay?"

"Sure," Escobar said as he stepped back through the door-way. "Let me know when you're ready."

"I didn't see any other doubloons," Gallagher whispered to Rita. "But there's treasure, including gold pre-Columbian ar-tifacts. That much I know."

"When you said on the radio Nick'd been right . . . and then Tim told me there was a wall of silver . . ." She held the doubloon between her thumb and forefinger and turned it slowly so that it gleamed in the soft light. They both gazed at the Jerusalem cross for a moment before she turned the coin again and placed it in the palm of his injured hand. "Jack," she said. "I'm sorry you . . ." She took a deep breath, stifled a cough, and exhaled slowly. "It's all been . . ."

He shook his head. "It was something I had to do," he said to her. Staring at the doubloon, he added, "I understand that now." Even in the room's half-light, the two lions, facing each other at the base of the castle, glinted against the white bandage.

40

An hour after he had finished giving his statement, Gallagher sat upright in the bed watching the hazy gray twilight supplant the darkness. He had explained everything exactly as it had happened out at the dive site, but he hadn't shared any of the conclusions he'd reached. Escobar had then left to file his report, and Rita had gone to visit Tim in the hospital's other wing. The rain had halted again, but beads dotted the window like some inscrutable braille message.

Hernández came into the room carrying an airline bag with clothes and shoes for him. Her floral sundress belied her fatigue; her eyes were both bleary and bright, as though she'd had too little sleep and too much coffee. Smiling wearily, she put down the bag and said, "Here's the stuff you asked for, Jack." She went over to the bed, gently traced the cuts on Gallagher's face with her index finger, and added, "I'm glad to see you."

Gallagher looked into her eyes. "I'm glad to be here, Josie," he said. "Believe me."

When he reached out and touched her shoulder, she leaned against the bed but looked away from him. "I'm sorry about what happened, Jack," she said. "If I'd told you Hugh was my source, none of this . . ." She rubbed her forehead. "Dewey might . . ."

He paused for a moment before saying, "Josie, I've thought about it a lot. It probably would've gone down the same even if you'd told me." He shifted his weight in the bed and then reached for her hand. "I figured out that Hugh was your source before I went out there with Tim. We were headed into harm's way no matter what."

She perched on the edge of the bed and looked into his eyes. "Jack," she said, "I was afraid . . ." She leaned down and kissed his swollen lips. "You've gotten into more than you, or any of us, bargained for." She clasped his injured hand with both of hers. "After that damned radio . . . After I heard the tape of you and Whitaker . . ." Her voice became quieter. "During the storm, I was sure you were lost. And I care . . . a lot." She smiled sadly. "No story is worth a life . . ."

He nodded but didn't answer right away. Certainly no story was, and no treasure, no matter how vast, was either. "Just the same, Josie," he said finally, "I want you to tell the story. Or at least part of it, anyway. According to Rita, Bee-cham's going to skate. And that's not right."

She patted his arm just above the rope burn. "The cops may not be able to touch him, but Beecham's involvement's not a dead issue. I got a friend at Ma Bell to, ah, *obtain* Hugh's phone records." She gazed at the empty glass for a moment. "There's calls to me, of course, but there's a bunch more to Beecham's home." Sucking in her breath, she moved her hand up his arm. "Two of them on the night we were . . . at the Doubloon office. And get this: After the break-in, a little before five in the morning, Whitaker called Beecham again. They talked for ten minutes."

He tried to decipher the runes beading on the window. Whitaker had even orchestrated Beecham's arrival at the office that morning with the list of demands. There wasn't really any end, he knew, to what petty and destructive and, ultimately, tragic things people would do for treasure. "Whitaker radioed somebody from *Sea Rover*," he said. "Probably with a message for Beecham."

She nodded. "I'll check it out with the coast guard."

Taking a piece of Kleenex from the box by the bed, he said, "Beecham must've about shit when Whitaker went after him at the hearing."

She nodded again. "Yeah. It looks like they'd concocted the compromise so Hugh'd get the leases to the deepwater sites in the spring. But there was no way he could let me take the stand." She smiled ironically. "I wouldn't have *testified* that Hugh was my source, but I would've said enough that you, at least, would've figured it out." Fingering her gold rope necklace, she added, "And Jack, Rita doesn't know it yet, but Doubloon's lease renewals are a lock. Findley, the new guy on the board, knew Beecham's report was tainted—some sort of personal vendetta—even before the hearing. Afterward, what with Tim's finding the statue and the truth coming out about Whitaker screwing the company, Findley guaranteed me your leases'll be renewed as long as Doubloon agrees to earmark a small percentage of the value of any artifacts recovered for an environmental fund to save the reefs."

"I wonder where he got that idea?" he asked as he cocked his head and looked into her eyes again. "I'll make sure the funding's there." He shook his head and added more to himself than to her, "It'll be no small chunk of change."

"Thanks, Jack," she said.

He folded the Kleenex in eighths and then pulled off the tape that held the shunt to the back of his hand. "Josie," he asked, "do you know where Señor Cardona lives?"

"Of course. Jack, what're you . . . ?"

"Good." He slipped out the IV, pressed the folded Kleenex over the point of blood, and retaped his hand. "Did you drive here?"

"Yeah." She squinted at him. "Is that why you wanted your clothes?"

He pulled back the sheet. "I need you to take me there."

She stood and stepped back. "Jack, you're in no condition to go anywhere. And anyway, he's not there."

As he swung his feet over the side of the bed, his ankle throbbed. "What?" he asked. "How do you know?"

She tugged at the spaghetti strap of her dress. "What's going on, Jack?"

"How do you know, Josie?" he repeated.

"Because I spoke to my father . . ." She turned and looked out the window. ". . . yesterday afternoon. And the maestro was with him. He'd taken his yacht up to the mainland to avoid Brenda."

He pressed his hands on the bed until pain shot up his arm. "Damn," he murmured.

"He might be back, though," she said. "My father asked if it was still too sloppy down here to run a boat into the Bight. I told him the charter captains were starting to return."

He stood up, and the room furled around him for a moment before settling down at right angles. Light-headed and beginning to sweat, he leaned against the bed, closed his eyes, controlled his breathing, and gathered himself.

"Wolf," she said, taking his elbow, "you can't leave. Look at you."

He pointed to the bag she'd brought. "Josie," he whispered fiercely, "I have to see Cardona."

She looked into his eyes for a moment before saying, "All right, Jack. Okay. I'll take you."

While he dressed, she left the room to find something to help him walk. As he folded the hospital gown and laid it on the bed, she returned with a pair of aluminum crutches. She propped them against the foot of the bed, looked him over, shook her head, and said, "I'll stop at the nurses' station. Draw their attention. The elevators are to your right."

"Thanks, Josie." He took the doubloon from the tray-table, rubbed his thumb over the castle and lions, and slipped the coin into the pocket of his khakis.

When Gallagher and Hernández reached the hospital's main reception desk, he asked where the recompression unit was. The receptionist, an older woman with a pinched face and scrawny arms, told him the location and then informed him that the area was restricted. Gallagher asked Hernández to wait in the lobby for him and then spent almost five minutes talking his way into the recompression unit, which was set off by a locked steel door. He explained that he had been aboard ship with Tim and that he, too, had later been transported by helicopter to the hospital—but it was only when he mentioned that he was Tim's brother that the orderly staring through the reinforced glass of the door's small rectangular window finally admitted him to the unit.

The recompression area, with its linoleum floor and bare green walls, looked more like a laundry room than a hospital ward. The recompression chamber was a twelve-foot-long gray and white cylinder just over five feet high. The exterior had a series of gauges; an airlock through which food, supplies, and medication could be passed; and a viewing port. Gallagher leaned his crutches against the chamber and gazed through the port at Tim, who lay on his back with his eyes closed, naval issue BVDs and a clean white T-shirt draping his long frame.

Gallagher pushed the intercom button and said, "How're you doing, buddy?"

Tim's eyes fluttered open. He squeezed his eyes shut, opened them again, reached over, and pressed his intercom button. "Stir-crazy, Jack," he answered. "Fuckin' stir-crazy." His amplified voice sounded deep and mechanical. "What're you doin' here?"

"Thought you might need a visitor."

"I do. Any time." Tim smiled. "Mom left a little while . . . Time fucks with my brain in here, Jack. Anyways, I didn't expect to see you 'til I got out. She said you went through hell."

"Something like that," Gallagher answered.

"Vogel was out at the site? Fuckin' shot Dewey and Hugh?"

Gallagher shook his head. "I'll fill you in later."

Tim reached up and tapped the port. "Thanks, Jack," he said, "for actin' so fast." He frowned. "I might not've made it otherwise."

Gallagher scratched the side of his nose. "No problem," he answered. "Had to, really. You're the guy that found *Magdalena*'s motherlode, and I sure as hell wasn't going to let you miss the celebration." He smiled at Tim. "Couldn't have the party without you."

"What's this I'm hearin' about a ton of pre-Columbian stuff?"

"A ton?" Gallagher smiled again. He guessed that as the news of the *Magdalena* treasure spread, the value of artifacts and the size of the silver wall, spectacular as they were in reality, would increase exponentially. "There's a chest full of 'em, Tim. And at least two other bronze chests."

Tim shook his head slowly as he said, "Holy fuckin' shit!"

"Tim," Gallagher said, his expression and tone becoming more serious, "there's something I need to know. Did Nick . . . Dad . . . ever . . . I don't know . . . leave the dive sites suddenly . . . not come back for a while? With Ozzie, maybe?"

"Ya got me, Jack." Tim shrugged. "Maybe."

Gallagher scratched his neck below his bandaged ear and waited for Tim to go on.

"Yeah, I guess," Tim said. "But everybody was always comin' and goin'. It's not like we had a set schedule or nothin'." He stared up through the port. "What's goin' down, Jack?"

"Nothing," Gallagher answered. "I was just wondering . . ." He tapped the port. "You get yourself out of here so that we can have that celebration."

Tim frowned again and then nodded as though he was lost in thought. "Yeah, okay," he said finally. "Forty fuckin' more hours, that's it. But you take care, too. I don't want you missin' the party either."

41

The wind had died, and a hot, dank stench pervaded Key West as Hernández drove Gallagher in her red Miata toward the Bight. He felt cramped in the sports car, and his whole body began to ache as well as itch. Brenda's full fury had missed the island, but more than six inches of rain had fallen and winds had gusted to sixty-five miles an hour. Electricity had gone out for almost ten hours, and the city's cisterns had been fouled. The foliage of many of the trees and bushes had been stripped, and a pasty, repellent mixture of windblown leaves, salt, garbage, and dead insects stuck to the trees and fences. Plywood sheets still covered the windows of many of the houses; downed branches littered the lawns and gardens.

They parked a block from the Doubloon, Inc., office. As he hobbled with her through the hazy humidity, he had trouble catching his breath—as if the storm was still somehow lodged in his lungs. Flies swarmed around a dead seagull impaled on the barbed wire atop the trailer court's fence. An old, bearded man in jeans and a red sleeveless T-shirt mumbled to himself as he swept debris from in front of the shed where before the storm he had sold T-shirts and conchs and wind chimes to the tourists. The fishnets and multicolored buoys were gone from the tavern's walls. Though the waterfront market was open, its windows were still boarded.

Waves ran against the outer seawall, but the Bight itself was calm. The water's surface was mottled with light and dark patches; the odor of decay permeated the waterfront. Dead parrotfish, their bellies bloated and their eye sockets empty, floated near the dock. The catamaran *Stars and Stripes* and the other tourist boats had not yet returned, but a dozen other boats, *Intrepid* and *Maestro III* among them, were moored at the finger piers. Hernández and Gallagher stopped on the wharf as he gazed at *Intrepid*, memories of his last hours on *Sea Rover* welling. Its hull and deck had recently been scrubbed, and the tug looked almost as though it had been refitted. A new white radar antenna was fixed to the top of the signal mast above the wheelhouse. He took a deep breath, shook his head, and led Hernández toward *Maestro III*. Canvas curtains covered the express cruiser's bridge and aft cockpit; a series of deep dings marring the port side of the hull testified to the storm's rage.

As he handed her his crutches, she asked, "Jack, are you sure you know what you're doing?"

"Absolutely, Josie," he answered. "Do you know what I'm doing?"

"No." She shook her head. "But it has something to do with the maestro and your father, doesn't it?"

He nodded.

"And my father, too . . ." She reached out and took his arm. "Jack," she said, "he always kept his political activities from my mother and me. But I'm not blind. I've known that

he and the maestro . . . and others . . . I've known that something . . ." She let her hand slip from his arm. "And I'd noticed
that your . . . that Nick and the maestro seemed to have some
unspoken bond."

"We'll find out," he said, yanking the canvas curtain free
of its snaps. He swung his bad leg up, swiveled on the gunwale,
and hopped into the stern cockpit. By the time he got his
balance, a wiry young Hispanic man stood on the deck pointing a .357 Magnum at his chest. A leather shoulder holster fit
snugly over the man's clean white T-shirt; his face was ex-
pressionless, and his dark eyes showed nothing. Recognizing
him as the man he had seen leaving the yacht the afternoon
of the Antiquities Board hearing, Gallagher said, "I need to
talk to Señor Cardona," turned, and reached back through the
opening in the canvas for his crutches.

Still training the gun on him, the man backed to the cabin
entrance and sidled down the steps.

Hernández had just clambered aboard when the man re-
appeared, waved the pistol's barrel at them, and grunted, "*Ade-
lante!*"

The salon was cool and bright and smelled of strong coffee.
Cardona sat at the curved sofa, his forearms resting on a shiny
black portable table set in front of him. He wore a burgundy
bathrobe, and though his hair was neatly combed, he looked
diminished—the skin of his face and neck droopy and his eyes
rheumy. His glasses lay on the table between a steaming china
cup of coffee and a copy of the *Key West Tribune*. The television was again tuned to CNN with the sound muted.

The young man slid the pistol into his shoulder holster,

folded his arms across his chest, and leaned against the bulk-head. Standing to Gallagher's left, Hernández ran her hands down the sides of her dress and stared at the engraved platter above Cardona's head. The sweat on Gallagher's neck and back chilled in the air conditioning.

"Jack, I am glad to see you," Cardona said, his tone stiff but cordial. "But it was not appropriate to bring María José here with you."

"She's not any part of this, Mr. Cardona?" Gallagher asked.

Fingering her necklace, Hernández glanced from one man to the other.

Cardona put on his glasses and looked Gallagher up and down. "No, Jack, she never has been. It was her father's wish. And now you have imprudently involved her."

"Dewey's dead," Gallagher snarled. "And Whitaker. And I'm betting Vogel is, too."

Cardona placed his hands over the cup so that the steam escaped between his palms. Blinking rapidly, he looked at Hernández instead of Gallagher. "María José," he said, "you must never publish what Jack and I speak about this morning. Is that understood?"

"Of course," she said, her eyes wide.

"If any word of what you hear becomes public knowledge," Cardona said, "people, friends of your father's, will be hurt, perhaps killed. You understand this?"

She hesitated for no more than a second before nodding.

Cardona shifted his gaze to Gallagher. "Yes, Jack. Unfortunately, men died. But it is all for the best. Señora Gallagher's company is saved. Our interests are protected. And Doubloon will, I suspect, be rid of Señor Beecham." He tapped his fingers on the newspaper. "You came in at the end of it, Jack. It was all inevitable."

Gallagher swung his right crutch up and swept it across the table, strewing the newspaper and shattering the china cup against the door to the forward stateroom. "Bullshit!" he shouted. "You *sent* Vogel out there!"

The young man drew the pistol and pressed it against Gallagher's neck.

"No!" Ozzie Millan loomed in the stern hatchway glowering at the young man. He stepped into the salon and snatched the gun, which looked small in his huge hand.

Cardona glanced at the coffee running down the door and staining the carpet.

"*Salga!*" Millan barked at the man.

The man looked at Cardona, who nodded almost imperceptibly. As the man slouched up the stairs to the aft cockpit, Millan flicked on the Magnum's safety and slid the pistol onto the counter. "Jack, *mi amigo*," he said, his voice soft, "what're you doin' here?" Gazing at Gallagher's cuts and bruises and bandages, he shook his head. "You should be in the hospital." His smile, more sad than happy, revealed his gold tooth.

Gallagher took a deep breath. "I'm trying to get the goddamned truth out of . . . your leader. He sent Vogel out to the dive site after us."

Millan looked over at Cardona. "*Qué?* Is this true?"

"Nonsense," Cardona snapped. "No one sent Señor Vogel anywhere. He was going to cause trouble no matter what."

"You equipped him," Gallagher said.

"Yes," Cardona answered, gazing past them for a moment at the television that showed images of Caribbean countryside ravaged by Brenda.

Millan stepped back as though he had been hit. *"Por qué?"*

"I anticipated contingencies," Cardona answered, gazing grimly at Millan, as though his authority should not be questioned. "It was not an operation that concerned you."

"It is my business, Maestro," Millan said. "Doubloon is partly my company . . ." He raised his hands and shook them in frustration. "Dewey was *mi amigo* . . . You should have told me . . ."

Cardona scowled at him for a long moment before his face became softer again. "Making Señor Vogel a limited—and temporary—partner in a salvage company enabled us to keep track of him and gave us potential future access to dive sites should Doubloon's leases not be renewed," he said, his voice low. "We did not inform you because we believed that you would not have been content to let events come to pass. And the decision, though perhaps not entirely wise, was necessary."

Millan nodded, but his eyes betrayed his residual ire.

"You knew what Vogel would do!" Gallagher said.

"I *knew* nothing," Cardona said.

"He shot Dewey and Hugh."

"Yes, Jack. And *you* shot him." Cardona took off his glasses and wearily rubbed his eyes. "You did what was necessary, and you survived. And your father's dream of discovering Spanish treasure is a reality."

"Vogel was still alive when . . . Where the hell is *Vengeance?*"

"In a safe harbor," Cardona answered. "She barely outran the storm. But Señor Vogel, badly wounded as you know, was lost overboard."

"Shit," Gallagher muttered. "You . . ."

"Understand this, Jack," Cardona said, his tone sharp. "My two men were aboard that boat to protect my interests, not Señor Vogel's. Events did not turn out as we anticipated . . . but it is far simpler this way." He paused, staring into Gallagher's eyes. "And, you must also understand that my interests and yours are really very much the same."

"Right," Gallagher scoffed. "And that's why your men left Dewey and me out there to die in the hurricane."

"That is not true," Cardona answered, his voice still sharp. "They returned to look for you, but they did not find you."

"Bullshit. They came back for two minutes before turning tail and hauling ass out of there."

"When they could not locate you, they radioed the U.S. Coast Guard in an attempt to find assistance for you."

Gallagher shook his head, glanced at the pistol on the counter, took a deep breath, and exhaled slowly, "And killing the burnout that attacked Josie and me?" he asked. "That was protecting your interests, too?"

Cardona put his glasses back on and looked at Hernández. "I simply saw to it that justice was served on worthless scum that had endangered the lives of the children of two of my good friends."

Hernández's eyes grew wide again. She began to speak and then shut her mouth and took hold of Gallagher's elbow. He sagged on his crutches, his energy waning. "Jesus," he said, "some goddamned justice." Looking over his shoulder at Millan, he asked, "My father brought Ozzie to you when he was wounded . . . but what the hell else did he do?"

Cardona sighed. "Nicholas Gallagher was a great friend. Ozzie was the first, but not the only one, Nicholas saved. As an American treasure hunter, Nicholas could go places and meet people that no *cubano* could. He helped us, risked his life." He stared into Gallagher's eyes again. "Do not misunderstand me, Jack. Your father acted out of friendship and loyalty. His only interest was Spanish treasure, not Cuban politics."

Millan stepped behind Hernández, knelt on one knee, and swept the china shards onto the soggy newspaper. Hernández slipped her arm around Gallagher's waist.

"And you reciprocated?" Gallagher asked Cardona.

"*Sí*, your father and I, we had an understanding."

"When Whitaker secretly sold you his shares, you told my father?"

Millan placed the newspaper and shards in the sink. Hernández brushed her hair back from her eyes and looked at Gallagher.

"*Sí*." Cardona nodded. "And then friends in Spain informed me that Señor Whitaker had extended his research beyond the Archive of the Indies. I did not know what he had discovered . . ."

"But you knew he'd found something," Gallagher said. "You should've told my father."

Cardona folded his hands on the bare table and studied them before cocking his head, glancing at Millan and Hernández, and then gazing at Gallagher. "I did, Jack," he said. "Why do you suppose Nicholas changed his will?"

Millan placed his hand softly on Gallagher's shoulder.

"Like me," Cardona went on, "he had to let events play themselves out. Of course, he did not know he would . . . what would happen to him . . ."

Biting his swollen and cracked lower lip until he tasted blood, Gallagher stared at the engraving of *La Fuerza*.

"I have already told you," Cardona said, "that he wanted you here to deal with the situation if he could not do it himself." He shrugged, as though Gallagher must finally and inescapably begin to accept the fact that sailing against the winds of time and fate was futile. "And, Jack, that is exactly how things have worked out."

Gallagher shook his head again, the anger ebbing but a deep sense of wrong remaining. *Things* may have worked out and the *situation* may have been resolved, but there were still casualties. "The company may be saved and your interests protected, Mr. Cardona," he said, "but Dewey and the others never knew what the stakes really were." As he turned on his crutches between Millan and Hernández, he added, "And they didn't survive. Dewey's dead. And the others. Their deaths . . . you have to live with that." Without looking back, he hobbled across the salon, up the steps, and away.

Epilogue

The next morning, Hernández's articles on the *Magdalena* treasure and on the latest South Florida political scandal involving Robert Lee Beecham were picked up by the wire services and splashed across the front pages of newspapers around the country. Beecham's denials became increasingly strident as the calls for his dismissal became more forceful. The Marine Antiquities Board convened and promptly renewed the Doubloon site leases, with the stipulation that five percent of the gross be donated to the newly created Nicholas Gallagher Memorial Fund for saving Florida's coral reefs.

Millan returned the following day with the *Magdalena* statue and the three brass chests. The first chest contained two hundred pounds of bullion—gold bars and disks stamped with royal seals and mint marks. The second held an array of personal items—etched gold plates and cups, hand-wrought gold chains, gold rings set with diamonds and emeralds, gold crucifixes engraved with images of saints, and a magnificent belt of ornately rendered gold links. The third, the one that Gallagher had discovered cracked open, offered up more pre-Columbian gold artifacts than there were in all of the world's museums combined. There were earrings and nose adornments, ritual masks and death masks of hammered gold, statues of monkeys and llamas, ornamental lizards and birds and spiders. And there was a solid-gold twenty-seven-inch wheel, an Aztec calendar swarming with archaic glyphs.

As the news of the gold artifacts and the pre-Columbian treasures spread, media estimates of the value of *Magdalena*'s cargo soared from two hundred million to four hundred million and then to over a half a billion dollars. Television crews descending upon Key West bustled about accosting anyone even remotely connected to Doubloon, Inc. All the network news programs featured interviews with Tim, even before his release from the recompression chamber; once he was out of the hospital, the prime-time news magazines vied for his "exclusive" story.

Thibodeaux's funeral was carried live on CNN. Hernández found herself granting more interviews than she was getting; unable to work without constant interruptions in the *Tribune* office, she hid in her publisher's fishing shack on Sugarloaf Key and e-mailed her stories to the paper. Braxton Finch waxed eloquent for anyone and everyone. Even the diver, Matt, still baffled by his encounter with Saint Elmo's fire, appeared on NBC's *DATELINE*. The *Magdalena* statue graced the cover of *Time*, and Millan, holding the Aztec calendar, made the cover of *Newsweek*.

Despite the fact that coast guard cutters and navy hydrofoils constantly patrolled the straits, Rita had to hire a marine security firm to keep poachers away from the dive site. *Intrepid* was anchored at the site as a permanent dive platform, and a new marine archeologist signed on, as did an additional eight divers. Rita finally escaped the media blitz by heading to the dive site to oversee the mapping of it and the long and arduous task of raising the silver bars and searching for more artifacts.

Newscasters and journalists hounded Gallagher, trying to turn him, despite his protests, into America's newest hero. They embellished his military record and exaggerated his role in the discovery of the *Magdalena* treasure. Anything anyone said echoed in his bandaged ear, and, by the third day, after he had recounted his survival of the hurricane more than a dozen times, he only answered the telephone in his hotel room when it had just rung twice and stopped—a signal from Hernández.

After Finch obtained copies of the English transcriptions of the documents the police had discovered in Whitaker's apartment, Gallagher spent much of his time reading through the material. A strong, almost eerie tingling ran along his spine as he read Bartólome de Alcala's narrative about *Santa María Magdalena*'s last voyage, the hurricane that sank her, and de Alcala's ride on a spar, half-drowned, until he was thrown ashore on one of the Far Tortugas.

Just after dawn the fifth morning, Gallagher limped along Margaret Street past an uprooted Spanish laurel. The sidewalk was ruptured, and the red bricks beneath it were strewn about. Muck squished under his shoe and caused the rubber tip of the cane he had exchanged for his crutches to slip periodically. The sky was overcast, the wind patchy. His shirt clung to his chest and back, and sweat ran down his neck as he scuffed across blossoms scattered on the cement. Remnants of the orange hibiscus grew through the chain-link fence near the cemetery's main gate. A pale green pickup truck with the town's conch seal stood along the roadway.

The storm had wreaked havoc in the cemetery, and many of the vaults had been resealed with new tops. A few vaults still had cracked walls and toppled lids washed to the side. Three workmen in dark green uniforms were using a forklift to rebuild a vault by the far wall. Gallagher stopped for a moment by the iron fence of the battleship *Maine* cemetery plot. A red-winged blackbird flew from the line of manila palms along the fence, and a striped gecko skittered across the walkway. Gazing at the statue of the sailor holding the tall oar in his right hand and shading his eyes with his left, Gallagher wondered what had really happened to the *Maine* that day in Havana Harbor in 1898 and what exactly had gone on at that same dock two and a half centuries earlier while the crew prepared *Santa María Magdalena* for her last voyage.

The royal poinciana to the left of Nick Gallagher's grave had strewn heavy black seed pods in the grass. Gallagher brushed the dried husks from the top of the vault. Below the chiseled image of a galleon on the grave marker was the inscription, "Like the waves and time, he is gone but not forgotten." As Gallagher stood there gazing at the vault, palm fronds clicked in the intermittent breeze. The rumble of the forklift and the voices of the workmen carried to him.

He wondered again about his father and the man's obsession with sunken treasure, an obsession so strong he had called seances and counterfeited doubloons to keep it alive. They had found the treasure where, finally, he had known it must be. But the treasure, as everyone now realized, had been gained at an extreme price, and he wondered, too, if his father would have thought it worth dying for. His father had certainly known that the sea, as Millan would say, was not only a benevolent mistress but also capricious and vindictive. The ocean had been giving and taking since before human history.

He picked up one of the royal poinciana's seed pods. Hard and black on the outside and brown-gold inside, it curved like the hull of a ship. The seeds that had lain in the grooves were scattered. He shook his head and smiled ironically. As a result of his father's quest for treasure, he, Jack Gallagher, would become wealthy—something he had not set out to be. And, perhaps, he would finally be able to stop wandering. In some sense that he was just coming to understand, he realized that he, too, was an end-of-the-roader. There was, for him, no going back to American and three-day trips and the apartment in Chicago. It was time to settle down in this rootless town among all of the rovers and dreamers. His father had altered his will shortly before his death, and that act had ineluctably brought Gallagher to this time and place and to this understanding of his father and himself.

As he reached into his pocket and pulled out the doubloon, a mottled lizard scrambled by his shoe. A song sparrow, its tail feathers quivering, lighted on the vault. The sun broke through the clouds, and heat seemed to radiate in swirling waves above the vault as the sparrow trilled. Gallagher gazed at the doubloon's shield and then turned the bright coin over and stared at the Jerusalem cross. He traced the sign of the cross with his finger and offered a long, silent blessing. Then, he stooped, scratched a hole in the crusty earth, and buried the doubloon. Finally, he stood before the grave, his head bowed, until a jet, streaking through the clouds, shattered the moment.

About the Author

Jay Amberg is the author of *Deep Gold* and *Blackbird Singing*. He also compiled a collection of poetry entitled *Fifty-two Poems for Men*. Mr. Amberg lives in Evanston, Illinois, and teaches English.